FLAMES OF TIME: BOOK ONE

SPLINTERED SOULS

ERICA LUCKE DEAN

Splintered Souls
Book 1: Flames of Time™
A Red Adept Publishing Book
Copyright © 2014 by Erica Lucke Dean All rights reserved.
First Print Edition: August 2015

ISBN-13: 978-1-940215-57-0
ISBN-10: 1940215579

Red Adept Publishing, LLC
104 Bugenfield Court
Garner, NC 27529
http://RedAdeptPublishing.com/

Cover and Formatting: Streetlight Graphics

*To
the doctor
who prescribed the medication
that gave me insomnia, which resulted in
three glorious weeks of unfettered writing.
Thanks.*

The Paradox of Time
Time goes, you say? Ah no!
Alas, Time stays, we go;
Or else, were this not so,
What need to chain the hours,
For Youth were always ours?
Time goes, you say?-ah no!

–Henry Austin Dobson

"Into every soul, love is born; it calls back the separate halves of our original selves and tries to make one from two and heal the wounds of the human heart."

–Plato, The Symposium

THE BLESSING

1654

A CHILL CUT THROUGH HER, AND Lady Catherine
Fairchild melted into her cloak. She forced herself to
keep to the shadows as she followed her maid along the
darkened path to the stables. Even with no moon to light her
way and wearing a pair of borrowed boots at least two sizes too
large for her feet, she lost her footing only once.

The girl hurried inside to retrieve the horse while Catherine
listened to the wind howling through the trees. Panic clawed at
her insides, and she fought to push it back. Foolish idea or not,
she would carry it out. What choice did she have? She feared
her husband dead—or worse. And if they implicated him in the
failed plot to restore Charles II to the throne... She shuddered
to think what that would mean for her unborn child.

"My ladyship, are you certain you won't permit me to
accompany you?" Tension lined the young maid's face as she
steadied Duchess, the anxious mare, and Catherine read the
unspoken words in her eyes. *A lady should never travel alone,
especially at night.*

With one foot in the stirrup, Catherine threw a shaky leg
over and climbed into the gentleman's saddle. She thanked her
good fortune that her brothers had insisted she learn to ride like
a boy. "I'm quite certain."

"Perhaps we could take the carriage. The sky is ripe with a
storm, and with you being so newly with child—and riding like
that." She nodded to Catherine's skirt.

Catherine's face flamed as she rearranged the fabric to cover her thighs. With her legs astride the horse, she'd exposed more skin than would have ever been considered proper.

Mary's eyes burned a hole through her. "What would Sir Thomas say if he saw you?"

Catherine flinched at her husband's name, that familiar feeling of dread seeping into her bones yet again. "Thank you for your help, Mary. But what I must do, I must do alone. Storm or no storm." A change in the wind sent a tremor through her, and she tugged her heavy woolen cloak tighter around her slight frame, keeping her flaxen curls hidden beneath the dark hood.

Catherine knew Mary had good reason to worry. She couldn't afford to forget the dangers awaiting her along her journey, but with her husband missing and England in an uproar, she needed to seek out the help of someone *not* under the influence of Oliver Cromwell's rule. She might not have sided with the old king, but poor Charles hardly deserved a public beheading. In the years since abolishing the monarchy—thus scattering the king's heirs to the wind—Cromwell had ruled her beloved England with an iron fist. And with the latest plan foiled, her child would be born the son of a traitor unless she took matters into her own hands.

"I'll be fine. You'll see." She gave Mary a faint smile and slid her hand over the horse's neck. The mare snorted, as if the anxiety straining just below the surface of Catherine's skin had worked its way from her delicate fingers and into the beast. Its sinewy frame shifted beneath her as it pawed the damp ground, making the saddle creak. "And God willing, I'll be home before sunrise."

"Then safe travels, Lady Catherine." Mary stepped back. She dropped her tortured gaze to her battered shoes before her head snapped back up, her eyes wide. "Be sure to keep to the main roads as long as you can. And don't pay her a single crown more than what I told you. She'll try to take you for more if you let her. And my dear lady, whatever you do, do not permit her to use the dark arts. *Nothing* is worth the price you'll pay for that."

Catherine clenched her thighs against the warm saddle and gave her maid a quick nod before reaching out with trembling hands to take the reins. Gripping the leather straps until her bare knuckles went white, she urged her husband's fastest mare forward until the sudden jolt sucked the air from her lungs. Giant hooves thundered down the path, kicking up mud like musket fire in their wake.

As if racing to catch her, a bitter wind rolled in from the south, bending bare tree limbs until they creaked and groaned, brushing their branches against the muddy earth. In the distance, bright flashes lit the horizon, and the sky rumbled its displeasure, dark clouds hanging like an omen.

"Faster, Duchess." After riding until her bones felt like jelly, Catherine clutched the reins tighter and nudged the horse's flanks with her heels. "We can't afford to be caught in this storm."

The inky-black mare snorted out a white breath as the first drops of rain splashed against her mane. With a lunge, Duchess increased her efforts, the corded neck muscles bunching and tightening as she bore down toward the thick woods and the tiny cottage hidden just beyond.

A twinge of fear gripped Catherine. Under normal circumstances, she would have never considered seeking out a witch. The penalty for getting caught would be far too harsh. But with her husband likely lost forever and her child's life at stake, she would risk the noose for even a whisper of white magic.

What was the harm? She shuddered, leaning forward in the saddle to grab ahold of Duchess's mane, and jabbed her heels into the horse's side again. She focused her attention on the pounding of hooves, ducking her head against the coming downpour. Rain sliced through the sky at an angle, pricking her exposed skin like pins. She was almost there, though she'd be soaked to the bone by the time she arrived. She could only pray the rain would wash away her sins—she could never confess such things in church.

CHAPTER ONE

2014

IN ALL MY EIGHTEEN—ALMOST NINETEEN—YEARS, I couldn't remember a colder day in August. Instead of drenched in sweat like usual, I'd woken to temperatures colder than a witch's tit. And in Annandale, Virginia, that was almost unheard of.

I shot off a few texts, responding to the handful of people who actually gave a damn that instead of taking advantage of my academic scholarship to my father's alma mater, the school I'd busted my ass for four years to get into, I was moving to bum-fuck Maine with my mom and my little brother. Then I unplugged my phone from the charger and crawled out of bed, twisting my honey-colored hair into a loose topknot before stalking off to the bathroom. The movers were due to show up at eight, and I still had to grab a shower and something to eat before diving into what would be the second-worst day of my life.

I only had myself to blame. It was my choice to go to a small local college—a branch campus of U-Maine—so I could stay close to Mom and Josh. After everything that had happened, I just couldn't leave them. But I would have done almost anything to take my mind off the move, even sit through one of Dad's exaggerated stories about his years as an Army brat, moving from one end of the globe to the other, all before he was my age. Then again, if he'd been there—if he hadn't *died*—we wouldn't have needed to move at all.

My cat-pee-yellow cap and gown and the brand-new red

bikini I'd ordered the minute the new swimwear catalogues showed up in the mail back in February taunted me from my empty closet. I couldn't decide what to do with either of them. Pack or pitch? Those were my choices. With one last lingering gaze, I wadded them together and shoved them into an open box along with the rest of my memories.

The air conditioning didn't kick in once while I stuffed my entire life—what was left of it, anyway—into two-foot-by-two-foot boxes, but I wouldn't have minded if the furnace had. Unfortunately, Mom'd had the gas disconnected a week ago, so I had to settle for one of my dad's old Georgetown hoodies and a pair of his thick wool socks. Somehow, I knew he'd sent the cool weather to take the sting out of packing or maybe to remind me of what was in store for me in New England: snow up to my eyeballs, from October through April.

So much for the red bikini.

One by one, I sealed each cardboard square with clear tape and stacked them by the door for the movers. Five boxes and one hot-pink duffel bag later, I stared at the vast emptiness of my room as if we were total strangers—every hint of Ava Elizabeth Flynn wiped clean. I shivered and pulled my hands into the sleeves of Dad's worn blue-and-gray Hoyas sweatshirt. The only clues that I'd ever lived there at all were the imprints in the carpet where the bed and dresser used to be and the clean spots on the wall where my classic rock posters had hung. I'd started collecting them when I was thirteen, and Dad introduced me to Zeppelin and the Stones. Soon, even those faint shadows of me would be gone like footprints after a fresh snow.

"Ava, you about ready?"

I flinched and spun around to find my mom leaning against the doorframe. Her haggard appearance made her seem much older than thirty-nine, especially without a stitch of makeup to cover the dark circles under her honey-brown eyes—eyes that were an exact match for mine—and with a new crop of gray peppering her dark hair. She'd obviously skipped her last hair appointment, and instead of wearing it in shiny waves over her shoulders, she'd taken to haphazardly tangling it into a loose bun at the back of her head. I guessed losing a husband would do that to a woman. Not that I knew firsthand, but I did feel as if I'd aged a dozen years after losing my father.

She must have felt my eyes dissecting her appearance like a science project and pushed a loose curl behind her ear. "Honey, did you hear me?"

"Oh, um, yeah." I pointed to the stacked boxes by the door. "That's the last of them, I think. Hard to believe my whole life fit into five boxes, huh?"

"Tell me about it. Though it took me a few more than five. And I have several more to donate to the church. I don't think we need to cart your dad's old clothes with us to Port Michael." Sadness leached the warmth from her voice.

Sharp pain sliced through me, and I swallowed to keep from crying out. "No. I guess not. Except maybe his old sweatshirts. I mean"—I glanced at the faded bulldog on my chest—"I like wearing them. And I'm sure the peanut will want a few... *someday*. When they don't swallow him up completely, that is." Imagining my eleven-year-old brother wearing our father's clothes like dresses triggered an unexpected giggle.

Mom's face lit up for a moment, and she nodded. "You're right. You and Josh should have something of your dad's. I'll drag the boxes with us, and we'll dig through them later. We can always donate some to the local church when we get there, right?"

"Sure. I'll bet they'd like that." Not that I had a clue what the churches in Port Michael, Maine, would or wouldn't like. I'd supposedly spent summers there when I was a toddler, but other than a few fleeting images of chipped croquet mallets and bloodred roses climbing a white trellis, I didn't remember a thing, not even the little shop on the square where Mom swore I had my first banana split—and where Jackie Kennedy supposedly bought ice cream cones for her kids when they were little. I remembered the story well enough—Mom had told it at least three times since she'd decided to pick up and move—but if I'd ever been there, that memory was as lost as Miley's innocence.

"Okay, good. The movers should be finished packing up the truck within the hour, and then I need to drop the keys off at the real estate office." Mom stared past me out the window and pushed another loose lock of hair out of her face. "After that, we'll hit the road. We have a long drive ahead of us, and I'd like to get there before dark." She studied me for a long moment, as if trying to see my future or something. She still worried that I'd regret my decision to give up my dreams and follow them to Maine. She never asked the question, but I saw it in her eyes every day.

I meant to ask her if I could help with anything, like scrubbing the bathrooms or vacuuming the cobwebs from the corners of the kitchen. The words were right there on the tip of my tongue. At the very least, I should have asked if my brother had packed up his crap or if he needed a hand. Instead, I watched as she turned and disappeared down the hallway then sat in my barren room, picking at the twisted strands of purple shag carpeting as if they were blades of grass in a field. I let my mind wander, running through eighteen years of milestones as I tried to commit every single detail—every whiff of nail polish, every bedtime story, every creaking floorboard—to memory.

As promised, the movers came to take my boxes sometime in the next hour. I didn't speak a word, just grabbed my pink duffel and left, scooping my phone and charger from the floor on the way out.

"I call shotgun." Josh bolted through the house and out the front door after my mother, a bright-blue backpack slung over his shoulders. "Can we stop at McDonald's?" He threw his bag into the back of Mom's new cherry-red Durango then ran around and climbed into the front passenger seat.

Mom loaded the last of her bags, glancing at him then at me before huffing out a breath and closing the hatch. "No."

With the front seat taken, I climbed in behind Josh and shoved my stuff to the floorboards beside my feet. Having the backseat to myself was hardly a sacrifice on a road trip.

"Burger King?" My brother bounced, making the entire car

rock from side to side. With each jump, the brim of his baseball hat crested the top of the headrest.

With an exasperated sigh, Mom climbed behind the wheel. "No." She turned the key, cranking the SUV to life.

"Wendy's?" With another bounce, his hat taunted me from the front seat, and I reached out, timing my movements to his bopping head.

Mom blew out a breath as I swiped for the cap, missing it entirely. "I told you, no fast food."

"But *why*?" My brother flopped back into his seat, putting my goal completely out of reach. "You won't let us eat anything good anymore." He continued to whine as Mom backed out of the driveway.

"Because I'd like to see you reach adulthood." Mom's voice wavered, and she shot me a pained glance in the rear view mirror. Moments like that were why I'd made the sacrifice. Even if she'd never say so, I knew she needed me.

Josh tossed his ball cap up and caught it, repeating the action a second time. "It's because of that stupid documentary, *Super Size Me*, isn't it?"

When the hat hit the air for a third time, I leaned forward, reaching out my hand to snatch it as it came down again.

"Hey! Give that back." My brother whirled around, grasping wildly for his hat, his fast-food fixation forgotten for now.

Mom mouthed, "Thank you," in the mirror, and I gave her a quick nod as I surrendered the Orioles cap to Josh. Ever since Dad had died of a heart attack at forty-two, Mom had become obsessed with healthy living. No more fried or processed foods and no sugary drinks. I hated it as much as Josh, but I got where she was coming from. She and my dad had been soul mates, and now he was gone. And because of that, we were leaving the only home I'd ever known. Without Dad, it was just a place, an empty shell, stripped bare of even the memories at this point.

I twisted around as far as I could without unbuckling and watched out the back window until we turned off Gallows Road, and the house disappeared from view. My eyes burned with tears, but I refused to let them fall. I'd cried every day since the funeral, but I didn't think I had anything left.

"Hey..." My brother stopped bouncing and turned a serious face toward Mom. "You are going to feed us, though, right?"

She reached across the console to ruffle his floppy dark hair. "Of course I'm going to feed you, Joshy."

"Okay." He turned around to smirk at me like some miniature supervillain. "But *I* get to pick the place."

We hadn't driven more than five blocks before the skies opened up, pelting rain down on us like tears, as if Annandale knew we would never be coming back, and it missed us already.

Other than a quick stop for food and fuel and a few more for bathroom breaks for the bladder challenged, we drove straight through. Even with lighter-than-usual traffic, close to nine hours of Twenty Questions and I Spy nearly pushed me over the edge. By the time the sun had melted into the horizon with a sizzle, leaving an orange glow across the sky, we'd reached Port Michael.

I didn't want to like it. In fact, I wanted to hate the quaint little harbor town. It had no business being so idyllic when Dad was gone. Life was utterly and completely unfair, yet I caught myself smiling as Mom wove the SUV through the narrow streets past rows of Colonial houses and cobbled walkways.

We pulled up to a battered gray three-story shingle house. I could almost taste the salt water that had been eating away at the siding for over a century. Overgrown rose bushes crawled across the front porch, and green and brown vines climbed up the side, devouring entire sections of the house. In the glow of evening, one of the two upper windows appeared to wink at us like a giant jack-o'-lantern.

"This is it?" I leaned out the window to stare at the ancient monstrosity from the safety of my seat. A curtain of vines hung in front of the porch. "It looks deserted."

Mom shut off the engine and climbed out of the Durango. "Nobody's lived here since... before your grandmother died."

"Well, that's a glowing endorsement of the place," I muttered under my breath, unbuckling my seatbelt but staying put, taking it all in.

"Can we go inside?" Josh hopped out and ran up the walk to the front porch.

"Hey, be careful." Mom fumbled with the keys as she hurried to catch up to Hurricane Josh. "Wait for me!"

The glint of sunlight reflecting off the third-story windows drew my attention again. Mom said no one had lived there for over a decade, and yet, it felt as if the house was watching me.

"Are you coming?" Mom called from the front porch. "You'd better stake your claim on a room before your brother does. He's still fascinated with the pocket doors between the living and dining rooms, but we both know it won't be long before he realizes the third-floor bedroom has its own bathroom."

I climbed out of the car and stood in a patch of weeds alongside the driveway. "Really? It does?"

"Yep. Even has a claw-foot tub. That's where your dad and I stayed when you kids were little."

"Oh." My shoulders deflated a little. It would have been nice to have my own bathroom, but of course, Mom would want that room.

She tilted her head and watched me from the front steps with a glint in her eye. "It's yours if you want it."

"What?" Shock held me in place as she made her way back to where I stood. "You don't want it?"

"Too many memories." Grief rolled off her in waves, soaking me with her pain. "Oh, don't look so sad. They're all good memories, but I think, maybe that makes it worse, somehow. Besides"—she flung an arm over my shoulder—"you're starting college in a few weeks. You should at least *feel* as if you have a place of your own."

"Thank you." I gave her a quick hug, fighting back tears. I understood all too well how good memories could be worse than the bad ones. Those were the ones worth grieving for. My attention drifted back to the third-story window as I imagined all the memories trapped within the walls.

I peeled back the draping vines and stared at an old porch swing. White paint flaked off old boards. *Would it hold me?* I didn't weigh *that* much. Deciding against it, I gave the wooden seat a shove with my foot and listened to the rhythmic creaking as I followed Mom inside.

I did a quick scan of the cracked plaster walls and the wavy window glass. Thick black skid marks stained the red brick fireplace surround and the chipped mantle. My footsteps kicked up miniature dust clouds, and I almost hacked up a lung breathing them in. The place reeked of mildew and old people and reminded me of an old black-and-white horror movie. "You call this renovated?"

"It *was* renovated." Mom flipped a switch, lighting a grungy crystal chandelier and bathing the shadows in a warm glow.

I spun around to take in my surroundings. I knew it was my grandmother's summer house, so I wasn't surprised the place came completely furnished. But white sheets draped the furniture like the ghosts of summers past, and several layers of dust coated every surface. I wondered if we could figure out how long the house had been vacant by counting the layers— like carbon-dating dinosaurs or something. "When? In the last century. Or the one before that? How old is this place, anyway?"

"Over a hundred years old. Maybe two." Mom eased back a sheet to reveal a gray linen sofa with rolled arms and plump cushions. "I remember work being done years ago, but that was probably before you were born. And when Grandma got sick back in 2002..." That devastated look washed over Mom's face again. "Well, I can't say if anyone bothered to air out the house after that. Your grandmother was the glue that held the family together."

I understood glue. Dad had been our glue, and his loss had the three of us clinging to each other to keep from breaking apart.

The sound of thundering feet from above shook the house just before Josh came barreling down the stairs. He charged through the glittering dust motes hanging in the waning rays of daylight, scattering them to the air. "I call the third floor!"

I had no idea how he'd made it up there without us seeing him. "Too late, peanut. Mom already said I could have it."

"No fair! I got there first. I already wrote my name in the dust!"

I bit back a laugh.

"Sorry, Josh. I guess you'll have to share the second floor with me." Mom caught Josh at the bottom of the stairs and wrapped her arms around his middle. She pretended to eat the side of his face as she towed him toward the car to get his bags, leaving me to explore on my own.

I ran my finger through the thick layer of dust on the mahogany handrail as I made my way up the stairs. Some long-lost memory must have come dislodged because my feet knew exactly where to take me, and before I realized it, I stood in a doorway, staring at my new bedroom. Or maybe suite would be a better description.

I didn't blame Josh for wanting dibs on this room. For an attic space, it was pretty amazing. Polished wood floors. An antique iron bed with what looked like handmade quilts and feather pillows. A glossy dark wood dresser and mirror. And the cherry on my bedroom sundae—a carved marble fireplace. *I could get used to this.*

Josh must have already uncovered the furniture because a pile of white sheets lay in the corner, and I couldn't find even a sprinkling of dust anywhere but the floor, where Josh had scrawled his name in giant block letters—*JOSHUA DAVID FLYNN, MASTER OF THE UNIVERSE.*

The little idiot.

After swiping my sneaker through the message, I wandered through the space to find the bathroom. White marble subway tile covered the room from floor to ceiling. The glossy claw-foot tub took up one side of the room, and the dainty pedestal sink and toilet shared the other. There was even an ornate silver mirror over the vanity. It couldn't have been more perfect.

With one last lingering gaze at the tub, I left the bathroom and continued my exploration.

Behind the bedroom door was another, smaller door that led to a tiny yet hugely creepy unfinished attic space running the length of the dormer. It was more like a long, narrow closet with a low, slanted ceiling, filled from end to end with dusty furniture and a few old trunks. I squeezed into the little room and peeked into the closest trunk.

Clothes. I ran my fingers over the cool, slippery skirt of a vintage floral dress. It looked like something straight out of *Downton Abbey*. Mom had forced me to sit through the first two seasons on Netflix, but I'd refused to admit I actually liked it. I closed the trunk and backed out of the closet, wondering how much I could get for the old clothes on eBay. Hopefully, enough for a down payment on a car.

As the exhaustion from the day finally caught up to me, I sank into the downy mattress as if falling into a cloud.

Oh, yes. I could definitely *get used to this.*

Loud honking wrenched me from my own personal utopia, and I shuffled to the dirty window to peek out. The sun had slipped below the horizon, and the streetlights were coming on, but the two men and their truck had pulled into the driveway and were already unloading our stuff. "Impressive."

I used the sleeve of my sweatshirt to wipe away some of the thick grime coating the window. That's when I noticed the guy leaning against the lamppost across the street. He couldn't have been much older than me—dressed all in black, from his leather jacket to his Doc Martens, with artfully disheveled dark, wavy hair and a sexy crooked smile.

A warm prickle started at the base of my skull and worked its way down my spine. I cupped my hands against the glass to peer down at him. It had to have been too dark in my room for him to see me, but I could have sworn his eyes locked with mine. I almost wanted to wait for the sun to come up to see if he'd catch fire... or sparkle. The guy was *that* hot.

"What are you doing in my room?"

I squealed and spun around to face the wrath of my brother. His blue eyes narrowed—the same sapphire-blue eyes as Dad's—

and his stick arms crossed angrily over his loose-fitting Orioles jersey, the signed Cal Ripken jersey Dad gave him, if I wasn't mistaken. The thing hung on him like a tarp, but he rarely took it off these days. If he hadn't scared the life out of me, I would have found his fury hilarious. "Sorry, peanut. Mom said I could have it."

"Josh… stop bothering your sister, and come get your boxes." Mom's voice carried up the three flights of stairs.

"I *will* get my revenge." With one last death glare in my direction, he spun on his heels, grumbling to himself as he stomped out of my room and down the stairs.

As soon as I was sure he wasn't coming back, I whirled to the window and the mysterious guy below.

But he was gone.

CHAPTER TWO

AFTER TOSSING AND TURNING THE entire night—images of the lamppost guy running through my head like an animated GIF—I finally fell asleep sometime before dawn. So when Josh's gangly body crawled across my bed like a daddy longlegs spider just a few hours later, I was in no mood for his antics.

"Wake up! Wake up! Wake up!" He punctuated each command with a bounce, making the bed groan.

I let out a groan of my own and swatted him like a mosquito. "Go. Away."

"It's almost nine." He leaned in until I could smell the peppermint toothpaste on his breath. "Mom said get up."

I shoved him hard with my foot, knocking him off the bed mid-bounce.

He landed with a thud. "God! You're such a *bitch*, Ava."

Mom poked her head in the door as I was about to let him have it, saving me the trouble. "Josh, what have I told you about the swearing?"

He sighed and recited the mantra Mom had drilled into him. "No more video games if I don't knock it off."

"Exactly. Now run downstairs and get ready. We're leaving in ten." She ruffled his hair as he bolted out the door as quickly as he'd come in. "Ava, you need to get up so we can head into town and get a few things. I figured you'd want to get your room set up sooner than later."

The idea had merit. But so did more sleep. I pulled the quilt

15

over my head to block out the light streaming in through the clean patch on the window. "Can't we do that tomorrow?"

Mom pulled back the blanket. "Nope. Tomorrow already has a schedule. And you, young lady, are messing with today's. I'll give you eight minutes."

"Eight?" I sat up and rubbed my eyes, wondering if parents took classes on torture methods. "You told Josh ten."

"Yes, and you've already wasted two." She gave me a smile that reminded me of the old Mom, the one from before Dad died.

"Fine, whatever. I'm coming." I pretended to be annoyed as I dragged myself out of the bed, but it was a pathetic attempt. Mom was smiling, and that was worth giving up sleep for.

Thanks to my bout of insomnia, I'd already unpacked my boxes, so it didn't take me long to find a clean pair of jeans and black shirt—my favorite vintage concert tee, my first concert tee, as a matter of fact. Dad had bought it for me just after my thirteenth birthday. Amazingly, it still fit, though a little differently than it used to before the boob fairy came calling.

After wriggling into the jeans and pulling on my top, I grabbed my hair to twist it into a messy ponytail.

What if I run into him *today?*

I caught my reflection in the large mirror leaning against the wall and shook out my hair until amber-colored waves tumbled over my shoulders and down my back, framing the giant red lips and juicy tongue of the Rolling Stones logo stretched across my chest. I gave myself two thumbs up.

As I was about to turn and walk out the door, a prickling at the base of my neck led me toward the window again. I had to see if he was out there. I didn't know why I thought he would be. Last night might have been a fluke. The guy was probably grabbing a cigarette on the sly or something. Maybe my rubbing a clean patch in the filthy glass had caught his eye. Whatever reason he had for staring up at my window could most likely be chalked up to a random coincidence. Nothing more.

I tried to sneak a peek without being seen—in case he *was* stalking me from below. But as I suspected, he wasn't there.

The street was quiet except for a girl jogging in a bright pink tracksuit and a man walking his Pomeranian. No uncommonly sexy guy dressed in black leather leaned against the lamppost waiting for me to show my face.

Disappointing.

With one last, lingering look at the vacant street below, I tore myself away from the window. I knew Mom wasn't kidding when she said eight minutes. Joanie Flynn was ruthless when her schedules were screwed with. I grabbed my phone from the charger and hurried out of my room. The prickling sensation—though not as pronounced—still buzzed at the back of my neck, and I tried telling myself it was only nervous excitement, some sort of weird crush brought on by the move or something. Nothing more.

I might have almost believed it.

"There she is!" Mom's overly dramatic tone made me giggle as I walked into the kitchen. She had a hand pressed to her chest as if my sudden appearance had knocked the wind out of her.

"Yeah, yeah. Here I am, ready to do battle with whatever tasks you've laid out for me today." I leaned against the white marble counter and hopped up, scooting my butt back as I shot her a mock scowl. "Our first day in a new place, I might add. Really, Mom, even soldiers get a damn day of rest before shipping out to war." Not that I knew much about going to war, but I had a feeling I was about to be put to work unpacking kitchen crap. Apparently, she hadn't been as wired as me last night because it didn't appear as if she'd unpacked a single box.

"War?" She rolled her eyes and waved me down from the counter as if she were afraid my hundred and fifteen pounds would crack the ancient stone. "I'd planned on something more along the lines of shopping. This house may have been completely furnished when we got here, but it's sorely lacking in the personality department. It could use a little brightening up, don't you think? And I don't know about you, but I'm starving, and there isn't a stitch of food in the fridge."

Josh thrust his fist into the air with a battle cry of "Food!"

"Well said." Mom laughed then rubbed her hands together as if she were about to impart her evil plot. "So we'll hit the cafe for breakfast, then the hardware store for a few gallons of paint and"—she swiped her finger through the dust on the island—"cleaning supplies. Then we'll grab some groceries before we come back here and turn this old house into a home."

A home. Sleep or no sleep, my day was looking up.

"What about this?" Mom held up a paint chip and gave me a hopeful smile.

I'd never been the typical moody teenager, but if she showed me another bubblegum-pink swatch, I'd go thermonuclear. "How many times do I have to tell you? I *hate* pink."

Mom puffed out her bottom lip in a glorious display of the parental guilt trip. "You used to *love* pink."

I let out a loud sigh. "Not since I hit puberty." Around the age of thirteen, I'd moved on to more sophisticated color schemes. Coincidentally, it was around the same time Dad introduced me to classic rock.

She turned the card around and frowned at it. "But this isn't *really* pink. It's more of a salmon."

I balled up my fists, trying to tamp down an unexpected burst of frustration. "Semantics, Mom. Can we please move to the blues? Or the greens?" Or black. Why couldn't I just paint my room black? *Paint it black?* I choked back a giggle. Mick would've been so proud. "Maybe a nice velvety—"

Her eyebrows went up at the same time as her hands found her hips.

Uh oh, this can't be good.

"Ava Flynn, I know what you're thinking, and you are *not* painting the attic *black*. That's just..." She threw her hands into the air. "I don't even know what that is."

"Cool? Modern? In keeping with my dark teenage moods brought on by fluctuating hormones and a deep-seated need to stand out from the crowd? In case you hadn't heard, I'm *supposed* to rebel against society—specifically my parents. I've managed to make it eighteen years with barely an outburst. You should be proud that I'm finally taking a stand." I pulled myself to my full height and gave her a triumphant grin. Let her push pink on me after *that*.

She didn't look proud. But she did look like she might want to laugh. "The answer is still no."

My shoulders deflated. "Come on. When will I *ever* get the chance to paint my room black again?"

She folded her arms in that judgy way she had when she knew she was winning the argument. "When you buy your *own* house, maybe?"

It was a losing battle, but I wasn't a quitter. "I know! How about red? Red would be pretty awesome too."

She turned her back to me and started picking through the blues. "I'm not turning my mother's house into a brothel. Here." She turned and shoved a stack of beachy colors into my hand. "We live in a harbor town. Let's stick with something a little more... *quaint*."

I had no idea what colors constituted quaint.

"Fine." I shuffled thought the stack like a deck of cards and pulled out a serene robin's egg blue. "How about this?" I hadn't really expected to get away with the Goth look. And honestly, I didn't know why I'd even tried. Not that I was going soft or anything, but I wasn't Goth, and I actually *liked* blue. I could pretend to be a rebel all I wanted, but my impeccable GPA ratted me out every time. My problem had nothing to do with paint selection and everything to do with one stupid boy and his stupid black-leather goodness. I hadn't even painted yet, and I was certain the fumes had affected my brain.

"Perfect." Mom flashed a haggard smile. "Now let's have them mix the color and find your brother before he breaks something."

I spun around, laughing, but almost choked on my own tongue when I caught a glimpse of a familiar leather jacket turning down the next aisle. I shoved the paint chip into Mom's hand and started toward where I'd seen him. "Um, how about you go get this, and *I'll* look for Josh?"

She looked perplexed but didn't argue. "Okay, that's fine, but don't—"

I didn't hear a single word she said after that because I was halfway down the next aisle, searching for Mr. Tall, Dark, and Dangerous. My flip-flops slapped against the concrete floor as I sprinted from row to row like some kind of crazy rock star groupie—exactly the sort of girl I'd always vowed *not* to be. I didn't even know for sure if it was him. Black leather jackets weren't exactly rare, even in Maine. But a certain prickling down my spine told me I was right. It just *had* to be Lamppost Guy.

The air shifted, and something moved behind me. I spun around in time to see a flash of black go around the corner, followed by a dark chuckle, the sound of which did something delicious to my body. Whoever this guy was, I would have been lying if I'd said I didn't thoroughly enjoy the effect he had on me.

As if playing a fast-paced game of monkey in the middle, I whipped to the left to dash around the opposite corner and ran headfirst into a blonde in a bright-pink tracksuit: the same girl I'd seen jogging past my house earlier.

"Oh my God, I'm sorry!" I jumped back, craning my neck to see if the object of my obsession had doubled back the other way. Damn it! I was going to lose him.

"Looking for something?"

I whirled back around to find the girl I'd nearly plowed over grinning at me—not in a bitchy, *Mean Girls* way, but in a genuine, friendly sort of way. Totally not what I would have expected from someone so... *pink*.

"I, um, was trying to catch up to—you didn't happen to see— ugh, never mind." I shook my head to clear it then tried to come up with something that didn't make me sound all kinds of crazy. But since nothing would come, I went with a loose version of the truth. "I'm trying to find my little brother."

"Oh!" The perky blonde scrunched up her perfectly arched brows and darted her eyes around the lower shelves. "What's he look like? I could help you. Is he like a toddler or something? Should we call the police?"

"No, he's eleven, so basically just your typical pain in the ass. But if I don't find him before he breaks something, my mom will kill me."

She laughed. "Gotcha. I have a twelve-year-old sister, so I totally get what you're saying. I'll bet your brother found the fish tanks in the back. Just make sure he doesn't try to talk you into buying him a turtle. Those things get huge." She grabbed my wrist and towed me behind her. "Come on, I'll show you." She looked like some sort of superhero weaving through the aisles in her Pepto-Bismol-pink outfit, blond ponytail swinging behind her like a tail, with me tagging along right behind her like the boring sidekick. "I'm Samantha Stone, by the way. My friends call me Sam."

"Oh, hey. I'm Ava. Flynn. Ava Flynn." I smacked my forehead to jar my brain back to where it belonged. Why did I have to be such a spaz?

"I've never seen you before. Tourist?"

I tripped on the toe of my flip-flop and had to grab onto her arm to keep from falling. "Uh, no. Just moved here yesterday. I'm starting at U-Maine next week."

She skidded to an abrupt stop, and I slammed into her again.

"Crap, sorry!" I jumped back with a nervous giggle. "I keep doing that."

As if she didn't even notice I'd almost tackled her in the hardware store for a second time, she smiled. "Port Michael campus?"

"Yep!" I went for an excited expression, but I think I floundered somewhere around confused.

She squeaked out a little gasp then pulled me in for a perfumed hug. "Oh my God! Me too! So you just *have* to come to the end-of-summer party Labor Day weekend at the lighthouse." Without taking a breath, she grabbed my wrist again, towing me to where I hoped we'd find the fish tanks and my brother. "Love your style, by the way. The Rolling Stones are the best. I mean, they're old enough to be my great-grandparents, but what the hell. Mick can still rock it out, right?"

My mouth dropped open, and I imagined I looked a lot like my T-shirt. Maybe I'd have to rethink my aversion to pink.

———◆———

Evening shadows angled across my new blue walls as the sun slipped lower into the horizon. I tossed the spent paint roller into the empty tray and flopped onto my bed. As much as I hated to say it, Mom was right. I loved the freaking color. It went perfectly with the antique furniture and patchwork quilt my grandmother had left behind. And it felt like a fresh start. No more sadness. No more painful memories. Not that I wanted to forget Dad, but like Mom said, sometimes those good memories hurt worse than the bad ones.

My phone buzzed with an incoming text, and I rolled over to snatch it off the nightstand.

Sam: You're still on for the lighthouse party, right? I already told Paige and Hannah. They're stoked to meet you.

I fell back against the mattress and laughed. Even in text, she talked a mile a minute.

Ava: Yes. I said I'd go. Sounds like fun.

Sam: Sweet! Can't wait!

I contemplated asking her about Lamppost Guy. She'd jogged past the house, so she must live nearby. And she seemed to know all the locals. Surely, she'd remember seeing a hot guy in a leather jacket.

I started typing out the words but stopped before hitting send. What if she not only knew him but liked him? As in *liked him* liked him. What if he was her boyfriend? My stomach plummeted. Sam *was* in the hardware store at the same time he was. If that was even him. I never did find him after we dragged Josh out of the fish aisle. But did I dare risk the only possible friendship I had in this town by staking a claim on her guy?

Crap. Being responsible was hard work.

I decided on a fairly neutral question to feel her out first.

Ava: Any cute guys in this town? She couldn't possibly get the wrong idea with that.

Sam: If you like crabs. And I mean that exactly the way it sounded.

Eww. Either she didn't know him, or he was a walking roach motel. I told myself she didn't know him. As much as it pained me to admit it, even crabs wouldn't keep me away from someone that delicious.

"Hey." Mom poked her head in my room. "Wow, the color looks amazing. You like it?"

I nodded, rocking forward until I sat cross-legged in the middle of my bed.

"I got the kitchen put together and even made dinner. You hungry?"

My stomach took that opportunity to rumble loud enough for her to hear it.

"I'll take that as a yes." She grabbed my hand and yanked me to my feet with a laugh. "Well, come on. I figured in honor of our new home, I'd cook something with a little local flavor."

"Cool." I followed her out of my room and down the stairs. "Whatever it is, it smells delicious."

Mom beamed. "I think you'll like it. I got the recipe from *Coastal Living.*"

I sat at the table beside Josh and waited while Mom plated our food—something so ordinary yet oddly profound after everything we'd been through.

"Okay, kids. Dig in!" Mom served us before sitting at the end of the table with her own plate.

"Is this what I think it is?" I picked up a tortilla chip and lifted it to my lips.

Mom flashed a wide smile. "Mmhmm. Shrimp and crab nachos."

Crabs. Perfect.

CHAPTER THREE

I STARED AT MY ANXIOUS REFLECTION, giving myself a pep talk. "This is a terrible idea. A seriously horrible idea." Okay, so maybe not as much of a pep talk as an intervention. I did *not* want to go to the party at the lighthouse.

And yet I did.

In the week since I'd met Sam in the plumbing aisle at the local Ace Hardware, I'd seen the lamppost guy exactly once. And that had only been a fleeting glimpse. I'd spied him out the window a few nights ago as I stepped out of the bathroom wrapped in nothing but a holey Mickey Mouse bath towel. It would have been as awkward as hell had I not been convinced I'd imagined it. Not that he would have been able to see all that much all the way up on the third floor, but still.

The longer I went without seeing him, the more I was able to convince myself the attraction was irrational. But in the back of my mind, he lingered like a headache brewing below the surface.

Sam and I texted daily, and I tried to bring up the topic of sexy mystery guy with her a few times, but the girl was either a master of subterfuge, or she had no idea what I was talking about. The sad thing was I didn't know which option bothered me more. And now, the stupid end-of-summer bash hung over me like a damn icicle, waiting to drop through my skull. I could think of only two possible outcomes. At best, I'd finally catch up with the guy in the black leather jacket, or at worst, I'd be stuck with a bunch of people I didn't know with no way to get home, since I'd agreed to let Sam drive me.

Sometimes, I worried about my so-called superior intellect.

"Ava! Your friend's here." Mom's voice carried up the stairs, making the hair on the back of my neck stand on end, and not for a good reason.

I glanced at the clock as I yanked off the Led Zeppelin T-shirt and pulled on the black tee with KISS printed across the front in big white letters. Quarter to six. She was early. "Okay! Be right down," I shouted back before changing my mind again and pulling off the KISS shirt to dig through my drawers for something else. *When did I become such a girl?*

"Hey, I liked that one." Sam stood in my doorway with an unapologetic smile on her flawless face. She didn't seem the least bit fazed that she'd caught me in nothing but jeans and a bra. "Your mom told me to come on up. I hope that's okay."

Was it okay? I debated the question for a minute before deciding I could use another girl's opinion. "Yeah, it's fine. Maybe you could help me decide what to wear."

Sam twirled a lock of her pale blond hair around her finger as she checked out my room from her spot by the door. She'd traded her usual uniform of head-to-toe pink for a pair of distressed jeans and a white thermal undershirt over a black bra. Once she seemed to have soaked up all the scenery, she pushed away from the door with what I'd come to realize was her signature smile—not a trace of snark to be found. "Sure. What are we looking at?"

Without saying a word, I stepped back so she could get to my dresser.

She picked through my concert tees before switching to the next pile. "Well, first of all, once the sun goes down, it'll get pretty cold, even with the bonfire. So whatever you decide on, remember to bring a sweatshirt or something for later."

I nodded.

"Oh hey, how about this?" She pulled out a black Audrey Hepburn T-shirt and held it up to me. It was one of my favorites with an image taken from *Breakfast at Tiffany's*. She bit her lip as if contemplating something. "Do you have something you can wear under it? A long-sleeve T-shirt or thermal like mine?"

An idea clicked in my head, and I nudged her aside to pull open the bottom drawer. I pawed through the stack of sweaters until my fingers glanced across the long off-white skinny tee. "What about this?" I'd never worn the shirt before, but I knew the lightweight fabric would cling like a second skin. "It's kinda long. If it was warm enough, I could almost wear it as a dress."

Sam let out a squeal. "Yes! Now do you have a pair of dark skinny jeans or leggings?"

Without saying a word, I scooted past her to the armoire and pulled things out until I found a pair of black Rag & Bone jeans. I held them up for inspection.

"Perfect! Oh my God, you're gonna look so hot. Hannah and Paige will *die* with envy." She emphasized each word as if she was itching for a funeral. "Okay, now hurry up and get dressed, we need to get our party on."

I giggled at her blissed-out expression. "You're crazy. You know that?"

"Yeah, I've heard that a time or two before." She wandered over to the window and stared down at the street below.

A twinge of jealousy clenched my insides at the thought of her seeing *my* lamppost guy, and I quickly pulled on the tight jeans before layering the snug tees. It wasn't as if I had a claim on him. And yet in a weird way, part of me felt as if I did, as if Sam's presence at my window had interrupted some imaginary intimate moment or something. I forced myself to sound disinterested. "Anyone down there?"

She cupped her hands against the glass and pressed her face between them. "Nope. It's as quiet as a cemetery down there." She turned back to me. "You ready?"

"As ready as I'll ever be."

◆

After swinging by to pick up Sam's friends, I had to listen to the teal-blue-haired Hannah bitch about me riding shotgun when I hadn't paid enough "dues" yet for that position. Then the ice princess Paige, with her long, silky black mane and perfectly arched bitch brow, lit up a cigarette in the backseat, accidentally-on-purpose singeing the ends of my hair.

Even after Sam cranked up AC/DC and the four of us sped up the coast toward the lighthouse in a bright-yellow Mini Cooper convertible with the top down, singing about shaking all night long, I had my doubts about those two.

Talking was impossible with the music turned up so loud, so pumping them for information was a no go. The whole way there, I stared out the open window, daydreaming about the stupid guy in the stupid leather jacket and hoping like crazy he would show up. There was something seriously wrong with me.

After several ear-bleeding performances of "You Shook Me All Night Long," we pulled into the park adjacent to the lighthouse. While everyone else climbed out of the car, I sat mesmerized, staring at the towering structure jutting along the craggy coastline overlooking Casco Bay.

I finally unbuckled and climbed out, caught up by the way the last rays of daylight broke through low-hanging clouds and danced off the ocean, making the whole scene feel like a moving painting. The relentless roar of waves crashing against the rocks, along with the siren call of the foghorn, had me under a spell. It was a sensory overload. Even from a hundred yards away, I felt the cool ocean spray coating my skin in a fine mist, the salty residue resting on the tip of my tongue like a secret.

"Will somebody help me carry this stuff?" Sam's sugary-sweet voice drew my attention back to the car. Baskets of food and drinks filled her trunk, and she stood, hugging a giant watermelon to her chest. "Hey, who am I? I'm carrying a watermelon." She giggled.

"Okay, *Baby*. You carry the stupid fruit, and we'll get the rest." Hannah rolled her kohl-rimmed eyes before grabbing the smallest of the baskets and a six-pack of Strawberry Fanta.

Paige threw me a shitty smirk as she tossed a couple of plaid wool blankets over her shoulder, leaving the huge wicker basket for me. The jury was officially in. I didn't know how or when, but the bitch was going down.

I stumbled over loose gravel, trying to keep up with them as we trekked from the car to the picnic area and half-moon beach. The Maine shoreline was nothing like the beaches of Virginia, but maybe that was why it appealed to me so much. I wanted to fall asleep to its sounds every night. "I had no idea Maine had so many lighthouses."

"Oh, yeah. There's tons of them." Sam's tone said she didn't share my fascination. "This is the only one I know of that will let us have a bonfire, though. The end-of-summer bash is some kind of tradition going back to my grandparents' time."

"When I turned in my books before graduation, I overheard Mrs. Davidson talking to Mr. Beck about the party. They were waxing poetic about the supposed significance of transitioning from adolescent to adult or some shit, but let's face it. This party is about getting drunk one last time before we all go off to college. If you can even consider the campus ten minutes from home 'going off to college.' But whatever." Paige rolled her eyes and made air quotes before flipping her inky hair behind her. It didn't take long for me to figure out the beach party was the consolation prize for all the kids *not* going off to college. Most of Sam's friends had either enrolled in the local campus like me or weren't destined for college at all. "Who am I to shoot down a perfect excuse to party?"

"You know it!" Sam shifted the watermelon to one side to give a not-so-high five to Paige. "My mom let it slip once that she lost her virginity here. I have no idea if it was my dad or not, though, and like I'm going to ask *that* question, right?"

"That's gross." Paige shuddered. "I don't even wanna think about my parents having sex with *each other*, let alone anyone else."

"Seriously," Hannah chimed in, crinkling up her nose until her ruby nose ring poked out like the pop-up timer on a Thanksgiving turkey.

I kept my mouth shut. I would've given anything to know my parents locked themselves in their room at night having crazy monkey sex until the sun came up because that would mean my dad hadn't died.

"Well, the point I'm trying to make is that this party is an annual tradition, and we're going to have a freaking blast!" Sam wiggled her hips like a spaz, almost capsizing her giant watermelon in the process.

By the time we reached the party, several people had already set up camp, stacking driftwood to build a fire and creating a wide circle around it using assorted blankets and folding chairs.

"Okay, put our stuff down wherever. Help yourself to the food. Once everyone else gets here, we'll have more than we can possibly eat." Sam glanced at the horizon then checked the time on her phone. "We have less than an hour 'til sundown, and that's when the really good drinks show up. So be sure you eat something." Sam directed her last comment to me, though I had no idea how she knew I was a total lightweight. The topic of liquor had never come up. She spun on her heels and turned back toward the parking lot.

"Where are *you* going?" Paige let her mouth drop open like a great big bitchy fish.

Sam whipped her head around and winked. "I'm going to see a boy about some music."

———◆———

Sam was right. I should have eaten something. But nerves were angry harpies, and mine had my stomach tied up in knots. The only people I actually knew had abandoned me—Sam, to flirt with a Ken-doll lookalike, and Cinderella's evil stepsisters took off to smoke weed behind the lighthouse with the rest of the stoners.

Depressing Nirvana tracks played quietly while I sat alone on the far side of the fire, wishing I'd listened to Sam when she told me to bring a sweatshirt and chain-drinking warm apple ale until I couldn't tell the difference between the crashing of the waves and the rushing in my own ears.

"Hey." A boy with floppy dark hair and a lip ring dropped

down beside me, invading my personal space. He might have been cute if not for the creepy grin and glazed-over eyes. "I don't know you."

"You're observant." I scooted over so his arm wouldn't rub against mine. He reeked of cigarettes and cheap beer.

He leaned in, closing the gap I'd created. He pressed his fat-shaming Abercrombie & Fitch hoodie-clad body against me, and I caught a whiff of weed. "I'd like to fix that."

"But it wasn't broken." I shoved him back where he belonged, channeling a bit of Paige's iciness so maybe he'd get the idea that I wasn't interested in "getting to know him," but he didn't seem to take the hint.

"Aww, come on. I don't bite." He put a hand on my shoulder, making me flinch.

"Well, maybe *I* do." I jumped up, the three bottles of ale I'd already consumed making me unsteady on my feet, and dumped the rest of the fourth one into his lap. "Oops."

"Shit!" He righted the bottle, shooting me a death glare. "You need to chill out. I was just saying hi. It's not like I was trying to rape you or something."

I searched the shore for Sam—even Paige or Hannah would have been welcome at that point—but instead I saw a god in a black leather jacket storming his way through the darkness in my direction. The prickling I hadn't felt in days was back.

He was there. He came.

I grabbed another bottle from the cooler and sucked half of it down in one swallow. I hoped the fresh infusion of alcohol would burn away my inhibitions on its way down my throat. I didn't know what I was so afraid of. I'd done everything short of using a Ouija board to conjure him up. So why did my blood turn to ice the minute he found me? Intense heat flared through my icy veins, reminding me of the time when I was six and I grabbed a pan on the stove. My brain had registered ice cold until I'd realized I was actually burning.

And God help me, but that boy set me on fire.

"You know what?" the floppy-haired intruder asked the back of my head.

I didn't know why he was still talking because I had no interest in hearing what he had to say. My focus had shifted entirely to the tense jaw and angry glare coming from Lamppost Guy as he closed the distance between us.

Lust spread through me like warm butter chased by hot syrup. I couldn't tear my eyes from his, and my feet started moving of their own accord, drawing me closer to where he stood, no longer moving toward me, curving a finger, beckoning me forward.

I froze, a wave of self-consciousness locking me in place as I scanned the disinterested faces around the crackling fire, lost in their own conversations. No one seemed to notice the boy in black leather or the way he fixated on me as if he wanted to devour me in a single bite. In fact, no one appeared to notice him at all, as if he were my own personal mirage, brought on by my soul's dehydration.

My soul's dehydration? Oh my God, I've had way too much to drink. Though, drunk or not, I couldn't shake the notion that I was the only one who could see him.

The little prickle spread down my spine, jolting my nerve endings back to life and propelling me forward until I stood close enough to brush my fingers down his cool leather sleeve. He towered over me as I gazed up into his dark eyes. Swirls of green and gold in a field of honey brown held me captive. "Are you real?"

His lips curved into a sexy smirk. "Do I *feel* real?"

Biting my lip, I gave his arm a little squeeze, and his smirk spread into a full-blown smile.

With a slow, deliberate determination I could've never managed with my heart hammering out its erratic rhythm, he placed his warm palm against my cheek. "I've waited a long time to do this."

I understood him completely. Every second I stood there,

feeling his pulse thrumming through his rough skin, felt like an eternity. I leaned into his touch, purring like a satisfied kitten.

"Ava." My name fell from his lips like a plea, and his long fingers twitched against my cheek.

"How did you know..." I froze and held my breath as his other hand cupped the opposite side of my face, surrounding me in warmth. I couldn't move for fear I'd spoil the moment and burst the fragile bubble we were in. He was touching me. Dear God in Heaven, he was touching me.

He rested his forehead against mine, his hot breath both relaxing me and twisting me into knots. "I need to... May I please...?"

I knew what he wanted. At least I hoped. The desperation to press his lips to mine was palpable. With the waves shattering against the rocky shore and the lonely cry of the lighthouse beacon, I felt as if we were trapped inside some sort of historical romance. And what good was a romance without the requisite kiss in the moonlight?

"Who are you?" My question caught me by surprise. That wasn't at all what I wanted to ask. I wanted to beg him to put me out of my misery and kiss me, but my subconscious needed to know his name so I could call it out at the appropriate time.

The as-of-yet-unnamed boy didn't answer my question, but he did answer my unspoken plea. Soft lips captured mine, their pliable warmth stealing my breath and making my knees buckle.

Just as I was about to slip to the ground, an arm came around my waist, holding me upright while his mouth worked its way into my erratic heart.

As his expert lips drove me to the edge of sanity, he held me captive against his hard chest, one hand pressed against my lower back, and the other cradling my throat as if he needed to feel my pulse beneath his fingers. The night air whipped around us, chilling me from head to toe, but his tender touch seared my icy skin. Hot and cold. Once again, my body didn't seem to know the difference. Part of me wanted to crawl inside his jacket, while the other part wanted to drag him closer to the fire so he wouldn't need clothes at all.

Too soon, he pulled his lips from mine, nuzzling my neck and nipping and sucking the sensitive spot behind my ear.

"Ava." His breath whispered through my hair, sending fresh ripples of want through me until my head swam, making the earth tip on its axis, taking me with it. "Ava, wake up."

My eyes snapped open, and I had to blink a few times to register my surroundings. My head rested on Sam's sneaker-clad feet, my body cocooned within a black-and-red plaid blanket in front of the charred remains of the bonfire. A sliver of sun peeked over the edge of the horizon, casting a warm pink glow across the ocean rising up to meet the sky.

I sat up, still clutching an empty bottle of apple ale like a teddy bear. *Had I dreamt the whole thing?* I'd known it was too good to be true, too perfect to be real. But I wasn't that girl who obsessed over boys until my conscious and subconscious blended seamlessly together. I didn't live in a fantasy world, because if I did, my father would be walking around, breathing. My mother wouldn't cry herself to sleep every night, mourning her soul mate. My brother would have a father to toss baseballs with in the yard.

Hot tears burned a trail down my cheek. I needed to go home. I didn't belong there.

"Holy shit, Ava. I didn't even see you with anyone. How did you end up with that?"

I whipped my head around at the sound of Sam's groggy voice. "What are you talking about?"

"Your neck. Right behind your ear. You have a huge hickey, you big slut." She giggled and gave me a playful shove.

My hand flew up to the spot she pointed to, and I could still feel his lips there.

Maybe it wasn't a dream after all.

CHAPTER FOUR

"**A**VA!"

My eyes snapped open at the sound of his voice echoing inside my head. It had been three days since the party, and I still couldn't shake the feeling of being in his arms, even if it *had* been an alcohol-induced dream.

After waking up in front of the charred remains of Saturday night's bonfire, I found myself faced with a host of questions I had no answers for. For starters, I still had no idea who my mystery guy was or why he wasn't there the next day. Unfortunately, I couldn't find a single other person who'd seen him that night, and the last solid memory I had involved one floppy-haired Abercrombie sycophant putting the moves on me.

And then there was the infamous hickey.

As far as I knew, dreams couldn't leave sucker bites. But no matter how hard I tried to piece the puzzle together, the damn thing still came out distorted. Every scenario I came up with led to the same unfortunate conclusion: I'd dreamed about Lamppost Guy to block out the fact that I'd made out with Abercrombie.

Just imagining Abercrombie's potentially diseased mouth and attached lip ring touching my skin twisted my stomach so hard my toes curled. And the horrifying thought of him giving me a hickey just... well, it grossed me out beyond words. To make things worse, for the next two nights in a row, I'd dreamed about my leather-clad mystery guy and woken up in a cold sweat.

The dream always started out the same, at the lighthouse, with Abercrombie rubbing up against me as if he was about to dry-hump my leg and Lamppost charging toward us in a jealous rage. Clearly, my subconscious knew I'd broken some unspoken commitment I'd made to my fantasy-slash-obsession. But by the time Lamppost reached me, he wasn't dressed in black leather anymore. He was clad in shiny armor and carrying a sword, which he promptly used to slay poor Abercrombie, who'd conveniently morphed into a fire-breathing dragon.

I made a vow right there and then to never drink again.

And to add insult to injury, today was the first day of classes, and I still had the lingering remnants of a hangover. Apparently, apple ale packed one hell of a wallop.

Who knew?

I rolled out of bed and checked the time on my iPhone. Sam was due to arrive in less than an hour, and the girl was never less than fifteen minutes early. I tied up my hair and took a quick shower, letting the hot water rinse away the tension in my muscles.

There was one positive thing to come out of the stupid end-of-summer bash. After having a good long laugh at what happened at the party, Sam felt so guilty for leaving me alone to fend for myself that she offered to drive me to school until I could get a car of my own. I was only too happy to take advantage of her guilty conscience, especially since Mom had started her new job the week before and only had time to drive one of us without the risk of being late. As the oldest, I drew the short stick. Without a ride, I'd be walking the one point six miles to campus every day. Rain or shine, uphill both ways, as my dad liked to say.

A horn sounded outside, and I rushed to the window to see if Sam had broken her own record. Mom's SUV idled in the driveway, and she waved up at me before backing onto the street and driving off. I watched her until the car disappeared from view then turned to finish getting ready.

A scream caught in my throat as something moved past my mirror. The face vanished as quickly as it had appeared, but I still spun around to see if someone stood behind me. It had to have been a trick of the light or my imagination, especially since it looked an awful lot like Lamppost, but I couldn't shake the feeling of being watched.

With a shudder, I tossed my quilt over the mirror before pulling on the long khaki skirt and white tank top I'd set out for the day. I wore my wavy hair down in hopes it would help hide the stupid hickey and prayed that if I ran into Abercrombie, he wouldn't remember me.

"Are you ready?"

That time I did scream, my heart jumping into my throat as I whipped around to see Sam in my doorway. "Oh my God, Sam. You scared the everliving shit out of me!"

She threw her hand over her mouth and giggled. "Sorry. Your mom told me to come on up. You look nice."

"Thanks. Have you been here the whole time?" I took a deep breath, willing my pulse to slow.

"Just a second or two. Why so jumpy?"

I contemplated telling her about the face in the mirror, but then I'd have to explain *why* I thought I saw his face. And who he was. Which would open up a whole new line of questioning. Which would lead to what I *thought* happened at the lighthouse party. Which would just remind her that I'd made out with Abercrombie. And I didn't want to remember that. At. All.

So I lied.

Schooling my features into a false calm, I waved a hand in front of me. "Oh, nothing. I had a nightmare last night. I can't seem to shake it."

She plopped down on my bed. "Don't you hate that? I had a super creepy dream the other night, too. I dreamed Adam Levine streaked the campus quad, but as he ran by, he turned into my grandpa Ray. And don't even ask me why I know what my grandfather looks like naked because trust me, you do *not* wanna know." She rambled on about her Maroon-Five-does-Bad-Grandpa dream all the way to the car, and I welcomed the topic change.

With one last fleeting glance at the lamppost, I slid into the passenger seat and buckled in.

"How about some Kid Rock? We'll say goodbye to summer in style." Sam perched her giant Jackie O sunglasses on the end of her nose and cranked the ignition.

I pulled my own sunglasses out of my purse and slid them on. "I thought we already said goodbye to summer."

"Yeah, well, as far as I'm concerned, until the moment we pull into a parking space on U-Maine property, it's still summer." She pulled onto the street and floored it before making the first left.

"Works for me." I held on for dear life as her tires squealed, then I flashed her a wide smile as she cued up "All Summer Long." We belted out the lyrics all the way to the school parking lot, where we pulled in beside a shiny red Honda.

"You're still here?" Paige stepped out of the driver's seat and arched an eyebrow as her matching red stilettos clacked against the pavement. "I was hoping you'd gone back to Virginia."

"Can't get rid of me that easily," I mumbled, climbing out of Sam's Mini Cooper and smiling at a bored-looking Hannah. "So do you all commute?"

"Duh," Hannah said, as if it was the most obvious answer. "We're townies. We could walk if we wanted. Why would we stay in the dorms?"

"For the full college experience?" A sudden twinge of regret hit me as I thought about everything I'd actually given up by trading Georgetown for the much smaller Port Michael campus.

I'd barely had time to feel sorry for myself when Sam came around the car and shot a glare at Paige before turning to me. "Okay, hand over your schedule."

I fished in my purse for my iPhone.

I'd barely gotten it out of my bag and open to the right screen when Sam snatched the device from my fingers. "Seriously? Intro to Molecular Biology? Intro to Neuroscience? History of European Civilization? Classical Literature? Why take so many tough classes first semester?"

"Oh, hey, I enrolled in that European history class too!" Hannah beamed.

"Monday, Wednesday, Friday at ten?" I asked.

Hannah nodded.

"I had to drop my philosophy class to get into that one." On a campus as small as Port Michael, they didn't schedule more than one of each class per semester.

"So you *were* in Philosophy at ten, but now you're not?" Paige asked.

Despite the urge to ignore her, I pressed out a stiff grin and turned to Paige. "Yep, that's what I said."

"Oh, thank God." Paige flipped her hair for good measure. "That's one less hour I'll have to see your—"

"What?" Sam shrieked as if someone had told her she had to surrender her favorite pink tracksuit, and I could have kissed her for cutting Paige off. "You have a class at one? We all agreed to take lunch at one. I mean, I guess we didn't actually know you then, but you can't have class at one!"

Instinct took over, and I stepped back from her rabid expression. "That's the only time they offer Classical Literature."

"So?" She waved my oh-so-breakable phone in the air. "Drop it. Take it next semester."

I fought to keep my mouth from falling open. "You want me to drop a class so I can have lunch with everyone else?"

"Of course! You'd rather have lunch alone every day? And seriously, what happened to taking all your Gen Ed classes first, like a normal freshman?" Sam handed back my device with a scowl.

I shrugged. "I'm a biology major. I wanted to get the hard stuff out of the way. And History of European Civilization *is* Gen Ed. So is French."

"French?" Sam grabbed my phone again and, after scanning my schedule, did a quick fist pump. "At least we have *one* class together. And lunch. You *will* drop that class."

I opened my mouth to argue with her but snapped it shut. I knew I'd probably do what she said. Sam was my only real friend in Port Michael, and I wasn't about to screw that up over a stupid lit class.

Hannah grinned at Sam. "So besides our mandatory lunch

hour, what classes did *you* sign up for? Music Appreciation? Basket Weaving One-Oh-One? Intro to Hot Guys?"

"No. But if you find Intro to Hot Guys on the registration page, let me know, I'll drop pre-calc and take *that* instead." Sam bumped Hannah with her shoulder, and they both laughed. "Seriously though, I'm taking normal freshman classes. Pre-calc, Intro to Creative Writing, Western Civilizations, Sociology..."

"French," I blurted before she had a chance.

She gave me the side eye before shoving me lightly. "Yes, *French.*"

"So you basically took all the easy shit first." Hannah dodged another of Sam's half-hearted attacks. Someone needed to work on her not-so-passive-aggressive tendencies. "I guess you'll be partying while the rest of us pull all-nighters."

"Hey..." Sam pointed at Hannah. "At least you don't have to get up and run first thing in the morning."

"Run?" I knew Sam liked to run in the evenings, but why anyone would choose to do that before lunch was beyond me.

"I'm on the cross-country team, and apparently, they like to practice in the mornings. Rain or shine. Sleet or snow. How is that even fair? Do you have any idea what that'll do to my hair?" She handed me my schedule, continuing her tirade about the inequity of being forced to sweat so early in the morning as we made our way toward the enormous two-story brick building housing freshman orientation.

The sound of tires squealing on pavement drew my attention to the parking lot behind me. A tall guy in distressed jeans and a gray hoodie jumped out of a black sports car, and I immediately recognized his dark floppy hair.

Abercrombie.

My fingers flew up to pull my own hair over my neck, and I quickly averted my eyes, whirling back to the building. Abercrombie was the last person I wanted to see on my first day of college—or any day, really.

Keeping my head down as if trying to memorize my class schedule, I followed Sam across the quad.

"Is that him?" Sam leaned down to whisper in my ear.

My head snapped up, and I searched the area for a hot guy in a black leather jacket. When I didn't see him anywhere, I turned back to Sam's grin. "Who?"

"The guy." She jerked her head toward the parking lot, where Abercrombie had hauled a petite brunette over his shoulders and was running her around in circles like she was a football or something.

"The guy?" I'd lost my ability to form coherent sentences, so instead I just repeated hers.

"You know..." She motioned toward my neck, keeping her voice down so Paige and Hannah didn't hear her. She'd promised to take my secret to the grave, and although I'd only known her for a few weeks, I had complete faith in her as she mouthed the words. "The hickey."

I turned around again, giving Abercrombie my attention one last time, and swallowed back the contents of my stomach. "Yeah. That's him."

"Oh, my God." She snorted out a laugh. "I can't believe you made out with Aaron Finch. He's such a douchebag." Her voice dropped so low even *I* barely heard her.

I winced and tried to hide my face behind a curtain of hair. "Ack, don't remind me."

"Oh, trust me, I'm never going to let you forget." She let out a loud giggle that time, and Paige spun toward us, giving me a death glare that made my whole body shrink into itself.

It wasn't easy, but I managed to pull my eyes from hers, ignoring the fact that she still stared daggers at me. I counted the windows on the front of the building... watched the other students filing in and out of the double doors... I even paused to read the "Welcome Freshmen" message on the sign.

That's when I saw him in all his glory—sun glinting off his shiny black leather—leaning against the sign. Watching me.

Holy mother of...

I froze in place, unable to do anything but stare. And stare I did—from the toes of his black Doc Martens to the top of his disheveled head—lingering on a few places in the middle. My mouth went dry at the sight of him, as if I'd inhaled an entire bucket of sand. And after stuttering a few times, my heart stopped for a full beat before racing out of control. Then the prickling was back. And with it came the feeling in my extremities.

The sides of his mouth tipped up in a cocky grin.

I took a steadying breath before whipping my head back around to Sam. "Go ahead without me. I'll be right back." I *had* to talk to him, had to know why he'd disappeared on me at the bonfire. Why I couldn't get him out of my head… or my dreams.

"Wait. Why? Where are you going?" Her face scrunched up as if she couldn't believe I'd have anyplace else to be.

And at any other place or time, she would have been right. But right then, at that exact moment, I only had one place to be, and it was wherever he was. I had to know if Saturday—*if our kiss*—had been real.

Keeping my eyes on him the entire time so he couldn't vanish into thin air again, I shoved my schedule back into my purse and took the first step toward him, saying my goodbyes to Sam. "I just need to see something. I won't be gone long. I'll catch up to you in a few."

"But," she called after me, "you're gonna be late for orientation!"

"Save me a seat," I yelled as I sprinted for the bushes framing the Port Michael campus sign.

As I closed the distance between us, his amused expression morphed into all-out delight, and I could almost hear his dark chuckle as he stepped out of my eye line. But there was nowhere for him to go this time. He wasn't going to avoid me again.

"Hey, new girl. Wait up."

A wave of sickness rolled through my stomach at the sound of Abercrombie's voice. "Go away. I thought I made myself clear at the party."

"What? Are you gonna spill another beer on me? I'm guessing you don't have one on you. Or hey, maybe you do. I wouldn't mind one myself. We can slip off to the bleachers and get to know each other better."

His invitation brought me to a screeching halt, and I whirled around, almost gagging at his hopeful expression. "Are you serious? 'Slip off to the bleachers'? What is this, an eighties teen movie? Give it up, Abercrombie. I'm not interested."

He laughed as he took another step toward me. "Aw, come on. I thought you liked me."

Using my hands as a wall between us, I backed away. "No. Just. No."

The hope drained from his eyes. "Fine. Be that way. But it's a long semester, and I'm not going anywhere."

"Gross," I muttered, turning to make a run for the sign.

I was out of breath when I reached the bushes and took a second to catch my breath before stepping around to find him. The static in the air around me crackled, but he was gone.

Again.

———◆———

After setting my tray on the table, I dropped into the hard plastic seat and stared at what the Port Michael campus cafeteria called food. *I paid five bucks for this?* I hadn't even taken a bite, and already, I'd lost my appetite. The cafeteria at my high school had offered a better selection. I expected so much more from a college dining hall. In fact, I'd expected so much more from the campus itself. The whole place probably could've fit within the walls of my high school. So far, all my classes took place in ordinary, block-wall rooms—a far cry from the grand lecture halls of Georgetown. But as I repeatedly reminded myself, the tiny Port Michael campus *wasn't* Georgetown.

I felt guilty as a wave of regret washed over me. "Is the day over yet?"

Sam threw back her head and laughed. "You wish."

"You're damn right I wish. I think I might be cursed." And very possibly losing my mind. "I can't believe you don't remember seeing a hot guy in a black leather jacket in the quad this morning. He was right out in the open." He was right there, and I'd let him slip through my fingers. With my luck, by the time I actually caught up with him, he'd have taken out a restraining order against me.

"Trust me, if I'd seen a hot guy in a leather jacket, I'd remember." She smirked at me. "What I *do* remember seeing is you running across the quad like your hair was on fire to meet up with Aaron freaking Finch."

I groaned and pushed runny creamed spinach around my plate with my fork. "For the last time, I wasn't meeting up with Aber-*Aaron*. I was trying to catch up to the guy in the leather jacket."

"What guy in a leather jacket?" Hannah's tray landed with a clatter across from me. The hippy chick was slowly growing on me.

"Never mind." I let out a loud sigh. "I was obviously hallucinating." *Again.*

Paige dropped down next to Hannah with a shit-eating grin plastered on her face. "So I heard you and Aaron are secretly dating."

"Oh. My. God!" I shouted, and my face flamed as the dining hall went silent and everyone turned to look at me. I waited until the masses had gone back to what they'd been doing before leaning across the table to whisper. "I am *not* secretly dating—or openly dating, for that matter—Aaron Finch. He creeps me out."

"Well, that's not what I heard." Paige picked up her fork and stabbed a piece of lettuce on her plate. "Aaron told the entire hockey team to stay away from his girlfriend, or he'd kick their asses. He's lucky none of them shoved a stick up *his* ass."

"You mean, he's lucky he dominated the state championships the last three years running," Hannah said with a bit of attitude. She blushed and added, "But he's still a dick."

"Could this day possibly get any worse?" I muttered.

"Ava!" Abercrombie shouted my name from across the room. I'd spoken too soon.

"How did he find out my name?" I darted my eyes between the only people in Port Michael who knew who I was.

"I told him."

My mouth fell open as I stared at Paige's unapologetic face.

"Oh, come on, *Ava*. We all saw you running across the quad to see him this morning. And Tory Phelps said she saw the two of you looking all cozy at the lighthouse party, so give it up. Your secret's out." She shoved another bite of salad between her viper lips.

"Hey, gorgeous!" Abercrombie sat in the vacant chair beside me and reached out for my free hand.

I clenched my jaw and spoke through my teeth. "Touch it and die. Do you hear me?"

He must have seen the fire in my eyes because his hand dropped to his side, and he turned to say something to Hannah.

"What the hell am I going to do now?" I whispered to Sam.

She almost choked from laughing so hard, and I couldn't decide if I'd bother giving her the Heimlich if she did. "I guess you'll have to wait for your leather jacket guy to show up and defend your honor."

She thought she was being funny, but that's exactly what I hoped for. Unfortunately, I'd begun to think I really *had* hallucinated him.

CHAPTER FIVE

ANGRY WAVES SHATTERED AGAINST THE *rocky coast as the god in black leather stormed toward me through the darkness. Sea spray soaked through my clothes, leaving me damp and cold, but the way he looked at me made my skin flame. His body vibrated with rage, his eyes flickering between my face and Abercrombie's hand resting on my shoulder as he closed the distance between us.*

With my mystery guy just a handful of yards away, Abercrombie let loose with a baleful cry, his bones cracking and snapping as he shifted from a normal frat boy into a fire-breathing dragon. He towered over me, nearly as tall as the lighthouse in the distance. I opened my mouth to scream, but no sound came out. I tried to wrench myself away from his side, but he wouldn't let go. His claws dug into my shoulder, and I felt the first hot trickle of blood as he broke the skin.

"Please, let me go!" I cried.

The dragon glared down, and his two glittering black eyes told me he wanted to consume me. Devour me. His giant mouth stretched wide, and I tasted the rot and decay on his breath. Before the monster had a chance to take the first bite, Lamppost surged in, his jacket melting away to expose a suit of shiny armor. He shoved me to the ground, and a huge sword sprouted from his outstretched hand. In one fluid motion, he lunged forward, sinking the blade between the dragon's ribs. The earth beneath my feet trembled as the dragon crumpled and fell in a cloud of dust.

After nearly a week of the same dream, my subconscious anticipated each scene before it happened. The dragon would fall, crumbling into dust, and my mystery guy would come to me. My body thrummed with anticipation as I waited for his rough hands to capture my face, for his lips to mold themselves to mine.

But that didn't happen.

Instead, I found myself spiraling down a dark tunnel, an icy wind whipping my hair around me like a cape. I reached into the abyss, my hands grasping for anything to stop my fall but catching nothing but damp air. I couldn't see. I could barely breathe. And it took so long to reach the bottom; I feared I would fall forever.

I landed in a pile of hay with a bounce.

A soft snorting to my left startled me, and I turned to see myself reflected in a single dark eye. But that couldn't be me, could it? The heavy dress weighed me down, making it difficult to move. A dress? And my long honey hair fell loose around my shoulders in thick waves that I would have never had the patience to style.

The dark horse pawed the stable floor, shaking its huge head as it grunted at me, and I scrambled to my feet, pressing my back into the wall to get away from it.

I heard his dark chuckle before he stepped into a sliver of moonlight. This time, he wore skin-tight riding pants and a long, loose shirt as if he were auditioning for a Renaissance faire. "Afraid of a little horse?"

I darted my eyes from his to the huge animal between us. "Th-that's not a little horse."

He laughed again. This time, it was light and happy. "Always such a girl." He stepped around the beast and reached a hand toward me, his eyes flashing with amusement. "Come on, you little coward. I'll protect you."

My hand went to his of its own accord, and my entire body relaxed as his warm palm pressed against mine.

"You're shaking. You were really afraid, weren't you?" He tugged me into his arms and stared down at me. His eyes were dark in the night, and as hard as I tried, I couldn't make out the

color. "Don't you know? I will always protect you. Not even death can keep me from you."

I closed my eyes as he dipped his head down to smash his lips to mine. Unlike all the others, this kiss wasn't gentle. My lungs burned as he continued to steal my breath, his mouth devouring mine as if he'd been starving for the taste of me. He didn't just kiss me. He possessed me.

His body shook as his hands ran over my clothes, heating my skin through the fabric like flames. He made it perfectly clear I was his, and I didn't care to argue. Again, my head swam, the earth tipping on its axis, ready to take me with it. I was mere moments away from losing consciousness. I could feel it.

Abruptly, and as if it pained him to do so, he pulled his mouth away, panting as he rested his forehead against mine. "Ava...wake up."

A scream bubbled up in my throat, but I swallowed it down. "Holy shit. What was that?" I sat up, pulling my arms around my middle and squeezing to hold myself in as I tried to make sense of that dream. I'd lost my mind, or I was heading in that direction. Every night, it was the same dream and now... wow.

Lamppost had a dominant side.

My iPhone chirped with an incoming message, and I scooped it off the nightstand.

Unknown: Ava baby. Why don't you ditch Barbie, and let me drive you today?

Me: Who is this?

Unknown: Duh, your boyfriend.

Ugh, freaking Abercrombie. How the hell did he get my number? The minute the thought manifested itself, I knew the answer. "Paige."

I tapped out another quick text, telling him he'd be my boyfriend as soon as hell put in an ice rink, then stalked off to take a hot bath before school. I'd almost survived my first week of college. I just had to get through one more day, and it would be the weekend.

But that stupid nightmare had me on edge.

I twisted on the taps and poured a cap full of lavender bubble bath under the stream. Before I knew it, bubbles filled the claw-foot tub, and fragrant steam filled the room. Every breath I took dragged me closer to tranquility. I pulled off my pajamas and stepped into the steaming tub, sinking down until my shoulders disappeared under the water. I'd come to the unfortunate conclusion that my mystery guy was probably just a figment of my imagination. But that didn't stop me from clinging to him like Saran Wrap on last night's leftovers.

I knew I shouldn't, but I wanted to see him around every corner. I felt drawn to him in a way I couldn't begin to explain. I rested my head against the edge of the tub and closed my eyes, almost drifting off to sleep.

A faint breeze blew across the water, making my skin pebble. For a second, I thought I heard soft footsteps against the marble floor, but when I opened my eyes, I was alone.

Closing my eyes again, I hummed "Wild Horses" by the Rolling Stones. The memory of the keyed-up horse in my dream replayed in my head. Then I heard it again, the muffled sound of bare feet on marble, and my eyes snapped open. I stood up and grabbed my towel, wrapping it around me as I stepped out of the tub. "Who's there? Mom? Josh? I'm naked in here, so quit screwing around." I poked my head into the bedroom but didn't see anyone. I reached up to wipe the steam off the bathroom mirror and noticed my name scrawled through the fog in elegant script.

My skin prickled as if coated in hot sand from head to toe. I sucked in a breath, and the gritty particles caught in my throat, choking me. This wasn't funny anymore.

❖

Sam paid for her venti iced caramel macchiato—with four heart-attack-inducing shots of espresso—and turned back to me. "Maybe you have a ghost."

I brought my half-caf vanilla latte to my lips to blow on it.

"I don't have a ghost." *More like an overactive imagination and a pain-in-the-ass little brother.*

"Come on, think about it. Your house is ancient. And old houses always seem to have one or two ghosts running around." She took a sip of her drink and moaned out her approval before holding the cup out for me to taste. When I shook my head, she continued. "My Aunt Betty has a ghost. It's always messing with the settings on her toaster, so her toast burns every time."

I held the door open and thought about what she said before following her out. "Ghosts don't care about toast. And it's probably just my little brother. He vowed to take revenge on me for snagging the best bedroom, and I wouldn't put it past him to play a prank like that."

"There's always that possibility. But I'm still going with the ghost theory. How else can you explain the invisible guy you were chasing in the quad Tuesday morning?" She paused, snapping her fingers and sucking in a quick breath. "Oh my God! *That's* why you were running around the hardware store the day I met you. You were looking for him, weren't you?"

My cheeks flamed, and I ducked my head to hide the evidence. "Yes."

She let out a squeal, her body practically vibrating with excitement. "I knew it."

I coughed out a laugh. "You did not."

"Well, I knew it was something. He must be a hot ghost if you tried to hook up with him at the lighthouse." She giggled as she got behind the wheel of her car.

I climbed in, banging my head against my seat and wishing I'd kept my mouth shut. "I never should have told you about that. You're going to think I'm some crazy girl hallucinating hot guys only to make out with assholes."

"Hey, I haven't known you long, but I think I know you well enough to know you wouldn't make out with Aaron Finch, no matter how many drinks you'd had. So obviously, it was the ghost you wanted." She smiled as if that was the most obvious conclusion. "And now, someone's writing in the steam on your mirror? Can your brother even reach that high?"

I shrugged and sipped my coffee.

She nodded. "Definitely a ghost."

Sam parked around the corner from the quad, but instead of dropping me off and leaving, she got out of the car. "No practice this morning?"

"Nah, we don't practice on Fridays. Lucky me."

"What are you two hookers doing here so early?" Paige came up behind Sam and gave me her best bitch brow over Sam's shoulder.

I matched her bitch brow with one of my own. "I have class."

Sam eyed her suspiciously. "I'm heading to the library, but what I'd like to know is what are *you* doing here this early? Shouldn't you be sleeping? Your first class isn't 'til ten."

"Oh..." Paige shrugged. "I volunteered to head up a group project in Philosophy."

Sam laughed. "Okay, who's the guy?"

Paige spread her ruby lips in a wide smile. "How'd you know?"

"Please. As if you'd ever just volunteer for anything. I totally know your game. You used to have your daddy call the principal with an excuse anytime you didn't want to participate in special projects—which was most of the time."

"Ha!" Paige hip-checked her. "I don't even know his name yet, but he's gorgeous, and as soon as I realized which one of the critical thinking groups he was assigned to, I volunteered to take the lead."

"Which group?" I asked.

"Oh, um..." Paige shifted on her heels. "The uh, economic inequality study. At the food bank."

"*You're* going to work at the food bank? For a guy?" Sam bit back a giggle.

I didn't know Paige as well as Sam did, but even I knew Paige wouldn't last a day without her smartphone or her Manolos.

"Go ahead. Laugh. But you didn't see him. He's totally worth it. And the way I see it, I'll have a captive audience for at least the next six weeks. It's up to me to make the first move. And believe me." Paige wiggled her hips. "I'll be making my move this afternoon."

Sam turned and backed her way across the parking lot toward the library. "You're so gross."

"You love it." Paige winked at her then, once Sam was out of earshot, turned her snarky smirk back to me. "Why are you still here?"

I pushed away from the car and stepped into her personal space. She might have acted tough, but I wasn't afraid of her. "Because I get off on making your life miserable."

She rolled her eyes before spinning around to head off in the opposite direction.

"Ava!" Abercrombie's obnoxious voice carried across the quad, making my stomach lurch. The half a banana I'd had for breakfast threatened to make a reappearance.

Without acknowledging his presence, I jolted forward, dodging and weaving my way through the cars to avoid him.

"Baby, wait."

He was gaining on me as I entered the building, and images of Abercrombie as a fire-breathing dragon flashed through my brain, making my natural fight-or-flight instinct take over. "Excuse me." I pushed between a pair of girls, knocking their books to the floor, but kept going. I had my History of European Civilization classroom in my sights and started bargaining with the gods. *Please let me get there first. If you help me beat him to the door, I promise I'll cook dinner for the rest of the week. I'll stop illegally downloading music, and I won't give Josh shit when he sneaks into my room to steal my CDs. Hell, I'll even give Josh my room if I never have to see Abercrombie again.*

I was almost to the door when he wrapped one of his giant paws around my arm. "God, girl. What's the hurry?"

I clenched my teeth and jerked away from him, panting. "Don't you ever give up?"

"Oh, he gives up, all right." Hannah poked her head out of the room and gave Abercrombie an icy smile. "About two seconds after he pulls out, he'll want nothing to do with you."

My mouth dropped open at the exchange, and I wondered if she was speaking from experience.

"Oh, hey, Hannah. Yeah, well. I gotta get to class." Abercrombie looked like *he'd* seen a ghost. "Call me later, Ava. Okay?"

"Not on your life, Abercrombie."

As if he'd already forgotten Hannah's comment, he flashed me his signature smirk. "Come on. You know I'm starting to break down those walls of yours." He turned and dashed down the hall.

"What a piece of work." I watched him until he disappeared around a corner then looked at Hannah and burst out laughing. "Thanks."

She grinned back at me, bumping me with her shoulder. "Don't mention it. And I mean that, Ava. Please don't mention it. To anyone. If Sam—or, oh God, *Paige*—found out about..." She closed her eyes and shook her head. "Never mind. Just don't say anything, okay?"

"I won't." I looked into her cautious expression and smiled. "Honest. I won't say a word."

"Thanks." Her lips quirked. "Because I would have so kicked your ass if you did."

And with that, I decided Hannah was okay in my book. Blue hair and all.

◆

"Mom?" I threw my bag on the kitchen table and snatched an apple from the bowl on the counter. "Mom, are you home? Josh?" A shiver ran up my spine. Stupid Sam and her stupid ghost talk, especially since the only sound in the house came from the grandfather clock ticking in the living room. The freaking thing creeped me out. Mom had wound it the other day, and ever since then it was like reliving *The Tell-Tale Heart* twenty-four-seven. It was so loud I could hear it all the way on the third floor. *Tick tock, tick tock.*

My stomach rumbled, and I pulled open the fridge. For half a minute, I contemplated making dinner. Then I remembered my bargain with the gods. If they didn't have to keep up their end of the deal, neither did I. So instead, I grabbed my bag and my apple and headed upstairs to do my homework.

Who knows, maybe I'll get lucky, and the ghost is good at molecular biology.

After cranking up the volume on my phone to blast the new One Direction album—my secret guilty pleasure—I flopped down on my stomach across the bed and pulled out my history assignment. Thanks to my recent nocturnal exploits, I'd recently developed a fascination for the Middle Ages. Frankly, Lamppost looked way better in his armor than the cavalry soldiers in the days of Charlemagne.

I got the brilliant idea to look up medieval armor on the Internet and pushed my book aside to flip open my laptop. I paged through the images until I landed on a painting that actually resembled the boy in my dream.

Maybe Sam was right. Maybe he *was* a ghost.

I rolled over and pulled myself up to a sitting position, crossing my legs in the center of my bed. "Spirit, if you can hear me, make yourself known." I waited for a minute but got no response. I tried again, this time closing my eyes and holding my arms out to my sides like they did in the movies. "I know you're here. I've felt your presence. If you can hear me, please make yourself known."

"You are so weird."

My brother's bored voice sounded from just inside the doorway, and I let out a bloodcurdling scream, jerking backward and rolling off the side of my bed to the floor. "Josh, I'm going to kill you!"

CHAPTER SIX

EXHAUSTION PLAGUED ME FROM THE moment I opened my eyes that morning. The weekend had practically flashed by. My recurring nightmare took Friday off, but it came back with a vengeance Saturday and Sunday. The dream always started at the lighthouse and ended in the stable. Saturday night, the horse turned into a dragon, and I had to stand by helplessly as he and my mystery guy battled to the death.

Some nights, the action looped through two or three times before his voice would whisper for me to wake up, as my alarm was about to go off. The dragons and medieval warriors battling it out in my head had me so strung out, I was afraid to fall asleep. As we walked across the quad Monday morning, I barely had the energy to toss verbal barbs back and forth with Paige.

"How are things going at the food bank?" Sam asked Paige as we reached the front doors.

Her flawless face twisted into an ugly scowl. "He didn't show up. I spent half the morning with smelly homeless people and a bunch of potheads."

"Aren't you a pothead?" I tried to pull back the question as soon as it flew past my lips.

She made a choking sound in her throat. "I may smoke the occasional joint, but I am *not* a pothead."

Hannah held up her hand. "I'm a pothead."

"We know," Sam and I said at the same time then quickly followed it with "Jinx."

"You're practically a poster child for why the youth of America shouldn't do drugs." Sam elbowed Hannah in the ribs, and they both giggled. "You've smoked so much pot your hair turned blue."

I spun around at the sound of sneakers slapping concrete.

Abercrombie stopped short, obviously not expecting me to catch him. "Oh, hey. You scared me."

"I sincerely doubt that," I muttered, pretending he wasn't still following me around like a lost puppy.

He let out a long sigh. "What will it take to get you to give me a chance?"

"A terminal illness with only three days to live. No, wait. A day and a half."

"Come on, Ava. Don't be such a bitch. I'm not that bad. I'm on the hockey team. I have a car."

Sam shoved him out of our path. "You also have crabs and probably several other sexually transmitted diseases I can't even begin to pronounce."

"That's just a rumor." He flashed a cocky grin, all traces of sincerity wiped clean from his face. "I started it myself to get rid of this clingy chick my junior year."

"Well..." I held up my hand between us like a force field. "Let's add that to the list of reasons I won't be going out with you."

"You have a list?"

"Oh, do I." I was about to run through them one at a time when Abercrombie threw his arm over my shoulder. I froze as the pricking started at the back of my skull. It had to be a coincidence. There was no way my body would react to Aaron Finch that way.

"Don't you two make a cute couple?" Paige pulled out her phone and made fish lips at us. "Come on, Aaron, give her a big kiss. I'll post it on Instagram."

I cut my eyes to Hannah, who was giving an Oscar-worthy performance over there. I would have never known she had a thing for the guy. I certainly had no idea what she saw in him. I ducked down, pushing his arm off me, and the prickling increased.

"Where you going?" Abercrombie winked at me, the asshole.

"To class?" I smirked at him. "Isn't that where we're all

going?" As if I could feel my ghost's presence, I whipped around and caught a flash of black going around the building. *Damn it.* The urge to go after him was almost unbearable. A week ago, I would have chased him down, but where had that gotten me? Nowhere. I had to keep reminding myself he wasn't really there. The guy was a hallucination or a ghost or, as the evidence might imply, a paranoid delusion.

"You okay, Ava?" Sam put her hand on my arm, and the contact calmed my racing heart.

"Yeah, I'm fine." I gave her a weak smile. "Just thought I saw something."

"The ghost?" she mouthed, and I nodded. "Did you need to go look for it?" The look of concern on her face touched me.

"No, it's fine. I'll be fine." I took a steadying breath and willed the tears to hold off, at least until I got home. Ava Flynn didn't cry over boys, especially boys who didn't even exist.

She gave my arm a squeeze then turned to laugh at whatever Paige had said.

Hannah caught up to me and gave me a sad smile. In some strange way, we were both in the same boat, pining after what we couldn't have. "Did you do the history assignment?"

"Uh, no. I started it, but my weekend just seemed to spiral out of control." That was an understatement if I'd ever heard one. The memory of me sitting in the middle of my bed attempting to conjure up a ghost flashed unbidden into my head.

She leaned into me, brushing my shoulder with hers. "You wanna copy mine?"

"Nah, I'm good. What's Professor Hurley gonna do? Put me in the dungeon for not completing an assignment?" We both laughed at that, and I had a sudden sense of belonging. Port Michael was actually beginning to feel like home.

Hannah and I were still laughing about Professor Hurley's possible medieval punishments when we wandered into the classroom ten minutes later, and I couldn't help conjuring up my armored hottie. The whole class seemed to be whispering as

I stepped through the door. The buzzing at the back of my neck flared, and my stomach clenched so hard I gasped.

Lamppost sat in the back of the room.

I looked around, but no one seemed to be paying the least bit of attention to the guy in the *black leather jacket*. Either the entire class was in on it, or I'd finally snapped. I was seeing ghosts in school. Our eyes locked for a second, and the corners of his lips tipped up before smoothing out again.

I took my seat near the front and opened my book while Professor Hurley went over his expectations for the upcoming project. A group project, of course. I couldn't catch a break if my life depended on it.

"Hey, are you okay?" Hannah whispered from the seat behind me.

I glanced back and caught the ghost's eye again before whipping my head forward again to nod. In truth, I wasn't at all sure I was okay. The minutes clicked by so slowly, I was certain the clock had frozen in place.

By the time class ended, my muscles were so tense, I was afraid I might not be able to get up. But stiff muscles or not, I bolted out of my chair and out of the building so fast it made my head spin. I had no intention of sticking around long enough to find out if the ghost was still in the back or if he'd vanished during the lecture.

Thankfully, I didn't see him in my next class, and my neck was prickle free all the way to the dining hall.

My crew was already sitting at our usual table when I set my tray down to eat.

"... and you should have seen her hair. That's the worst highlight job I've seen since my mom had me pull her hair through a cap in middle school." Sam snorted. "Oh hi, Ava. Where the hell have you been?"

"Class?"

"Well, duh. But I haven't seen you all day. You were supposed to meet me in the library after bio. Are you feeling all right?"

"Yeah, I'm fine. I…" I exhaled on a sigh. "It's not important."

"Ghost problems?"

My thoughts flipped back to the guy in the back of my European history lecture, and I shrugged.

"Well, I know how to cheer you up." She took a sip of her lemonade, and I raised my eyebrows and waited. "Will Clark—you haven't met him yet, but he graduated with us. He's having a party this weekend. It's an annual tradition. The first party of the school year."

I bit back a groan. "Didn't we just go to a party? Last party of the summer? Another annual tradition, if I'm not mistaken."

"That was summer. This is fall." She laughed, pointing her fork at me. "You seriously need a boyfriend."

That time, I laughed. A boyfriend was the *last* thing I needed.

"You should have seen the guy checking her out in our European history class." Hannah dropped into the seat beside me and nudged me with her foot. "He was super cute. I'm surprised you didn't notice."

"Nope. I was paying rapt attention to Professor Hurley's fascinating lesson on the characteristics of medieval society." Or I was too busy avoiding the ghost in the back of the room to notice some random guy checking me out. So unless the cute guy happened to be a leather-wearing ghost, I didn't want to hear it.

Hannah stole a fry from my tray. "Right."

"I was!" I reached over and snatched it back, stuffing the fry into my mouth.

"You fell asleep, didn't you?" Sam asked. "I fell asleep in biology sophomore year. I woke up wearing a dead frog as a hat. Mr. Burton had a sick sense of humor."

As Sam went on about the pranks her high school science teacher played on his students, I realized something. "What happened to Paige?" Not that I missed the bitchy ice princess, but her absence was almost as disconcerting as her presence.

"Oh, she's still trying to score with food bank guy. She texted me and said she saw him crossing the quad. She was in pursuit."

Hannah shrugged. "I think it's become more of a challenge than anything. She's never had a guy ignore her before."

"Never?" The more I thought about it, the more it made sense. Paige might have been a total bitch, but the girl was gorgeous.

"Never," Sam whispered.

After lunch, we split up and headed in different directions. Once or twice, I thought I caught a glimpse of my ghost on campus, but my eyes could have been playing tricks on me. Everywhere I looked, I saw something that made my breath catch in my throat. It seemed as if nowhere was safe from my delusions. If I didn't find a way to get past my crazy obsession, I was going to drive myself completely insane.

———◆———

"Bonjour!" Madame Finkelstein greeted the class with her typical enthusiasm. Her ability to maintain that level of positive energy all the way through a late-afternoon class amazed me. Not that I was complaining. It didn't seem to faze her in the least when Sam and I slipped into the room five minutes late.

We took our seats in the front, as usual, and I fumbled to pull my book out of my bag before the professor called on me to recite something in French. On a normal day, that wouldn't have been an issue, but after hallucinating Lamppost more times in a single day than all the others combined, my brain was fried.

I glanced over at Sam. She looked like I felt. Her cheeks were flushed, and she was making faces at me that I felt sure had to be some sort of teenage girl code. But despite my current status as an *actual* teenage girl, I didn't speak the language.

"What?" I mouthed, keeping my head down as much as possible and pretending to pay attention to the page we were supposed to be following.

I swear she mouthed the word "toast" before pointing to the cell phone hidden in her lap. I shook my head and nodded at the NO CELL PHONES sign tacked up on the front wall. Sam let out a frustrated grunt and pointed at her lap again.

I rolled my eyes and worked to dislodge my phone from my

jeans pocket without alerting the professor. Just as I'd pulled it all the way out, it buzzed in my hand, startling me. After fumbling with the damn thing for what seemed like an eternity, I dropped it. With a little fast thinking on my part, I shoved my book off the desk, making an even louder smack against the floor.

"Mademoiselle Flynn, *es-tu bien*?" Madame Finkelstein glared at me from the front as if she'd caught me breaking her only posted law, but relaxed her features when she saw the book lying face down at my feet.

"Um, *oui*? Just clumsy." I flashed an innocent smile as I scooped up my phone without detection.

"Nice save," Sam whispered, and I shot her a death glare. "Hey, it's not my fault you dropped the damn thing."

After flipping my book to the right page again, I pulled my phone out and checked the messages. The first one was from right after lunch.

Abercrombie: Meet me in the stacks at three. I wanna show you something.

As if.

The next two were from a few minutes ago, and both were from Sam.

Sam: Cute guy alert. Back right corner. I'm gonna need a cold shower.

Sam: Tell me what your ghost looks like again.

Those two messages couldn't have been more unrelated. I tried to peek over my shoulder, but without turning completely around, I wouldn't have been able to see the so-called "cute boy." But since my current obsession was fresh in my mind, I had no trouble conjuring up his image.

Me: Tall. Hard muscles but not bulky and gross. Messy dark hair, like after crazy sex. Sexy smirky smile. Dark dangerous eyes. And that black leather jacket.

I stopped before I got carried away, hit send, then tucked it away so I wouldn't get caught.

I ignored the phone buzzing in my pocket.

"Ava." Sam's ability to whisper was slipping. "Ava!"

"Mademoiselle Stone?" Madame Finkelstein had finally lost the battle with her good humor—all because of Sam. "*Pourquoi continuez-vous d'interrompre ma classe?*"

"Uh, I was just going to ask Ava—"

"*En Français.*"

"*J'ai besoin...*" Sam huffed out a breath then snatched a sheet of paper from my notebook and waved it in the air, flashing her orthodontically enhanced teeth in a wide smile. "To take notes."

Madame Finkelstein slid her electric-blue glasses down her nose as she scrutinized the two of us. She blew out a breath and seemed to give up the idea of trying to get us to speak her language. "There's no need for notes yet. Just pay attention. And no more talking."

Sam pressed her lips into a tight line and nodded.

I was fine with that. I had nothing to say.

Sam stared a hole in the side of my head, trying to get my attention. Ignoring her had actually become somewhat of a game. But the longer I ignored her, the more my phone buzzed in my pocket. There was a serious risk of her head exploding if I didn't check my messages.

Keeping my eyes on the professor, I slid my phone out of my pocket, this time, making certain it didn't slip through my fingers. I'd only gotten as far as the first text when an attack of palpitations hit me. Was it possible for someone to die of heart failure before the age of nineteen?

The prickle shot down my spine and branched out through my extremities. I felt it in every pore of my body. Maybe I was having a stroke. My entire face had gone numb.

"Are you sure?" I whispered, keeping my head facing forward. I didn't dare look for myself.

"Pretty sure." Her response was so low, I wasn't certain if I actually heard it or just imagined it.

I read the text again to be sure I hadn't passed out and was dreaming or something.

Sam: I think your ghost is sitting in the back of the room.

I sucked in a breath, holding it for as long as I could before blowing it back out. I needed to stay calm. If Lamppost *was* in the back of the room, that meant Sam could see him. And I wasn't imagining him. And he was real. I'd just gotten used to the idea of him being a figment of my imagination, and now, faced with the possibility of him being real, I didn't know how to react.

My phone buzzed again, and I peeked down at the new message.

Sam: What are you gonna do?

I had no idea, but I figured the first thing would be to turn around and see if it was really him back there and not some *other* leather-wearing, palpitation-inducing guy.

My knuckles went white from the death grip I had on my desk as I worked up the nerve to look. But what did I have to be afraid of? The guy turning out to be real should have been the least frightening thing I'd dealt with since moving. No. Since before Dad died. But somehow, the prospect of having a crush on a ghost was way less scary. Real guys terrified me.

"If it's not him, can I have him?" Sam's whispered question snapped me out of the throes of an anxiety attack, and I had to cough to hide my laugh.

"If it's not him, yes." I bit back a giggle before steeling myself for what I was about to do.

As soon as Madame Finkelstein turned to write something on the board, I whipped around to check out the guy three rows behind me. My eyes zeroed in on him like a laser pointer, and the corners of his mouth curved into a slow smile. He winked at me, and I spun back to face the front, anxiety pouring off me in waves. He was here. In my classroom. In the actual flesh, it would seem. The same lips I'd tasted nearly every night for over a week in my dreams had grinned at me. *Holy shit, what do I do now?*

"I guess that's him then?"

I nodded without looking at her.

"Damn. You think he has a brother?"

That did it. As the professor announced the end of class, setting off a symphony of chairs scraping against the old wood floors, I lost the fragile grip on my control and burst out laughing. Madame Finkelstein shouted out one last addition to our assignment as everyone filed out of the room.

Sam waited for me as I got up and shoved my book into my bag. I couldn't decide if I should just walk back there and talk to him or wait for him to come to me. The more I thought about it, the more I realized the guy had played me all week. Sort of. I'd seen him several times and even pursued him once or twice, and he let me think he was a freaking hallucination.

I spun around, channeling the feisty kitten inside me—arched eyebrow at the ready, fists balled at my sides—prepared to give him a piece of my mind.

And he was gone.

I deflated like a popped balloon.

"I was just going to tell you. He snuck out the instant class ended." Sam twisted her lips to the side, giving me a sympathetic smile.

"Well, damn." I stared at his empty chair and sighed. So much for him sticking around. "At least he's consistent, right?"

"*And* we know you have wicked good taste in guys." She came to a complete stop in the doorway, and I ran straight into her. She spun on me, gripping my shoulders so hard I feared she might draw blood. "Do you know what this means?"

I winced, shrugging out of her death grip. "It means my brother wrote on my mirror while I was naked in the tub."

"Oh, yeah, that too. Eww. But no, I was going to say, that means hot leather jacket guy is the one who gave you the hickey!"

Oh, my God. "I really *did* make out with him at the bonfire." And so help me, I wanted to do it again. And soon. "Thank God! I can permanently erase the image of Abercrombie kissing me from my brain."

All it took was one look from Sam, and we let out matching squeals. I didn't even care how ridiculous I looked jumping up and down in the middle of the hallway until I heard a throat clear behind me.

I felt the color drain from my cheeks as I turned and faced the literal guy of my dreams.

He looked almost shy as he pushed away from the wall and took a step toward me. He stopped and gave me his signature smirk before turning to walk away. "See you tomorrow, Ava."

CHAPTER SEVEN

OR THE FIRST TIME SINCE the lighthouse party, I made it through the entire night without a single dream. There were no obnoxious teenage boys shifting into dragons, no leather jackets transforming into medieval armor, and not a single lamppost in sight. I didn't even dream about Annandale... or Dad. I slept like the dead and woke up completely refreshed.

And then I panicked. For the first time since I'd moved to Port Michael, running into my mystery guy would be a certainty. He'd said it himself. *See you tomorrow, Ava.* And his last words to me—his only words to me, in fact—played through my head like the chorus of my favorite song. There would be no more wondering if I'd imagined him or if he was a ghost, no clandestine chases through the quad or seeing him disappear around corners before I could catch up to him. No. Today, I would actually *see* him, maybe even touch him, and not just in my dreams.

I only hoped the reality lived up to the illusion and that I hadn't made a huge mistake in pursuing him.

"Are you really wearing that?" Sam stood in my doorway, staring at my half-nakedness as if I'd committed the biggest crime in the fashion world.

"Jesus, Sam! You really need to stop doing that." I clutched the Ziggy Stardust concert tee to my chest and willed my pulse to go back to normal.

Sam flopped into the center of my bed, laughing her ass off. "Sorry. Your mom—"

"Sent you up, I know." I shot her a scowl and pulled the

T-shirt in question over my head. "Either knock or make some noise next time."

"You're always so jumpy." She sat up and crisscrossed her legs in front of her. "And don't pretend you didn't hear me—you can't wear that today."

I glanced down at the image stretched across my chest then back to Sam's bored expression. "What's wrong with Bowie?"

She rolled her eyes as if it pained her to have to spell it out for me. And maybe it did, but I still had no idea what was wrong with what I'd picked out. "You can't expect a super-hot guy to kiss you while you're wearing an androgynous rock star across your chest. It's dating one-oh-one."

"We're not even dating." A little voice in the back of my head asked if I even wanted to date him. My skin prickled at the thought. Yes. Yes, I did.

She leaned back and propped herself up on her hands. "Well, you never will be if you don't listen to me. Do you have anything a little sexier? Don't get me wrong. I love your vintage rock style, but today we need something a bit more *bow chicka wow wow.* Ooh, like that!" She jumped up and snatched a baby-blue ruffled peasant blouse from my open drawer. She inspected it before throwing it back at me. "Wear this and the long pencil skirt you wore on the first day." She moved her inspection down to my freshly pedicured toes. "Ghost guy is tall, so you can wear heels if you want to, but I'd stick with something more comfortable so you don't trip and bust your ass while you're hoofing it across campus."

"Thanks for the vote of confidence," I muttered.

She winked at me. "Hey, I just call 'em like I see 'em."

As soon as I'd dressed in the clothes she'd picked out, Sam grabbed a lock of hair from either side of my face and twisted them until she'd created two cords. She pulled them back and secured them behind my head in a style that reminded me of my dream. Then she stood back to admire her work.

I turned from side to side, checking myself out from every visible angle. "Well? How do I look?"

"Beautiful." She rested her hands on her hips, beaming at me with pride. "He won't be able to resist you."

———◆———

"Are you sure I don't look like I'm trying too hard?" I caught my bottom lip between my teeth and checked my reflection one last time in the visor mirror.

She unbuckled and pushed her door open. "You worry too much." When I didn't get out of the car, she leaned back in again. "You look fine. Better than fine. You look amazing. And no, I don't think he's going to think you're trying too hard. He's a guy. He's gonna notice how big your boobs look in that blouse. Now get out of the car. And stop making that face. Didn't your mother ever tell you it would freeze that way?"

I smoothed out my features and climbed out, careful not to snag my skirt on the door.

True to his word, Lamppost waited for me on the other side of the parking lot. He looked like sex on legs in his leather jacket—this time with a pair of faded and distressed jeans and a gray V-neck shirt—leaning against a flame-orange motorcycle. He looked good enough to lick.

I gnawed on my lip as I walked toward the quad, keeping him in my sights the entire time. I wasn't sure if he wanted me to come to him or wait for him to come to me, so I played it safe, throwing him as many signals as I could give off without looking too desperate. Didn't he know I'd been waiting for this day for almost a month, ever since that first night I saw him beneath my window like some tragic Shakespearean hero?

"Tone down the pheromones there, Juliet."

I whipped my head around to see Sam smirking at me, her eyes dancing with humor.

She hooked her arm in mine, towing me back toward the others since I'd somehow managed to get pulled off course by some crazy sort of voodoo magic. "You just mumbled a line from Romeo and Juliet."

"I did?" My voice squeaked, and I cleared my throat. "How

the hell am I going to get through the morning, let alone the rest of the day? What am I supposed to do? He's just standing there, watching me. How is that living up to his promise of 'I'll see you tomorrow, Ava'?"

"Oh, trust me," Sam said. "He sees you."

"But I wanted to *see* him. As in talk to him. Up close and personal."

Sam giggled. "You're just a little addict over there, aren't you? Jonesing for a taste of whatever he's offering."

I shrugged, tossing a look over my shoulder. He was still leaning on the damn motorcycle, staring at me as if he could see directly into my soul. With a little whimper, I hoped no one heard, I gave Sam a vigorous nod. "I've got it bad. And trust me when I say, that's not good."

"What are you two whispering about over there? You'd think you were a pair of lesbians the way Ava's hanging all over you, Sam." Paige's voice dripped venom, and I flinched back so I wouldn't get burned.

"So what if we *are* lesbians?" I said. "Nothing wrong with that, if it's what you're into."

Paige scoffed and tossed her perfect hair over her shoulder like a matador flipping his cape. "I'm just making an observation. I didn't say there was anything *wrong* with it."

I let out a silent battle cry and charged in with my horns out. "Well, for your information, we were talking about something that doesn't concern you. Is that quite all right with you?"

"Geez. Bitch much, Ava?" Paige turned around to talk to Hannah.

Score one for me.

"Don't look now, but he's coming this way." Sam whispered in my ear then released my arm and skipped ahead to catch up with Hannah and Paige.

But could Paige leave well enough alone? Of course not. As soon as I was out of Sam's protective sphere, Paige wheeled on me, and I could tell by the laser beams shooting from her eyes, whatever she was about to say was going to be brutal. Then she stopped and stared—not at me—at something over my shoulder. And her bitchy facade melted into the sweetest, sugariest smile I'd ever seen on the girl's face. It was almost creepy.

Oh, hell no!

"Well, hello. I knew you'd come around one of these days." Even her voice changed into something eerily *Stepford*. Thankfully, he didn't respond, and her smooth, sophisticated demeanor slipped. "Aren't you going to say something?"

His lips brushed my ear from behind, and I had to force myself to stay still. "Good morning, Ava."

I turned just enough to see him smiling down at me and opened my mouth to say something, but the words wouldn't come. The smug smile, however, refused to be ignored.

Without taking his eyes from mine, he reached out and tucked a lock of my hair behind my ear. "See you in class." He turned and walked away.

Just like that.

"What the hell was that?" Paige's face turned so red I thought her head might explode. "Why is my food bank guy saying good morning to you?"

"*That's* food bank guy?" Sam threw her head back and laughed. "Oh honey, you lost that battle before it had even begun." She grabbed my arm and towed me toward the building, still giggling about Paige and her group project drama.

I wondered if it was possible to die from extreme sexual tension. I had no idea how he did it, but Lamppost had managed to get himself reassigned to all of my classes, a fact I considered disturbing yet oddly wonderful. And when I wasn't in class, he was waiting for me in the library. Or the coffee shop. No matter where I was, he was there, sitting off to the side, setting my skin on fire with the intensity of his stare. I could feel his eyes roaming over me the entire time. Rationally, I knew his unparalleled stalker skills should have freaked me out, but the inexplicable pull I felt toward him took precedence.

And I still didn't know his name.

What I *did* know was he liked to chew on the end of his pen while he read. His mouth moved when he took notes as if he were reciting them in his head. And he smelled like the sky after a good hard rain—fresh and clean—and all boy. I might have *accidentally* brushed up against him a few times.

Getting close to him wasn't easy, though. Despite what I'd hoped, he didn't walk me to class. Instead, he hung back several paces, keeping me in his sights, of course, but never getting close enough for conversation. It was pure torture.

By midday Wednesday, I was ready to explode. The prickling down my spine had spread throughout my entire body, and I felt like I'd been grasping a live wire all morning. If his plan was to kill me, he was doing a damn good job so far.

I followed the lunch crowd to the campus cafeteria, sensing his proximity as he trailed several paces behind me like a sparkly stalker. I'd ignored every safety precaution my father had drilled into me from my preteen days. It was as if the very core of my being *screamed* to be with him, and that simple fact defied logic. Why hadn't he spoken to me yet? What sort of game was he playing?

I filled my tray with more food than I could possibly eat on a nervous stomach and made my way to our table. Sam and Hannah were already there with their heads together as if they were sharing a juicy secret.

"Dare I ask?" I dropped down into the chair across from Hannah.

"It's nothing." Sam gave Hannah a funny look.

"Okay." I could play it cool too. Besides, I had way more to worry about than whatever those two were cooking up.

"So..." Hannah dragged out the word then left it hanging.

"So?" I picked at my mystery-meat loaf, keeping my eyes on my plate.

"Has he told you his name yet?" Sam leaned across the table, resting on her elbows as she finished Hannah's thought.

70

I stabbed a hunk of the slippery loaf and held it up like a weapon in front of me. "Nope."

"Interesting." Sam looked at Hannah again, and they seemed to be having a conversation with their eyes alone.

I dropped my fork with a loud clatter. "Would one of you just spill it already?"

Hannah chewed on the inside of her cheek until Sam nodded. She took a deep breath and started talking. "I was outside the registrar's office this morning. It's a little-known fact, but they have the only vending machine on campus that stocks Little Debbie Swiss Rolls and Twinkies, so of course, I'm heading there after..." She brought her thumb and forefinger to her lips and took a hit from an invisible joint.

"Skip the charades, and get to the point." Sam scooted forward in her seat and motioned for Hannah to pick up the pace.

"Fine. Ruin the best part of the story." Hannah dropped her hand into her lap with a sigh. "Take a wild guess who walks in while I'm stuffing my purse with snacks?"

I resist the urge to glance over my shoulder.

"Bingo! So of course, I followed him in. I mean, it's not like he's a stranger to creepy stalker behavior, right?"

"Right?" I sort of agreed.

"He was arguing with the lady behind the desk. He spread the charm like creamy peanut butter, but man, was she giving him a hard time. The whole argument had to do with—and you're gonna love this..." Hannah choked back a giggle. "Getting out of the food bank thing. He'd already dropped the class, but they still had him down for the stupid project. Something about throwing off the numbers and the school had made a commitment. I didn't get all the details on that part, but I *did* happen to catch a glimpse of his name written across some document." Her eyes flashed to where Lamppost sat across the room. "Okay, it wasn't an accident. I practically leaned over the counter. I mean, I just *had* to look because I knew he hadn't told you yet, and I figured you'd want to know. In case he was hell-bent on keeping it a secret or something." Hannah finished her monologue then sucked in another deep breath.

I turned to Sam. "You knew about this?"

She shrugged. "For like ten minutes."

I glared at her, crossing my arms in front of me. "Were you ever going to tell me? *Are* you ever going to tell me?"

Hannah tipped her head to the side. "Tell you what?"

I threw up my hands. "His name!"

The dining hall got quiet for a few seconds before everyone went back to chattering again.

"Damn it. I didn't mean to yell." I tucked my hair behind my ears and leaned back in the chair. "This has easily been one of the most exhausting weeks I've ever spent, and it's only half over."

"Do you want to know his name?" Hannah bounced in her seat, her smile threatening to split her entire head open.

"Yes, of course I want to know what his name is."

"Maddox Fairchild." Hannah's mouth moved, but it wasn't her voice I heard.

I whipped my head around and came face to face with a ghost—or rather, one Maddox Fairchild, former ghost. Though I guessed he was never really a ghost at all. He held his hand out to me, and seemingly, of its own accord, *my* hand reached out to meet his.

"Maddox." I said his name, trying it on for size.

He nodded but didn't say anything. He simply lifted our joined hands to his mouth and brushed his lips across my knuckles.

"What the hell? Again?" Paige slammed her tray down, making her dressing splash all over the table.

"God, Paige, get over yourself." Sam voiced what I could only imagine we were all thinking.

Maddox squeezed my hand, and I darted my eyes back to his.

"I have to run, but I'll see you in molecular bio, right?"

I nodded, but somewhere in the back of my mind, I wanted to ask him all the questions he hadn't answered, like how he managed to change his schedule a week after classes started.

Not why—I could guess why—but *how*. And molecular biology? *What are the odds?*

"Good. Enjoy your lunch." He walked away. Again.

"What the hell was that?" Hannah's eyes stretched wide as she watched Maddox cross the cafeteria and collect his things from his table on the other side of the room.

"I have no idea." I kept my eyes locked on his as if some magic I didn't understand had taken control of me. He was attractive. God, he was gorgeous, but it wasn't like me to completely lose myself in a guy. I shook my head to clear it. "Did someone drug my Kool-Aid?"

Even Paige laughed at that, and gradually, our table went back to business as usual. Sam reminded me about the party I didn't want to go to on the weekend. Hannah offered to score some weed if any of us were interested. And Paige still couldn't believe her food bank guy was fawning over me as if I was a Victoria's Secret model or something. The only thing missing was—

"Ava, baby. I haven't seen you all day. Have you been dodging me?"

Abercrombie.

"Didn't you know? I'm always dodging you." I took a bite of my rehydrated mashed potatoes to keep my mouth busy and avoided looking into his puppy-dog eyes.

As usual, Abercrombie couldn't take a hint, and he dropped into the seat beside me, draping his sweaty arm over my shoulder. "Are you going to the party Saturday night?"

I pushed his arm off me and shuddered. "That depends. Are you going?"

He flashed a lazy smile. "Yep."

"Then I'm definitely *not* going." I scooted over as far as I could in the tight space.

"God damn it, Ava. I'm not one to give up easily, but you make it hard." The expression on his face told me he wasn't saying I was difficult.

"Gross, Abercrombie. When will you take a hint? I'm not interested. I will never be interested. End of story."

"Just one kiss. Come on. One." He leaned in, sticking his lip ring in my face and breaching the limits of my personal space with a vengeance.

Then he was gone.

I spun around to find Maddox towering over Abercrombie, who was sprawled out on the floor like a hockey player rug. Maddox clenched and unclenched his hands at his sides, and I could feel the rage rippling off him. "Learn to take a hint." His reaction should have terrified me, or at the very least, given me pause. But fear was the absolute last emotion to manifest itself. I jumped out of my seat and took a step in his direction. I didn't know what I'd planned to say, but the guy had just defended my honor in the campus dining hall. I had to say something. But before I could form the words, he'd stalked off again, this time bypassing his table and exiting through the double doors.

Somehow, I knew he wouldn't be in biology.

CHAPTER EIGHT

MADDOX DIPPED OUT ON THE rest of our classes. At first, I thought he'd just skipped bio. I would have skipped right along with him if he'd given me half a chance. And that wasn't like me. I'd always been the sort of girl to toe the line, get good grades. I didn't ditch.

But then he didn't show up in French. Instead of conjugating verbs with the rest of the class, I'd spent the entire hour watching the seconds tick by on the big silver wall clock, desperate for class to be over, desperate to find him. And that wasn't like me either.

The instant class ended, I was out of my seat like a shot, pushing past the crowds in the hall, bursting through the double doors, running full out through the quad to the parking lot. I think I knew he wouldn't be there, but that didn't stop the devastation when I looked for his motorcycle, and it was gone. He was gone.

Again.

I rode home with Sam in silence. Somehow, she knew not to bring it up, not to mention his name. And for that, I was thankful. I had nothing to say on the subject.

My heart skipped in my chest as we passed a billboard for the lighthouse. Strange, unexpected tears threatened to fall. But why? I'd just met him. Why did I feel such a strong pull toward him already? I had no explanation for my scattered emotions.

For the first time in days, I thought of my dad, and not just a fleeting moment or fragmented memory, although those came at me unexpectedly all the time. This time, I really thought about him. I remembered the way his eyes crinkled up at the corners when he laughed. The way he smelled when he leaned down to tuck me in at night. Watching him tear Mom away from the hot stove to dance with him in the middle of the kitchen, just because. Their love had filled our house with so much happiness. And so much devastation when he died.

I wanted to find a love like my parents had had. I wanted to feel so connected to someone that I would know when he was in the room without even looking. I felt that spark with Maddox. And when he looked at me? My entire body could go up in flames, and I wouldn't notice.

"Are you going to be okay?" Sam's voice cut through the silence, shocking me just a little. Those were the first words she'd spoken to me since lunch.

I looked up from my hands, clenched together in my lap, to Sam's concerned face. "Yeah. I'll be fine." I knew I was lying, and she probably did too. But it hadn't taken me long to learn that in Sam's world, that's what friends did. *Fake it 'til we make it.* And I *would* be fine. Eventually. It wasn't as if Maddox had left town. God, I didn't think so anyway. He'd just left school. And he would come back. He had to.

But that little niggling voice in the back of my head wondered if he thought Abercrombie meant something to me, if maybe he thought I'd led him on or encouraged his attention. It was a ridiculous idea, but what did I know about how boys thought? For all the crazy emotions coursing through me when he was near, I didn't really know Maddox at all.

"Okay, well, I'll see you in the morning. Call me if you wanna talk... or anything." Sam forced a smile, and I realized it was the first time since I'd known her that she'd actually faked it. Everything about her had always been so spontaneous and natural. It made the weight of the situation that much heavier. Maddox had swept into my life like a nor'easter, and he could easily blow out just as quickly.

I dragged myself out of her car and wandered into the empty house. Mom must have taken Josh somewhere because the only sound greeting me was the incessant ticking of that stupid grandfather clock my mother loved. I climbed the stairs as if walking to my death, chastising myself the whole way for acting like such a teenage girl. I was almost nineteen. It was time I started acting like an adult, not a lovesick child.

Later. For now, I needed time to grieve and maybe just a little time to convince myself I was overreacting, and he'd be waiting for me when I showed up in the morning. Still leaning on that stupid motorcycle as if he owned the world.

———◆———

Sleep didn't come easily. In truth, I just didn't want to dream. I knew if I did, he'd be there, waiting for me. And I wasn't ready to see him yet. So instead, I took a long hot bath, letting the steam surround me like morning fog, and disappeared for a while.

I listened to Bowie on repeat, wishing I'd hadn't ditched my favorite band shirts to dress up for a boy who couldn't even take the time to talk to me after stalking me for days. I should've never listened to Sam. Changing my appearance had put too much pressure on the situation and given too much importance to our nonexistent relationship. *I'd* put too much of myself into something that never panned out. And I'd let him rip my heart out when he left. I needed to pull myself together. I'd spent too much time looking for him. Thinking about him. Dreaming about him.

Tick tock. Tick tock.

Damned clock.

Tick tock. Tick tock. Plink plink plink.

"What the hell?" I sat up in the tub and wrapped my arms around my legs to listen. Interspersed between the ticking of the clock were little *plinks*. The cadence was off. The rhythm all wrong. But the sound didn't stop, and despite my better judgment, I was about to investigate.

I stepped out of the tub and grabbed a towel, wrapping it around me and securing it at the front. The old floorboards groaned beneath my feet as I stepped into my dark room. The single votive candle I'd left burning on my nightstand cast eerie shadows on the walls, and I contemplated locking myself in the bathroom until sunrise. I heard the *plinking* again, coming from somewhere near the window, and took cautious steps in that direction.

I glanced down at the wash of light under the lamppost, half expecting to see Maddox standing there, dark eyes riveted to my window. But the street was deserted.

I cupped my hands against the glass, pressing my face into them to get a better look.

Nothing.

A loud bang rattled the glass, and I jerked back, landing on my ass and swallowing a scream. I blinked a few times, waiting for the glass to shatter from the impact, but nothing happened. And then the light *plinking* started again, like pebbles against my window. I sat frozen for half a minute, listening to the clock and the *plinking*.

That is *pebbles against my window.*

I tugged the towel tighter around me and crawled over to look down again. This time I saw him as clear as day, standing in the shadows below, picking something from his hand and pitching it toward my house.

I pulled myself to standing and tugged on the sash, worried that years of nonuse and paint would have sealed the window shut, but after struggling for a minute, it ripped open with a groan. "What are you doing?" I whisper-yelled down at him.

"Trying to get your attention," he whispered back at me.

I tried to look angry, I really did. But staying mad was impossible when my insides felt like they were bursting with joy at the sight of him. "Well, you got it. Now what do you want?"

"I wanted to see you. And to apologize for ditching you this afternoon. I-I had to do something." His eyes pleaded with mine, and I struggled not to give in so easily. Being around him was dangerous for my self-control.

I rested my stomach on the windowsill, making sure the towel didn't fall open, and leaned out. "Something suddenly came up? Do I look like the sort of girl who believes things like that?"

My scowl left something to be desired if his smug expression was any indication. "Maybe not, but you look like a girl who would be willing to accept a heartfelt apology when she hears one."

"When I hear one, I'll let you know." I forced myself to climb back inside and reached up to close the window.

"Ava, wait! I'm sorry. Please. I really need to see you." He'd wiped the cocky grin from his face and actually looked as devastated as I felt. Maybe he could feel it too—the overwhelming pull—like gravity. I was the tide, and he was the moon. I couldn't stop myself from flowing toward him.

My hands trembled on the sash. "Fine. I need to get dressed. Give me five minutes."

His smile could have lit up the whole town.

With one good sharp tug, the window slammed shut, the glass still vibrating as I walked away. I grabbed the Ziggy Stardust shirt from my drawer then remembered what Sam told me about boys and kissing and tossed it onto my bed to find something else. I wasn't taking any chances.

Something Dad once said about how he loved when Mom wore his clothes popped into my head, and I dug to the bottom of the drawer to find a threadbare white T-shirt that had belonged to my father. I pulled it on and knotted it in the back so it would cling to my chest, then dove back in to find my loosest pair of jeans. They were distressed, with holes at the knees, and hung just a little low on my waist, but they were perfect. I didn't want Maddox to think I'd gone to any effort to look good for him, but I absolutely wanted him to take notice.

Then I pulled my hair into a ponytail before grabbing my keys. For the first time ever, I was about to sneak out. I crept down the stairs, careful to avoid the loose boards at the top— and again at halfway down—that I knew would make noise. But as soon as my hand gripped the doorknob, I panicked. What was I doing? I barely knew him. Nearly every moment I'd spent with him had occurred in my dreams, for crap's sake! I hadn't even known for sure if it was really him I'd kissed at the lighthouse party until two days ago. And I'd spoken more words to him while hanging out my window than I had any time before that.

I rested my head against the door, trying to get my breathing under control, but the prickle in my neck made it difficult. Maybe I *didn't* know him, but I *wanted* to know him.

And just like that, I'd made my decision.

Before stepping outside, I yanked the elastic band out of my hair and shook my head until loose waves fell over my shoulders. Such a girl thing to do. And until recently, I didn't act like a teenage girl. I didn't fall victim to my hormones. But I'd almost embraced the fact that, for this boy, I would always be a total girl.

With one last deep, cleansing breath, I eased the door open and closed it behind me with a quiet *snick*. Across the street, Maddox stood under the light, waiting for me. He stared up at my bedroom window as if he expected me to shinny down the drainpipe at any moment.

I studied him for a minute from the safety of the porch as he paced back and forth, combing one hand through his dark hair and jiggling his keys in the other. He darted his eyes toward the shadows, and I followed their path to the motorcycle parked along the curb. His eyes made several circuits between my window and the bike before he'd stop to lean against the lamppost. A moment later, he'd start the whole thing over again. Even from my hiding spot, I saw his lips moving as he talked to himself.

I giggled, and his eyes snapped to mine.

He blew out a long breath and smiled. "I didn't think you'd come."

"I wasn't sure I was going to." That was a lie. Whether I'd be willing to admit it or not, I'd decided the instant he'd asked me.

"Well, I'm glad you did. I owe you an apology." He took a tentative step toward me until he stood on the edge of the road while I waited on the sidewalk on the other side.

"A heartfelt apology," I reminded him, biting down on my lip in a pathetic attempt to keep from smiling. It was no use. He caught me and flashed the cocky grin that made my heart flutter every time.

Then he wiped the smirk off his face and walked forward, stopping to fall to his knees in the middle of the road. He folded his hands together and looked up at me. "I'm truly sorry for leaving you today. I hope you can forgive me."

Several feet separated us, but he held me in his grasp as easily as if he were actually touching me. My fingers twitched to reach out to him, so I clutched my hands together behind my back and stared down at my feet, willing them to stay put. I couldn't speak. I couldn't move. Afraid the smallest action would break the spell.

All humor drained from his face, his eyes pleading with me. "Say something, Ava. Say you forgive me. Say you hate me. Say *something*."

I cleared my throat. "I don't hate you. But I don't understand what this is." I unclenched my hands and waved one between us.

The tension drained from his shoulders, and that brilliant smile I'd grown desperate for was back. "You feel it too?"

I reached up to touch the back of my neck. "I do."

"Come on." He held a hand out, and a set of headlights came around the corner and blinded me. He jumped to his feet, practically landing in my arms as he dodged the oncoming vehicle. The car blew its horn at him, and we both laughed. "That was close."

"You idiot. You almost got yourself killed. Are you okay?" I glanced down to where his hands flexed at my waist.

He rested his forehead against mine, and his sweet breath washed over me. "I am now."

"Maddox, I—" I took a step back. I couldn't think with him so close. I'd have to work extra hard to keep my wits about me when he was around.

He cupped my face in his hands, holding me in place as he searched my eyes. "Take a ride with me?"

"A ride?" My heart hammered out a new rhythm, and I knew he could feel my pulse thrumming like a frightened bird under his palms. "Where do you want to go?"

"It's a surprise." He must have known the power he had over me because his hands fell away from my face, and he reached out to grab my hand, towing me toward the bike. "Trust me, okay?" The utter joy in his expression was contagious.

I'd never been on the back of a motorcycle before. It both thrilled and terrified me. I hadn't even climbed on yet, and my legs were shaking.

"Here, put this on." He handed me his leather jacket, helping me slide my arms into the sleeves and zipping me in with a smile. "There. I think I like you like this."

Wearing his coat was like being held in his arms. His warmth and his scent enveloped me, and I had to stop myself from sniffing the collar. "What about you? Won't you be cold?"

"Don't worry, I'll be fine." He leaned forward and kissed the tip of my nose, stunning me into silence. He pulled on a shiny black helmet and handed me its duplicate. "Safety one-oh-one."

I twisted my hair into a loose knot and tucked it inside before fumbling with the strap. "I-I don't know what I'm doing."

"Relax." He reached up to still my shaking hands, securing the helmet before helping me climb behind him on the bike. With a quick glance over his shoulder, he kick-started the engine. "You ready?"

Too scared to speak, I nodded.

"Hang on." And he took off, accelerating down the block.

I clung to him like a second skin, my arms wrapped around his waist in a death grip as we flew through the town, heading north. I had my front pressed so tight to his back I could feel his heartbeat in my stomach. Or maybe that was just butterflies. I'd never experienced anything so amazing.

Even his leather jacket couldn't protect me from the cold while we traveled at eighty miles per hour down the dark highway. Icy air stung my hands and face. My hair worked free and whipped behind me like a scarf. God, was it exhilarating. I imagined birds feeling this way when they soared above the clouds. I was flying, and Maddox was with me.

That was the only thing that really mattered.

CHAPTER NINE

FROM THE MINUTE WE TURNED off the main road, I knew where he was taking me. Even in the dark, I recognized the shapes created by the outcropping of boulders as we turned off Shore Drive and headed down the narrow access road. The towering shape of the lighthouse came into view, and my tummy fluttered.

Since it was after hours, Maddox switched off the headlamp and maneuvered the bike around the locked gate before driving to the other side of the deserted lot where the shadows would hide us from view.

He parked and helped me off the bike and out of the helmet.

"Are you sure we won't get in trouble for being here?" I stumbled on loose rocks as he led me the rest of the way to the shoreline, but he caught me before I fell.

He held me for a moment longer than he needed to, and I thought I might have to restart my heart. But I wasn't complaining. He bit the inside of his cheek, holding back an obvious smirk. "We'll be fine as long as we don't get caught."

"Okay then." I glared at him, and he laughed. "So you never said what it was you had to do this afternoon."

He took my hand to steady me as we climbed down a jagged rock formation to sit on the cluster jutting out into the bay. "Just a stupid family thing."

"Oh."

"Yeah, you know how it is… dealing with family drama." He leaned back on his arms and smiled, but his jaw clenched, and his eyes tightened. "The time juggling gets old after a while, but what can you do, right?"

"I was afraid it had something to do with me. And that idiot Abercrom—I mean Aaron Finch."

That time, his laugh was genuine. "I've been meaning to ask you why you call him Abercrombie."

"Because he always wears that stupid hoodie. I don't think he's ever washed it." I pulled a face, remembering Abercrombie's sweaty scent, and took that moment to discreetly sniff the collar of Maddox's jacket. His fresh rain smell filled my lungs, washing away the sour memory.

Maddox sat up, wrapping his arms around his bent knees, a dark shadow passing over his features. "Well, he'd better stay away from you if he knows what's good for him."

His sudden bout of protectiveness made my stomach clench in a good way.

"I have another question." I chewed on my bottom lip and watched his reaction cautiously, the wind whipping my hair across my face. Every minute we spent out there, the colder it got. Angry waves rolled in, spraying me with icy sea mist, but I didn't care. I would have ridden out a hurricane for the chance to spend time alone with him.

"Go ahead." His brow furrowed, and he tilted his head to one side.

I let the hair flutter around my face, taking any excuse to hide from him while I asked my question. "Have you been stalking me?"

He threw his head back and laughed. "I guess it might have looked that way, huh?"

I pushed my hair back and nodded.

"I wasn't stalking you, per se." He winked, making my stomach flutter again. "But I *was* watching you. I happened to be riding past your house when you pulled up that first day and..." Even in the dark, I could see the flush in his cheeks. "Well, you looked so lost... so beautiful, and I was immediately drawn to you." He leaned forward and brushed his cool fingers over my cheek before capturing my flyaway hair and tucking it behind my ear. "I probably shouldn't have, but I stood under the streetlight and watched you through the window. I guess I'd hoped you might come down and talk to me."

"I wanted to," I said as his hand continued to play with my tangled hair. This touch sent tingles over my skin, and I had to choke back a moan. "But the next day at the hardware store—"

"Ah, yes. The hardware store." His hand dropped to his side, and he sat back. "Your mother was there, and I don't exactly come off as the sort of guy mothers want to see with their daughters, now do I?"

I scoffed. "Why? Because of the leather jacket? Maddox, my *dad* owned a leather jacket. I'm fairly certain my mother could have looked past your clothes."

He raised his eyebrows, and I realized how that statement might have come across.

"I mean, she wouldn't have been bothered by the way you dress. Not if I liked you. She actually trusts my judgment."

"Unless you decide to paint your room black?" His eyebrows went up as he waited for that statement to sink in.

"You were listening?"

He chuckled. "I might have been listening for a minute."

"Well, what about the lighthouse party? My mother wasn't there." Just thinking about that night sent my pulse racing. What I wouldn't give for a reenactment of that kiss.

"How do I explain that night?" He groaned and tipped his face up to the stars while he put the words together. "I can't believe I'm about to admit this." He locked his eyes on mine. "I saw you talking to your friend *Abercrombie*, and it made me jealous. It was ridiculous because we hadn't even met yet, but I felt like he'd taken that chance away from me. Then you pushed him away, and he wouldn't take the hint, so I charged in to rescue you. You know the rest."

"I-I don't remember much." My skin flamed as the memory flared in my mind. "I think we kissed. I have vague memories, but I don't know how I ended up wrapped in a blanket, sleeping on Sam's sneakers."

He smiled. "You kind of passed out. So I wrapped you up and left you with your friends. I stayed for a while and watched over you while you slept." He laughed at my horrified expression and held up his hands in surrender. "Hey, I wanted to make sure that idiot didn't try anything while you were out cold. As soon as he took off with your blue-haired friend, I left."

"Hannah?" I had to pull my chin from my chest after he dropped that bombshell. "*Abercrombie* left with *Hannah*? That's so weird." But it did explain a lot. No wonder she seemed so anxious around him.

"Is that her name? I don't know. I only saw him shoving his tongue down her throat as they walked toward the parking lot."

"Wow. I knew she'd slept with him, but I had no idea there was still something going on between them." A shiver ran through me, and it wasn't from the cold, though the frigid mist had nearly saturated my clothes. I could even taste the salt on my lips.

"Cold?"

I shrank further into the warmth of his jacket. "A little."

"Come on." He took my hand and pulled me to my feet. "We can walk around a little. Get out of the wind before we have to go back."

"Okay." I had to shake my head to keep from getting lost in his eyes.

He threw his arm over my shoulder and nestled me against his side. "Is this okay?"

"Mmhmm." More than okay. Fantastic. Amazing. I never wanted to leave.

He led me toward the lighthouse, and I watched the sweeping path of the beacon as it swirled around. "So tell me why you moved to Port Michael."

"My, uh, dad died." The words were bitter on my tongue, and I suddenly didn't want to focus on anything other than the tops of my shoes.

He stopped walking and turned to look at me. He cupped my face in his hands and forced me to look at him. "Ava, I'm sorry."

I shrugged, swallowing back the instinct to cry. I didn't want to cry in front of him. "Heart attack. Six months ago."

He pulled me into a hug. "That must have been hard."

"It was." I pressed my nose to his chest and breathed in more of his intoxicating scent. "My dad and I were close. Really close." The minute I opened the floodgates, I couldn't stop. I told Maddox about my obsession with classic rock and how Dad started collecting the vintage tees that eventually became mine. And then I told him about Virginia, my little brother, and my mom and how the devastation of her loss had completely changed her—until we'd gotten to Port Michael and somehow, the light was back in her eyes again.

"Maybe your mom just feels safe in Maine. You said she spent summers here as a kid?"

I nodded. "My grandmother left her the house in her will."

"Well, that makes sense. The memories here are different from the memories she had in Virginia. She can probably think about your dad without getting overwhelmed. I-I imagine it's not easy to go on after losing your soul mate." He gave me one last squeeze then turned so we could continue forward. "My mother got sick when I was young, probably before I was born, actually. It wasn't cancer, but it was equally devastating. She lost touch with reality, as if something had eaten away her soul, day by day, little by little. But I don't think she and my dad were ever really in love."

"That's horrible. How could you marry someone you didn't love?"

He shrugged. "It was just how things were done where they were from. I think they had affection for one another, but there wasn't that spark." He took my hand, and I felt the very spark he spoke of.

We'd reached the door to the lighthouse, and I somehow wasn't surprised when Maddox opened it without any trouble. "After you." He let go of my hand to rest his on my lower back as he followed me into the dimly lit room. Light filtered down from high above, highlighting over two centuries of yellowed paint, chipping and flaking from the brick walls like a snake shedding its skin. A winding flight of ornate iron stairs twirled up through the massive tower. Maddox sat on the bottom step, waving me to join him.

I sat beside him, but my thoughts were still on his mom. "I'm sorry. Did she... is your mom..."

"Dead? Yes. But she didn't die until I was much older. She slowly went crazy until she died alone, lost inside her own damaged mind."

"Oh, Maddox. That's terrible." I pressed my hand to my chest. My heart actually ached for him. I wouldn't wish that on anyone, especially to watch someone he loved deteriorate right in front of him.

He rested his forehead to mine, and I tasted a faint hint of minty toothpaste on his breath. "Don't be sad. It was a very long time ago."

I nodded, but I wondered what he considered a long time ago. He couldn't have been much older than me.

"So..." He cupped my chin, lifting my face up to his. The playful grin on his lips told me he was about to change the subject. "You really didn't remember our kiss that night?"

I swallowed before answering in a whisper. "Oh, I remembered it. I-I just wasn't sure if it really happened."

"Well then, I clearly didn't leave much of a lasting impression on you, did I? I definitely think I deserve a do-over." He glanced at my lips then back to my eyes as he waited for me to respond.

I sucked in a jagged breath and went back to gnawing on my bottom lip. My ears buzzed. Whether it was the roar of the ocean or something coming from inside my own head, I didn't know. But my entire body vibrated with excitement. "A do-over, huh?"

"Yes, I'd like a chance to burn the memory into your brain this time. My fragile ego is slightly bruised at the thought of you finding our last kiss so forgettable."

I didn't tell him I'd already irrevocably burned the memory

into my brain. Even if I had thought it was all a dream, I would likely never forget that kiss. "Why is it boys are always so worried about—"

Without preamble, he captured my face in his warm palms, pinning me between his hard chest and the iron railing behind me. Before I could even take a breath, he closed his mouth over mine, silencing the rest of my thought. I moaned and felt a tremor go through him. His soft, pliable lips coaxed mine open, and he slipped his tongue between them to tease the tip of mine. As if someone had run a lit match over my skin, I was burning up and out of breath. Operating on pure instinct, I reached out and grabbed the front of his shirt, tugging him closer—as if that was even possible. Lack of oxygen made my head spin.

His arm came around my waist, yanking my entire front against his. We were so close I could feel his heart beating in my chest as if we were one person. One soul.

And then he was on his feet, pacing the floor in the tight space. "I, uh. I'm sorry." He glanced at me with genuine pain reflecting in his eyes. "I didn't mean to take it that far. I would never try to take advantage of you, Ava."

I licked my lips and tried to smile. The bitter taste of rejection slowly faded away. "It's not taking advantage if I'm a willing participant, right?"

He laughed. "I still shouldn't have done it. You deserve better than that."

I stood and took a step in his direction, careful not to move too quickly. "Why don't you let me decide what I deserve, hmm? Maybe I liked the way you were kissing me. Maybe I liked having your body against me. If that makes me a—"

He silenced me with his mouth, turning me and pressing my back against the brick wall and raising my hands above my head in one of his. "Don't ever disrespect yourself like that," he whispered as his lips burned a trail over my chin and down my throat. "God, you make me so crazy. I can't seem to help myself. I lose control when I'm around you."

Lose control? Until that moment, the boy had exhibited more control than a Franciscan monk. "Let go just a little bit. I'm not ready for... you know. But I want you to kiss me."

His lips found mine again, and I let my arms wrap around his neck as he kissed me into oblivion.

———◆———

"You *will* be in class tomorrow, right?" My teeth sank into my swollen bottom lip as I looked up at him under the streetlight in front of my house. We were right back where we'd started three hours ago. *God, three hours had flashed by in an instant.*

"You mean today?" He gently pulled my lip free and flashed me a smug grin. "I think that's taken quite enough abuse for one night, don't you?"

I shrugged and gave him a smug smile of my own. As far as I was concerned, he could abuse my lips any time—preferably sooner than later. He wasn't even gone yet, and I already missed him. "Oh, I almost forgot." I begrudgingly relinquished the warmth of his jacket and shivered in the cool night air.

"You're cold." He eyed my pebbled skin before leaning down to kiss me again. "You should go in."

My brain knew he was right, but my heart couldn't hear it over the hammering in my chest. "You never answered my question."

"Yes. I'll be in class tomorrow. I'll even get there early and wait for you in the parking lot."

I wanted to ask him to pick me up in the morning, but I wasn't that girl. I'd already given in to the teenage beast too many times in one night. I'd let things evolve naturally. "Okay. Good night."

I backed away until my feet hit the asphalt then turned and ran all the way to the house, stopping again to tiptoe up the porch steps to the front door.

I turned my key in the lock and slipped inside, but not without taking one last peek behind me at the boy who'd somehow managed to steal my heart.

CHAPTER TEN

H IS WARM HAND CLUTCHED MINE *as we darted through a field of wildflowers. My billowing skirts slapped against the tall stalks, kicking up millions of dandelion seeds as we ran. They floated through the air on tiny parachutes, sticking to the glistening sheen of sweat on my skin.*

"Stop. Stop," I panted through giggles. "I can't run anymore. I need to rest."

The musical sound of his laughter kept me going until he tugged me down, pulling me on top of him on a soft bed of flowers. I struggled to sit up, but he held me close. "You said you wanted to rest."

I stopped struggling but didn't quite relax. "But what if my father sees us?"

"He won't." His smile was as bright as the sun. Without moving from his place beneath me, he plucked a bouquet of snowdrops from the ground and presented it to me. "We're very well hidden."

"What if he comes looking for us?"

"He won't. You always worry too much." He rolled until I was under him and brought his lips down to mine for a quick kiss. "He knows I'd never harm you."

I laughed at the lascivious look on his handsome face. "Oh, I don't know about that. I think you mean to give me a raging fever."

"It's only fair. I already burn for you." His mouth captured mine again, sucking the breath from my lungs. No matter how many times I kissed him, I would never get used to the unbridled thrill of it.

Like practiced perfection, our lips moved together. He had me breathless and drunk on his affection. I never wanted him to stop. I needed his touch more than oxygen—the feel of his weight above me, pressing me into the warm earth, his strong hands gripping my hips to keep me still. I would rather suffocate than stop him.

Without warning, he pulled back. He didn't say a word, just stared down at me with a look I couldn't decipher.

"What is it?" My breath caught in my throat. "What's wrong?"

His eyes burned into mine for a long moment. He smiled. "I love you."

"I love you, too." I laughed, grabbing his shirtfront and tugging him back to me.

He kissed me again, nipping and licking my lips. Then he shook his head and pulled away, sitting an arm's length from me. "Wait."

I crawled to sit beside him and pouted out my bottom lip. "No waiting. Just kiss me. We only have until sundown."

He looked into the hazy blue sky then turned his eyes back to mine. "Marry me."

"What?"

"Please. I want to know you're mine forever. If your father won't give us permission, we'll run away together. I'll make all the arrangements if you'll just say you'll marry me."

My smile was so wide I worried my face would crack. "All right. Yes. I'll marry you."

"You will?"

"I will. I love you, Maddox."

As if I'd stabbed him in the chest, he wrenched himself away from me, a look of horror marring his perfect features. His voice cracked on a single word. "Laith."

"What?" I scrambled to my knees, terrified by the wild look in his eyes.

"My name is Laith." He ripped a flower from the ground and proceeded to crush it in his fist. "And I'd almost rather see you die again than let Maddox have you."

A scream bubbled out of me, and I bolted upright in bed as it tore out of me, making my ears ring from the shrill sound.

My heart had clawed halfway up my throat, and I swallowed

it down as I worked to get my breathing under control. *Only a dream—a nightmare—nothing more.* I wasn't surrounded by a field of flowers. I was safe in my bed… at home, though I could still smell the sweet fragrance of the bluebells and the beautiful boy by my side. I licked my lips and still tasted him there. But Maddox *had* kissed me, hadn't he? Last night at the lighthouse. And again outside. For whatever cruel reason, my subconscious was playing tricks on me again, as if my own brain was hell-bent on ruining my happiness.

"Ava!" My mom's voice shouted from the distance, but I couldn't bring myself to respond. I was still too shaken up. "Ava, baby, are you okay?" She came barreling into my room, her eyes frantic until they rested on me. She pressed a hand to her chest. "You screamed. It scared me half to death."

An unexpected laugh worked its way out of me. "A nightmare scared *me* half to death. But I'm fine now, really. It was just a bad dream." I took slow, steadying breaths, trying to convince myself as much as her.

"Well, all right. If you're sure you're okay…" She shook her head and made a noise in her throat. "I think you just gave me a few new gray hairs, kiddo."

I hopped out of bed and gave her a quick kiss on the cheek before walking over to the window. "Not that anyone would know if you still colored it." Part of me hoped Maddox would still be down there, staring up at me. But he wasn't. The man with the Pomeranian paused to let the dog pee on the lamppost.

"Smart ass." She barked out a laugh. "I haven't found a new hairdresser yet. Oh, while I have a chance… I'm going to be late getting home tonight. Your brother has a meet and greet at school, and I promised him fast food. So can you fend for yourself for dinner?"

Fast food?

"Mom?" I turned around as she was walking out the door.

"Great." She disappeared down the stairs. "Have a good day at school, honey."

"Yeah, sure. I'll be fine." But I wasn't thinking about school.

The dream still had me wrapped from head to toe like a pervasive vine. And the name *Laith* played on a loop inside my head.

"He threw pebbles at your window?" Sam spun around to gape at me. Her bubblegum-pink lips parted in a perfect O.

"Yes, now watch the road!" I braced my hands on the dashboard as she took the next corner too sharply. "Eyes forward if you want to hear the rest."

She scowled at me, but kept her eyes on the road. "Fine. Keep going."

"I opened my window, and he was standing beneath it, pleading for me to forgive him." The memory made my insides flutter.

"Oh my God, that's so Romeo and Juliet. How freaking romantic. You made him beg, right?" She glanced at me, and I pointed to the road in front of us. "Whatever. Never forgive a guy right away. Always make him work for it."

I giggled at her serious face. "Yes, I made him beg a little." I left out the part about him falling to his knees in front of me and almost getting run over by a car. She didn't need to know *all* the details. I didn't want her to faint when she saw me with him at school. "But once he explained everything, I did end up forgiving him."

She didn't respond right away, as if she was thinking about it. Then she nodded once. "Well, I would have made him sweat it out for a while, but if you're sure, then I'm happy for you."

Was I sure? A faint sliver of worry worked its way under my skin. What if after everything that happened last night, he still didn't show up? What if the nightmare was some sort of subconscious warning not to trust him? I had to stop thinking like that, or our relationship would be doomed before it even got started. *Relationship?* I didn't even know what our status was. After last night, was I his girlfriend? Were we just friends? Would he even acknowledge me in front of other people? And the voice inside my head whispered, *"Laith."* The unknown was eating me alive.

"Earth to Ava." Sam waved her hand in front of my face, and I realized we'd stopped moving. "There you are. I thought I'd lost you for a minute."

I shook the fog from my head and searched the parking lot for the familiar flame-orange motorcycle and the boy in the black leather jacket. "Sorry, I guess I zoned out for a minute."

She tilted the rear view mirror down and applied another coat of pink lipstick. "He's not here. I already looked."

My eyes snapped to Sam's, and she grinned. "Oh, you've got it bad all right. But don't look so worried. We're a few minutes early. Maybe we beat him."

I pulled my lower lip between my teeth and nodded. "Right. Of course. He'll be here." *He promised.* My stomach churned, and I immediately regretted the runny eggs I'd eaten for breakfast.

"Come on. Hannah and Paige are waiting." She nodded toward my window, and I turned to see Paige tapping out a rhythm with the toe of her fancy red stiletto. Hannah stood beside her, twirling a lock of blue hair around her finger, a bored look plastered on her face.

"Okay, fine." I blew out a breath. "At least I can always count on Paige to distract me."

Sam was still laughing as we reached Cinderella's wicked stepsisters, although I didn't really think of Hannah that way anymore. I didn't know *what* to think of her after hearing about her weird relationship with Abercrombie.

"What's so funny?" Paige glared at me, curling up her lip as if she'd smelled something bad.

"Ava is. She always cracks me up." Sam nudged me with her shoulder.

"Oh, yes." Paige's grimace twisted into a fake smile. "Our little Ava is such a comedic genius."

Hannah rolled her eyes. "Shut up, Paige."

"What?" Paige tried to look innocent, but she wasn't fooling me. "Fine. I have to go anyway. I need to talk to my philosophy professor."

"Trying to get out of the food bank thing now that you know

he's off limits?" I batted my eyelashes at Paige, and she snarled at me. She turned on her overpriced heels to walk away. "Bitch," I muttered under my breath.

The growl of a motorcycle engine snapped me back to my senses, and I whipped around as Maddox rolled to a stop beside Sam's car. The urge to go to him was like a living, breathing creature, and I had to steel myself to keep it from bolting across the parking lot.

"Keep cool, and let him come to you," Sam whispered as if she could read my thoughts.

I watched him secure his helmet to the bike and sweep his eyes around the perimeter. As if he was as tuned in to me as I was to him, his gaze landed on me, and his face split in a wide grin. He didn't run, but he moved swiftly as he closed the distance between us, never taking his eyes from mine.

Every drop of anxiety I'd felt since the moment I walked away from him in the wee hours of the morning melted away like a snowman in a greenhouse. By the time he reached me, I couldn't contain my smile anymore. The expected "next day" awkwardness was nowhere to be found as he cupped my face between his hands and pressed his mouth to mine.

Ignoring everyone around us, he finally pulled his lips away but didn't release me. "Good morning."

"Morning." I closed my eyes and leaned my face into his touch, drawing in his scent until I felt whole again. How'd he have so much power over me after so short a time? It was as if I'd been possessed or something.

And by the way he nuzzled my neck, I could tell he felt it too. "Did you sleep well?"

His question caught me off guard, and I opened my eyes, feeling my body tense as the heavy scent of bluebells and sunshine flooded back to me.

"What is it?" he asked, and I knew from the set of his jaw that my uneasiness had leached into him. The last thing I wanted to do was spoil the moment with my stupid insecurities.

I shook my head, forcing my nerves to quiet. "It's nothing. Not enough sleep, I guess. *Someone* kept me up very late."

He nodded, but something in his eyes told me he didn't quite believe me. "You'd tell me if something was bothering you, right?"

I swallowed back my confession and smiled. "Of course. But there's nothing to tell. I didn't get enough sleep, then my mom woke me up early."

He brushed his lips against mine again. "Remember, you can tell me anything."

For an instant, I debated telling him about the stupid nightmare but shook off the urge. It was a *dream*, nothing more. I'd had bad dreams a lot lately. A therapist would probably tell me my subconscious was still dealing with the loss of my dad. And the move. And the mysterious stranger who was or wasn't my boyfriend.

Not to mention a raging case of hormones. When I thought about it, I realized I'd gotten off easy. I flashed him a genuine smile. "I promise to tell you if something bothers me."

"Good. Now we'd better get to class, or we'll be late." He took my hand and pulled me across the deserted quad.

"Where is everyone?"

His body shook with laughter, and he squeezed my hand. "They took off while we were..." He stopped walking and turned to me, a serious look in his eyes. "I guess they got uncomfortable watching the unbridled passion sparking between us."

Something about the way he said the words made my stomach flip, and I felt it all the way to my toes. The sparks between us were no joke. We could probably set fire to the entire building if we kept the skin-to-skin contact going.

As if he'd read my mind, his face lit up in a brilliant smile. "Now come on before I say to hell with the History of European Civilization."

———◆———

Our first official lunch as a couple—or whatever we were—was shaping up to be a disaster. I had no idea where to sit. We'd kissed, but we'd never defined our relationship, and I felt like a complete idiot for letting it get to me. My hands gripped the sides of my tray as I contemplated my options. Since Maddox hadn't said anything and I was too afraid to ask, I found myself torn between sitting with my group at the big table in the center of the room and sitting at the quiet table in the back where Maddox had chosen to sit the only time I'd seen him in the dining hall.

"Everything okay?"

"Yeah, fine."

"Because, if something's bothering you, you know you can tell me." He chuckled as he sidled up beside me and whispered, his lips over my ear. "You always worry too much."

I whipped my head around to face him. "What did you say?"

He took a step back and scrunched up his face. "I said, 'you worry too much.'"

"No, you said *always*. I *always* worry too much." My knees threatened to give out on me. I'd heard those words before. In my dream.

"You must have misheard me." A tight smile stretched his face. "You were standing here as if you were lost in thought, and I—"

"I, uh..." I blinked away the image of Maddox in a field of wildflowers. "I wasn't sure where I should sit."

He let out a breath and nodded to the table where Sam was waving at us like a lunatic. "Don't you usually sit over there with your friends?"

"Uh, yeah. I do." We were blocking the aisle, and several people had lined up behind us, grumbling to make their annoyance known.

"Well there you go. Problem solved." He let the conversation drop and stepped around me on a straight path to my usual table. He sat his tray down, leaving room between him and Sam, then turned around as if to ask what I was still doing across the dining hall.

"Yeah, what am I still doing over here?" I mumbled to myself, and the girl behind me snorted out a laugh.

Maddox met me halfway and took the tray from my shaky hands. He acted as if nothing had happened, as if he hadn't just quoted a line straight from my subconscious. "You're acting really strange today. Are you sure nothing's bothering you?"

"I'm fine." But as I followed him back to the table, I couldn't manage to push his words out of my head. No matter what he'd said, I knew what I'd heard. Even the air around me seemed to shift with tension only the two of us could feel—and only one of us would acknowledge.

Maddox turned toward me and dialed up his smile to full volume. "Good. I'm starving."

I nodded and waited for him to start walking again. The urge to ask him the significance of the name "Laith" ate at me. My emotions seemed to be very much on his radar. And at the risk of sounding like every bit the teenage girl I was, I had a desperate need to know where I stood with him. But these things required finesse. Surely, *as an adult*, I could bring up the topics with some level of tact, couldn't I?

Maddox stopped again in front of our table and let out a sigh. "Ava, you really need to say what's on your mind. I promise it'll be okay. Whatever it is."

I drew in a deep breath. Then before I could stop myself, I blurted out the words, "Are we... I mean, are you... God, why is this so hard?"

"Just spit it out," Sam whispered from my left.

"Are you my boyfriend?" As soon as I got the question out, I slapped my hand over my mouth, wishing the floor would swallow me whole.

He set my tray on the table then turned to take both of my hands in his. "I sort of hoped after... well, after last night, you were. But if you'd rather not be my, uh, girlfriend—" He hid it well, but I still saw the flash of hurt in his eyes.

Before he could stop me, I wrapped my arms around his neck and silenced him with a kiss. Once the shock wore off, he responded by snaking his hands around me, lifting me off the floor and against his chest.

"Get a room!" a deep voice bellowed from a nearby table.

He set me back on my feet, and I hid my face in his chest until the catcalls died down. "I guess we shouldn't do that in public," he whispered, tugging me to sit beside him.

"Yeah…" I took a sip of my drink to cool off. "Probably not."

Sam leaned over from the other side of me. "Nice. I think I might need a cigarette after that kiss."

I coughed over a laugh. "You don't smoke."

"Well, honey, you *do*." She bumped my shoulder. "I could see the fireworks sparking from a mile away like a four-alarm fire in a tire factory. Totally unnatural."

I didn't bother telling her she was less than a foot away, because that was hardly the point. She'd hit the nail on the head. My skin prickled around him. I dreamed of him, I ached for him. I burned for him. And we barely knew each other.

But she'd gotten one part wrong. My feelings for him were as natural as breathing, as if we were destined to be together.

The prickling at the base of my neck flared, and Maddox captured my hand in his under the table and squeezed. I had no doubt he felt it too—the strange, electric connection between us.

It didn't matter how it had happened, I knew I didn't want it to end.

CHAPTER ELEVEN

1654

"COME IN, COME IN. I expected you some time ago." The old woman waved a gnarled hand toward Lady Catherine, and Catherine flinched away from her touch. The woman shook with laughter, exposing a scattered row of dingy teeth. "Afraid of an old woman?"

"No, of course not. I'm sorry. The weather is bad, and the ride has made me jumpy." Catherine stepped inside, shoving away the feet of several dead black birds hanging from the low ceiling as she wandered into the small cottage. A heavy curtain divided the room, and she wondered what the woman hid on the other side.

She forced a smile and tried to avoid pinching her nose to block the sharp scent of herbs, rot, and something else that she suspected emanated from the steam of a large pot simmering on the hearth. The sour odor didn't smell like any soup she'd ever been served, and the pitiful flames were barely large enough to give off heat.

The woman nodded. "A fine lady such as yourself shouldn't be out in this." She gave a quick peek out at the deluge before slamming the door shut. "So what brings you to see me? Not a social visit, I suspect."

Dragging the sodden hood from her head, Catherine shook out her curls in an attempt to avoid eye contact. "No. Not exactly." She smoothed the wrinkles in her skirt. "My handmaiden, Mary Black, bid me come see you. With my husband gone and the future uncertain..." Catherine stared at a wall of shelves as she struggled to come up with the words.

The flimsy boards sagged from the weight of all the jars lined across each one. So many jars of all different sizes. Several contained what appeared to be dried herbs and plants, but others brimmed with what looked like small animal parts floating in cloudy liquid. A throat clearing drew her eyes from her surroundings and back to the woman.

The old woman chuckled and locked her foggy gray eyes with Catherine's bright-blue ones. "I know why you're here. The same reason anyone of your rank comes to see me. You're looking for a blessing."

"I am." She rested her hand on her stomach. "But not for me."

"Ah, you're looking for guarantees for the baby's well-being?"

"Is it possible?" Catherine's eyes implored the woman.

She let out a loud laugh. "It is if you've brought your purse with you."

Catherine smiled, fishing into her cloak for the silk bag at her waist. "Yes. Of course. Here." She thrust the coin-filled pouch into the woman's hands. "Ten crowns."

"Just ten?"

Catherine's delicate face fell. "Is it more? Mary said—"

"No, no. Ten will do nicely." The woman tore into the bag, pulling out a coin. She put it between her rotten teeth and bit down, grinning from ear to ear before dropping it back into the bag with a clink. "Though I'd gladly relieve you of more if you have it."

Catherine said nothing and waited.

"Very well." The woman gave a terse nod. "Have a seat, and tell me exactly what it is you want from me."

She perched herself delicately on the utilitarian chair across from the old woman and folded her hands across her lap. "I want my child to be brought safely into the world. I want him healthy."

The woman leaned forward until her stale breath washed over Catherine's face. "You're certain it's a boy?"

"Well, no. Not certain. But I do hope. And if my instincts are correct, I want to be certain no one attempts to punish him for his father's choices."

"And what of your choices?" The woman narrowed her eyes.

Lady Catherine blanched. "What of my choices? I've done nothing to be ashamed of."

"If you say so." The woman nodded. "Continue."

"And I want to be certain he's comfortable. Financially. My husband is a very wealthy man, but if the tide should turn away from his favor, I want to be sure my child is still protected."

"Is that all?"

Catherine felt the woman's eyes boring into her soul and shifted her attention to her lap. "There is one more thing I would like."

"There always is. Go on."

With a determination that surprised even her, Catherine raised her eyes to the woman. "I want my son to know great love. But not just know it. Possess it. I want a guarantee that he'll be reunited with the other half of his soul. I believe the Greeks called it the split apart. I want to know that no matter what happens, my child will find his soul mate. I want them bound together for all time."

The woman shook her head, an uneasy look on her face. "The first part I can do. A simple blessing for good fortune is easy enough. The rest... I'm sorry. You've come to the wrong place."

"Why?"

"Because the Greeks were wrong!" the woman snapped. "And the consequences of such things are simply too great. Anything I do comes back in threefold. I won't take responsibility for that. No."

Catherine jumped to her feet. "I'll take full responsibility. I know for a fact soul mates exist. I found mine once, but my father forced me to let him go in deference to an arranged marriage. I don't want that future for my child—one of loneliness and longing."

The woman backed away, shaking her head. "You don't know what you're asking. What we do is about intent, and beneath all your love, the true intent of your heart is fear. No good magic comes of fear."

"I-I have more gold. I can give you two sovereigns for your trouble."

The old woman's face lit up before she tamped down her reaction. "Despite what my circumstances may imply, I can't be bought."

"But that's so much money. More than most people see in a year."

The woman scoffed. "Money means little to me if I'm not around to spend it."

"I'll do it." Another voice sounded from behind the torn drape. The curtain pulled back, and a woman no older than Catherine stepped out. Her dress was simple gray linen, and her dark hair hung in loose tangles about her shoulders, but she carried herself like someone born to privilege. And she was lovely.

"No! Jane, you mustn't." The old woman rushed to the younger girl, her eyes wild.

"Yes, Aunt Bess, I must. And if you won't take her money, I will. It may come to be that those two sovereigns are the only thing between you and a burning stake!"

"Lest you forget, there are far worse things than *that*," the woman barked at her niece then turned to Catherine. "You should leave. There's nothing for you here."

"Wait. Please!" Catherine begged.

"What you ask for is impossible. Now go."

"Dear aunt, be reasonable. We need the money. And the woman is desperate."

The old woman shook her head. "She'll be worse than that if we agree."

"I'll assume all responsibility." Jane clasped her aunt's mangled hands in her own.

The old woman gasped. "You'll do no such thing! Jane, take it back. Promise me you won't agree to something so foolish."

"If you won't have me do it here, I'll meet her elsewhere and make the deal. You can't stop me." Jane stood tall and jutted out her chin defiantly.

"Fine." The woman glared at her niece for a long moment then directed her icy stare to Catherine. "You have the gold on your person?"

Catherine nodded.

"And you'll accept the threefold consequences that the spell will bring forth?" Her clouded eyes flashed.

"I said I would, and I will."

The older witch gave a nod. "Very well, then. I'll do it."

CHAPTER TWELVE

I YANKED ON A PINK FLOYD concert tee and ran a hand through my tangled waves before flying down the stairs. I was late. "Mom, I'm leaving! Be home before sunrise." I'd almost made it to the front door before she caught me.

"Not so fast." Mom stood in the doorway between the living and dining rooms with her arms crossed and her famous bitch brow in place. I hadn't seen it make an appearance since the "paint it black" incident. She made Paige look like an amateur. "I'd like to set down a few ground rules before you go."

I deflated my lungs with a groan. "Come on, Mom. I'm nineteen and in college."

My birthday had come and gone without much fanfare. Mom baked a cake and gave me a two-hundred-dollar Amazon gift card. The peanut decided only one thing in his budget would make for a good present and relinquished all claims to the third-story bedroom. But since Maddox and I had only just made our relationship official, I didn't even tell him it was my birthday. I figured in a week or two I'd let it slip, and by then the awkwardness would have passed. Sam either didn't remember or was too preoccupied with the "first party of the school year," and that was just fine with me. I'd already gotten what I wanted, and he was probably waiting outside.

"You may be in college, but you're still living under my roof, and at nineteen, you're legally entitled to join the military if you don't like my rules."

"Really?" I let my mouth fall open as I stared at her harsh expression. She almost looked serious this time. "You're pulling the military thing again? It's not as if I'm going on a killing spree. I'm going to a party. With my *boyfriend*." Ever since Maddox had declared himself in the dining hall, I took every opportunity to say "my boyfriend." I'd dated a little in Annandale, but I'd never been anyone's girlfriend before.

"That's *exactly* why I wanted to make sure you understand the rules." With the light from the dining room behind her, Mom looked almost dangerous as she stared me down.

I sighed and sat down on the bottom step. For some unknown reason, I'd managed to get caught in Joanie Flynn's parent radar, and there was no sense even trying to escape until she'd said her piece. I waved her on. "Go ahead."

She relaxed her stiff posture and leaned against the doorframe. "First of all, I don't like you riding on the back of his motorcycle—"

"Mom! Maddox drives a motorcycle. But he's very careful, and in case you didn't know, I've already been on it, and I'm still alive, so the point is moot." If she'd only known where we'd gone on the back of that bike. I was sure after-hours visits to the lighthouse would be against her rules.

"You didn't let me finish. I don't like it, but I'll let that slide. But I do expect you to check in with me when you get there, and let me know when you leave so I don't worry."

I narrowed my eyes and tried to see through her poker face. "That's it?"

"Almost. I'd better not find out you, or especially Maddox, were drinking tonight."

"Drive safely, and no drinking. Got it." I gave her a stiff salute, biting the insides of my cheeks to keep from smiling.

"And have fun, but not *too* much fun. Remember, I was a teenager once, too." She smirked, and I knew the lecture was over.

I hopped up from the step. "So... you couldn't have covered all of that in a text message?"

"What? And miss the look on your face? No way." She swatted my butt with the dishtowel I didn't even notice she was holding and went back to whatever she'd been doing.

After watching until she'd disappeared into the kitchen, I turned to leave. As I reached the door, my cell phone chirped with a message.

Maddox: Something came up. Can you catch a ride with Sam? I'll meet you there.

I texted Sam to see if she could swing by and get me then sent a message to Maddox letting him know I had a ride.

Me: Everything okay?

Maddox: Yeah, just more of that family drama I was talking about. I should have it figured out before you even miss me.

Me: Too late. ;) See you there. Don't take too long. I'm wearing a miniskirt!

Maddox: You're killing me!

The urge to type those three little life-changing words was unbearable. My fingers hovered over the touchscreen for a half a minute before I changed my mind. We hadn't gotten to the "I love yous" yet, but it was only by sheer willpower that I managed to hold back. I didn't want to be the first one to say it. And not in a text message.

Sam pulled up a few minutes later, and the music thumping from her speakers reached me all the way inside the house.

"Mom, I'm riding with Sam, so you don't need to worry about seeing my body parts spread across Main Street. At least not until later. Love you!" Without waiting for her reply, I slipped through the door and ran the whole way to Sam's yellow convertible. I jumped into the passenger seat with a giggle.

"Wow. You're in a hurry." Sam laughed as she backed onto the street. Then she let out a squeal, burning rubber as she tore off down the street.

Will Clark lived on a deserted stretch of road in a waterfront building overlooking Casco Bay. According to Sam, the house was originally some sort of World War II warehouse. Rumor had it that it had housed a military armory, and I couldn't help imagining rows and rows of warheads stacked against the walls like furniture.

Not even a single streetlight illuminated the long, narrow

drive, but perimeter lights made the house glow in the distance. The angular shapes gave the building an industrial vibe, but it had supposedly been converted into a family home somewhere at the end of the last century. Vehicles squeezed into every available square inch all the way from the street to the sidewalk out front, but Sam managed to sandwich us between a hedgerow and the mailbox without getting a scratch on her car.

"Impressive." I gave her a nod as I inspected her parking job.

"This isn't my first rodeo, you know." She flashed me a grin then cut the engine and pocketed the keys. "Okay, you're gonna wanna stick with me. This party can get pretty *intense*."

"Intense?" I followed her out of the car, but a ripple of anxiety made my stomach clench.

"You'll be fine. Just don't take any unsealed drinks from anyone but me. And don't eat the Jell-O. Oh, and don't go upstairs. If you have to pee, there's a bathroom right off the kitchen."

I swallowed the urge to climb back into the car and sit there until Maddox showed up. "Is that it?"

She twisted her lips to the side. "Pretty much."

Somehow, her lack of confidence didn't make me feel any better.

Sam grabbed my wrist and towed me toward the house. The pulsing beat made the ground beneath my feet vibrate, and we followed the sound all the way down the walkway to the front door. Sam didn't bother knocking. She just pushed the door open as if she lived there and shoved her way past the sea of drunken coeds with her eyes fixed on the wall of windows in the back.

Inside, the house looked nothing like a military fortress. Decorated in muted colors and expensive art, the living room would have looked more like a magazine layout if most of the furniture hadn't been shoved against the walls to make room for dancing.

"Where are we going?" I shouted over the techno beat, but it was a useless effort. A wall of sound swallowed my voice.

Sam mouthed something I couldn't understand then gripped my wrist tighter as she led me through the crowded room, making a quick stop along the way to grab a few bottles of apple ale. We bumped into a few people I'd seen before, but other than a quick wave, they barely acknowledged my presence.

By the time we reached the back deck, my ears were ringing, and I discreetly checked them for blood. I'd been to my share of rock concerts but had never been exposed to music so loud. Even from outside, standing less than a hundred yards from the shore, I could barely hear the waves crashing against the rocks.

"Oh my God, that was loud." Sam handed me a bottle of lukewarm ale then stuck a finger in her ear and wiggled it around. "I'm seriously going to be deaf before I'm thirty."

"So now what do we do?" I twisted off the top and took a sip of the drink I'd promised my mom I wouldn't have. I leaned against the railing and stared out at the ocean, regretting my decision to let Sam drag me to the party. It hadn't seemed like such a bad idea when Maddox was going to be with me, but being there without him made my skin prickle. In a bad way.

Sam brought the bottle to her lips and sucked it down without taking a breath. "First, we're going to get a buzz while we wait for Paige and Hannah. Then we're—"

"Can I ask you something?" I turned to face her, taking a big gulp of my drink as I worked up the courage to speak the words in my head. "Why do you like Paige? I mean, she's pretty and smart, but most of the time she's…"

"A bitch?" Sam shrugged with a laugh. "Yeah, I know. But I've known her since I was seven, so I guess it's mostly just a habit. She isn't *all* bad, you know. Give her some time. She'll grow on you."

Like a wart, maybe. "Yeah, I'm sure you're right."

"So…" Sam held up her empty bottle. "You want another drink?"

I shook my head. "I promised my mom no alcohol."

"Oh come on. You had one little drink. It'll wear off way before it's time to leave." She flashed me her sugary grin. "She'll never even know."

"Fine. But just one more." Once again, I'd fallen victim to peer pressure.

While Sam braved the eardrum-shattering music, I watched the sweeping arc of light from the lighthouse beacon down the bay. I polished off the last of my drink and thought of Maddox. *Where is he?*

"You look beautiful with the ocean as your backdrop."

I spun around to the sound of his voice, and my mouth fell open. He looked sinfully good. Not that he didn't always look good—he did. But standing in front of me sipping an imported beer and wearing a pair of destroyed jeans with a white Imagine Dragons T-shirt stretched across his solid chest, he was almost too good to be true. I didn't even miss the leather jacket he'd obviously left behind. He stole my breath. "You made it."

Maddox handed me another bottle of apple ale and leaned down to brush his lips against mine. "You couldn't have kept me away if you'd tried."

"Where's your jacket?" Okay, so maybe I missed the smell of leather a little.

He shrugged then nuzzled my neck. "It's a warm night." His voice, so close to my skin, did things to me. The day's growth of stubble on his chin rasped over my skin, sending tingles all the way to my toes.

"You didn't shave." I leaned into him, mesmerized by the attention he was lavishing on me and feeling the calming effects of the alcohol in my system.

"Do you mind?" he whispered. "I was a bit preoccupied."

"With your family thing?" He had me breathless, trailing kisses down the column of my neck.

He chuckled against my throat. "Yeah, I had to do something about my family."

"Is everything okay now?" I pulled back to look up into his dark eyes. Something unfamiliar flashed in them, but I chalked that up to the crazy circumstances.

"Everything's perfect." He smirked before closing his mouth

over mine. His lips tasted faintly of beer, but the waves of intoxication coursing through me had little to do with alcohol.

I opened my mouth to speak, but he stopped me with his tongue, massaging it against mine. The prickling in my neck spread like a brush fire as Maddox drove me to the edge of reason. I felt him everywhere at once. His hands skated over my hips then down and around until he rested them on my butt. Despite wanting to kiss him more than I wanted oxygen, my lungs burned. I wrenched my face away to steal a quick breath, and he lifted me off the ground, wrapping my bare legs around his waist.

"Come on. I wanna show you something." He carried me down the steps to the patio below.

Before I realized what was happening, he had my back pressed against the rough brick wall, scraping my skin through my clothes. I ignored the pain, too caught up in the sensations created where his body lined up with mine. I had no idea what had gotten into him, but I liked it. A lot. Too much for my own good, in fact. I almost managed to push Sam from my thoughts. *Almost.*

"I've missed you so much, baby." He dove back in with a groan, fusing our lips together.

He practically vibrated with tension, his grip on my thighs almost painful as he rocked against me, building toward something new and exciting but also completely terrifying. He repositioned my legs, and a spark flared inside me. We hadn't done more than kiss before, and things were quickly moving far beyond kissing. I couldn't believe we were doing this. Here. Out in the open. Any more pressure and I'd fall apart where we stood.

Maddox's hand slid down the length of my leg, caressing my calf until I couldn't think straight, before making the trip back up. He paused just below the hem of my denim skirt, then his long fingers made the slow climb up my thigh.

My pulse quickened, and my head spun as he reached my

panties and traced the elastic leg band. "Wait." I tried to pull away, but he held me tight.

"I don't want to wait. Tell me this is okay," he begged as his other hand skated up my side, passing dangerously close to my breast before sliding into my hair. The fingers under my skirt glanced over the silk covering my crotch, and my breath caught in my throat.

"Okay." I panted out the word, too drunk on his touch to argue.

He slipped under the thin fabric, exploring me with the pads of his fingers. Every time he moved, he pushed me closer to the edge. *Almost there. Don't stop now.* I knew what came next, and I really wanted to be ready.

"Damn it, Ava." He groaned, bucking his hips into me. "I need to be inside you."

Fear shot through me, and I ripped my face away from his. No matter what I *wanted*, no matter how badly my body begged for release, I wasn't even close to being ready. "What's gotten into you? Are you drunk or something?"

He had the audacity to laugh. "What's wrong with *you*? Don't pretend you don't feel this too. And you know as well as I do we belong together, so why wait?"

I tried to squirm out of his grip, but he held on tighter, and I was certain I'd find finger-shaped bruises marking my skin come morning. That pissed me off more and managed to strip away the last of my longing like a layer of old paint. "Maybe because we're at a party, standing outside someone's house for all the world to see."

"Let them see." He ran his nose down my neck. "Are you afraid they'll be jealous?"

"You're acting completely crazy." I finally managed to unwrap my legs from around his waist and struggled until I stood firmly on my own two feet. My eyes burned with unshed tears, but I wasn't going to cry in front of him. "I wanna go home."

His anger flared. He paced, gripping his hair in both hands. "Fine, I'll take you home."

I shoved my shirt down from where it had ridden up to just under my bra. "Oh, no. I'm not riding with you. You've been drinking. Just go find a quiet room and sleep it off. I'll get Sam to take me. And if she won't take me, I'll call a cab."

"No, please don't go." The pleading tone in his voice broke through a bit of the ice, but I was still too mad to listen.

"I'll talk to you tomorrow." I pushed past him to run up the steps, barely beating him into the house. Tears blurred my vision as I shoved bodies out of my way to get inside. It didn't take long to find Sam. She had her mouth attached to some random guy's lips across the room. "Great. There goes my ride home."

"Ava?"

I spun around to face Paige and quickly wiped the trail of tears from my cheeks. "What do you want?" My voice came out nastier than I'd intended, but it was Paige. I didn't care if I'd hurt her feelings. If she even had feelings.

She held up her hands in front of her and took a step back. "Hey, I'm just trying to see if you're okay."

I screwed up my face, trying to swap the dagger in my chest for some good old-fashioned venom. "No, I'm *not* okay. I needed a ride home, but it looks like I'll be calling a cab." I pulled my phone from my back pocket and searched for a signal to look up the number.

"Oh. Well… I can drive you." She said it as if it was the most natural suggestion in the world. And that made me suspicious.

My eyes snapped up from my phone. "You? But you hate me."

Her bubbly laughter caught me off guard. *Paige? Bubbly?* Maybe *I* was the one who was drunk. "Listen, I know I can be a bitch, but that doesn't mean I can't do something nice once in a while. I only came so Hannah could get wasted if she wanted to and still have a safe way to get home. I can run you home really quick and come back. She won't even know I'm gone."

The tears were back, this time for a completely different reason. "You'd do that for me?"

"I'll deny it if you tell anyone, but yeah, come on. I'll take you home." She winked. Paige—the ice princess—*winked.*

Never in my wildest dreams would I have expected Paige to rescue me. Throw me to the wolves, maybe. But drive me home? Never. I managed a weak smile. "Thanks, Paige. I owe you one."

"And believe me, I'll collect." She tried to hide her grin, but I caught it just before she smoothed her features back into her resting bitch face. "Otherwise, people will think I've gone soft."

"You're okay in my book. But I'll totally deny it if anyone asks." I nudged her with my shoulder. "I'm thinking—just to make sure we don't upset the delicate balance of nature or anything like that—we should go back to being enemies on Monday. You know, at least in public."

She threw her head back and laughed. "Deal."

CHAPTER THIRTEEN

M Y PHONE LIT UP WITH another text, and I ignored it like all the rest. The messages had been coming in like clockwork since midnight, the alert tone chirping every few minutes. I knew Sam had to have been worried since I left without telling her, but I couldn't respond to her without seeing *his* name pop up on the screen. And without question, I wasn't ready to talk to Maddox, not when simply thinking about him brought me to tears.

After Paige dropped me off around eleven, I dragged myself to my room, took a long, hot shower, and retreated to safety beneath my covers. I had no idea what to do. My brain ached with all the questions floating around in there.

What could have possibly happened to make Maddox drink so much? And it wasn't as if I didn't want to have sex with him. I'd thought about it more times than I cared to admit, but I certainly didn't want my first time to be under the deck in the middle of a party. How could he think I'd want that? How could *he* want that? Did I really know him at all?

The opening bars of "Paint It Black" by the Rolling Stones played, and I rolled over so fast I almost spilled myself onto the floor. I fumbled with my phone, trying to press the ignore button, but somehow hit speaker instead. I meant to end the call—wanted to end it—but before I could stop it, Maddox's voice echoed through my room, and I froze in place.

"Ava? Hello? Are you there?" He groaned. "Ugh, I can hear you breathing. God, Ava, please say something. I'm dying out here. I really need to talk to you. To explain what happened. I'm so sorry about—"

I couldn't listen to him rehash our evening over the phone, so I ended the call and rolled back over, pulling the blankets over my head. I didn't want his attempted apology to affect me, but the pain in his voice managed to work its way under my skin like a splinter. And unfortunately, the only cure for a Maddox hangover was more Maddox.

I reached up and switched off my phone before punching my pillow a few times. With a groan, I did a face plant straight into it, hoping sleep would take me fast, but knowing it wouldn't.

———————◆———————

Plink... plink... plink.

I reached for my phone to silence it then remembered I'd already turned it off.

Plink... plink... plink.

Damn it. Someone was throwing pebbles against my window again, and I had a pretty good idea who. I jumped out of bed and crept to the window, keeping to the shadows so Maddox couldn't see me.

He stood below my window, dressed in his usual black from head to toe, and I wondered why he'd bothered to change. He reached up to throw another pebble but stopped mid-throw. Our eyes locked.

"Ava?" He mouthed my name, and even without hearing the sound, I could feel the pain in his expression.

I hoisted my window open and leaned out. "What?" I tried to keep my voice down, despite the urge to scream at him at the top of my lungs.

"Can you please come down? Just for a few minutes? I really need to talk to you."

"We *talked* plenty already." The irony of that statement wasn't lost on me.

"What?" He screwed up his face and shook his head. "Ava, I'm really sorry about tonight. I didn't mean to—"

"Listen, I'll see you tomorrow at school, okay? You can beg forgiveness then." I had the window halfway down before he yelled up.

"Wait! Please just come down and talk to me." The words ripped out of him, and he seemed to deflate with the effort. "Please."

"You're gonna wake my mom, and then she'll ground me so I *never* get to see you again." I should have closed the window and stuffed cotton in my ears. The sound of his voice, the look on his face—he had to have known he was getting through. The chinks in my armor were big enough to park a motorcycle in.

He stood straighter, a determined look in his hypnotic eyes. "I guess you'd better come down, because I'm not leaving until you do."

"Stupid stubborn boy," I muttered. "Fine. I'll come down, but you've only got ten minutes, so you'd better make it good."

I grabbed my keys from the nightstand and headed downstairs in my pajamas. I might have given up, but I wasn't giving in. If he wanted my forgiveness, he'd have to work for it.

After making it past the loose floorboards in the stairs and tiptoeing past my mom's room, I slipped through the front door and closed it behind me. Then I dashed across the damp grass in my bare feet to where he waited on the other side of the street, leaning on his motorcycle in the shadows.

"If you think I'm going for a ride on your bike, you're sadly mistaken." I folded my arms over my chest to keep out the chill in the air and regretted not grabbing a sweater.

"Are you cold? Do you want my jacket?" He had it off before I could say no and draped it over my shoulders, enveloping me in his warmth. He fought dirty. "I wasn't going to ask you to go for a ride. I just wanted to come and tell you how sorry I am about tonight."

"Well, you should be sorry. You can't treat me like that. If you want me to be your girlfriend, you can't just—" *Act like every other college boy looking to get laid on a Saturday night.* I didn't say it, but I thought it hard enough to send the message through, I was sure of it.

"I know. I'm sorry. It's just that the thing with my family got out of hand tonight and—"

"That's not my problem. But you can't act like—"

"Like I have no respect for you. I know. Can you forgive me?" He seemed sincere. He looked as if he'd learned his lesson. But it was too easy. Too quick.

I shifted my weight, turning a half circle so I wasn't facing him anymore, but I could still see his reaction in my peripheral vision. "I don't know. First you make me think you're an illusion, then you disappear on me, and now this."

He took a tentative step toward me and wrapped his arm around my shoulder, waiting until I relaxed to tug me all the way in. "Ava, I'm sorry. I should have… I don't know."

"You *shouldn't* have had so much to drink." I turned the tables again, regaining the power in our argument.

"I haven't had anything to drink." He laughed as if my statement was the most ridiculous thing he'd ever heard.

I scoffed. "Don't lie, Maddox. I could taste the beer on your breath."

"When?" He stepped back and held me at arm's length. Something that looked suspiciously like fear flashed behind his eyes. "What are you talking about?"

"Are we pretending nothing happened now? I mean, I get it. I lose control around you too, but I thought for sure we'd talk about it rather than pretend nothing happened." I let the frustration flow out of me. I'd had enough of the games for one night.

He shook his head, and for a second I thought, maybe, he really didn't know. But that was ridiculous. It wasn't as if he had amnesia or something. "Pretending *what* didn't happen?"

I spun away from him and threw my hands into the air. "Oh my God, Maddox. You either had *way* more than I thought you did, or you're being intentionally obtuse."

His muscles tensed, ready for action, and he stood stock still, his jaw clenched so tightly I feared it would shatter. Then, as if a blanket of calm fell over him, he crossed his arms, and his lips tipped into a frosty smile. "Why don't you spell it out for me then?"

Exhaustion had gotten the best of me. My brain was frazzled, my body tense and anxious. I'd had less than a few hours of sleep, and he wanted me to relive our first argument?

After taking a moment to consider it, I decided I owed him that much. It wasn't that long ago he'd had to tell me what happened at the lighthouse party after I'd drunk my weight in apple ale.

I chewed on my lip while I worked up the courage. The strength of my anger seemed to fade with each breath I took. I dropped my eyes to my naked feet, freezing in the dewy grass. "Fine. Since you don't seem to remember what happened, I'll tell you." I started rambling. "We, uh. Though how you could possibly forget that we almost had sex is beyond me. Well, I guess not quite *almost*, but if I hadn't come to my senses, if I hadn't stopped you, we probably would have."

"No. Ava, please don't..." The words tumbled past his lips like a prayer. If I hadn't known better, I might have fallen for the anguish reflecting in his expression, as if I'd just destroyed his entire world with that revelation.

I lifted my head, imploring him to understand my feelings. "Trust me when I say, I *want* to have sex with you, Maddox, but not against the wall at some random guy's party while you're drunk."

"I'm so sorry. I should have... " He choked back a sob and took a step toward me only to stop in his tracks.

"And if my mom ever finds out you tried to drive me home after you'd been drinking, she'll never let me see you again."

When I finished, I waited quietly for him to say something. Anything. But Maddox seemed frozen in place, as if he'd had some kind of seizure. Or a stroke.

"Maddox? God, are you okay?" I reached up to brush my

fingertips across his flaming cheek. He didn't have a fever, but he definitely looked like he was burning up.

"I-I don't know what to say." He clenched his jaw as raw fury warred with the utter devastation in his eyes. They seemed to glaze over, and he looked almost as if he were about to cry. "I'm very sorry that happened to you."

What the hell?

My eyes widened. "You're sorry that happened to me? Are you serious, Maddox? That's all you have to say?"

He swallowed hard and seemed to stagger on his feet. He looked lost and broken. I knew he'd been lying about drinking. "Ava, I think you need to sit down."

Despite the gravity of the situation, I laughed. "*I* need to sit down? *Me*? I barely drank anything tonight. *You're* the one who looks like you're about to keel over. Or throw up."

"Please!" he snapped then ran a hand over his clean-shaven face.

"Wait, you shaved? Since the party?" I took a moment to really examine him, and the differences started to add up. "And you changed your clothes, too." I took a step back and had to catch myself after stumbling over the edge of the curb. "Maddox, you're scaring me. What the hell happened to you tonight? Something really strange is going on, and either you tell me, or I'm going back inside and locking my doors behind me."

He licked his lips and stepped toward me, his eyes pleading with me to—I didn't know what. But I held up my hands between us. "Oh no, you stay over there until you explain yourself."

"Just... can you please sit down?" The weight of the evening seemed to catch up with him, too, and he looked as exhausted as I felt. "I really need you to sit down." He crouched down beside me and dropped into a seated position on the sidewalk. "See? I won't touch you. Sit beside me, and I'll tell you everything."

I nodded, pulling his jacket around my shoulders as I sat cross-legged beside him. "I'm sitting. Start talking."

"I wasn't lying when I said I had to deal with a family matter tonight. God, if you only knew how messed up my family is." He took a deep breath then closed his eyes and pinched the bridge of his nose before making eye contact with me again. "I-I was trying to work out a little *problem* I have with my brother. He's not... he's not a good guy. Not someone I'd *ever* want around you. I went to the place I expected him to be but he, uh, never showed up. So I went looking for him. I spent the entire evening looking for him, in fact. By the time I got back to town, it was obvious you'd already left the party, so I came here to talk to you." He sucked in another breath and reached his hands out to me. He waited until I nodded to take my hands in his. "Ava, I never made it to the party. I came here to apologize for ditching you again."

"But..." I stared into his dark eyes and tried to find the lie in his words. "That's just not possible. I was *there*. I saw you. Kissed you. I didn't imagine that." My cheeks flamed at the memory of how much more than kissing we'd done.

He shook his head, but I didn't understand what he meant by it.

"What? I didn't kiss you, or I didn't imagine it?"

"No, you didn't kiss me. But you didn't imagine it either." His eyes shimmered in the lamplight like tears waiting to fall. "Ava, I-I think—no—I'm *positive* you met my twin brother. And you have no idea how sorry I am that I wasn't there to protect you from him. I hope you can forgive me."

As if someone had sucker-punched me, the air in my lungs rushed out with a whoosh. "Twin brother? You have a twin brother?" *Oh my God, Maddox's brother had his hands all over me. And I liked it. A lot.* Guilt swelled, and I had to tear my eyes away from his. "Why didn't you tell me? Has he been walking around campus with your face this whole time?" I wondered how many times I'd seen him around a corner, thinking he was Maddox.

"I doubt it. We do our best to avoid each other, so he steers clear of the places I frequent." He barked out a hollow laugh. "And trust me, if you knew him, you'd know why I don't talk about him. God, Ava, I'd hoped you'd never have to meet Laith."

I scrambled to my feet, my heart skipping and jumping in

my chest like a broken clock. I knew that name. "*Laith*?" I tried to lick my lips, but my tongue went dry and shriveled up in my mouth like stale beef jerky.

"Yeah, Laith." He scratched his neck as he followed me to his feet. "We, uh, had a major falling out a long time ago, and we've never managed to get past it."

"And you're *sure* you never mentioned him before?" I could taste my heartbeat; it was so loud. How could he not hear it? I'd kissed Laith in a dream. Now I'd done it for real. And God help me, I wanted to do it again.

"Like I said, we don't get along. I try to forget he exists, if you wanna know the truth." He let out a forced chuckle, as if trying to make light of the situation. But there was nothing light about this situation.

"How did he know about me? Your brother? How did he know I'd be at that party?" I tried to drag the information out of him, but he wasn't cooperating.

Maddox averted his eyes. "I-I don't know."

I charged toward him with my heart in my throat. "Yes. You. Do! Stop lying to me. How the hell did he know I'd be at the party?"

He flinched back then reached out to me, but I wasn't having any of that. "Damn it! I don't know how to explain how he found you at the party."

My mouth fell open. "He's been following me, hasn't he? Maybe not on campus, but everywhere else." I knew the answer before I'd even formed the question. I'd dreamed about Laith. And whether or not he was stalking me in the daylight, he was most certainly stalking me in my sleep. "Answer me!"

"Yes, I think he probably is." He grabbed ahold of the front of his jacket and pulled me until I landed in his arms. He locked his arms around me and held on tight. "But, Ava, you need to stay away from him. He's dangerous. There's way more to this than you know. It's complicated, and I honestly don't know how to explain it all."

"You keep saying that, but what does that really mean? You

know what's going on, but you don't want to tell me?" I was sure I'd have bruises from the violent hammering going on behind my ribs. The secrets, the dreams, the inexplicable pull that held me tethered to Maddox, and now his brother—it was all too much for me to process.

He reluctantly nodded. "That's part of it. But before you assume I'm playing some kind of game, let me assure you I'm not. I care about you." He squeezed me to his chest. "God, you have no idea how much I care about you. But it was inevitable my brother would find you."

"I've been dreaming about him." The words tumbled out of my mouth before I could stop them.

"What?" Maddox tensed again, his body vibrating with anger. "Why didn't you tell me?"

I wrenched myself out of his arms again. "Tell you what? I've been having dreams about you, but it's not you? I thought I was going crazy or that my subconscious was having doubts about us. Not in my wildest imagination would I have guessed my dreams were premonitions."

He shook his head as if it hurt him to do so. "Not premonitions."

"What?"

"They're not premonitions, Ava. They're memories."

CHAPTER FOURTEEN

I WOKE UP IN A COLD sweat, dark memories swirling around in my head like a bad dream, a bad dream that came with a horrible hangover. I'd barely had anything to drink last night, but my headache thought differently.

Unfortunately for me, last night *wasn't* a dream. Unlike the boy slaying the dragon and boy in the field of flowers, *this* Laith was all too real.

It would figure, just when something in my life started to go right, my boyfriend's twin brother would waltz into town to mess things up. Laith was like a category five hurricane, blowing into shore and battering everything in his path into a pile of rubble. I'd spent less than thirty total minutes with him, and I couldn't shake his overwhelming presence from my thoughts. Or the taste of him from my lips.

Oh, God. How would I tell Maddox about the attraction I felt for Laith? How could I explain that the pull I felt for his brother was just as strong as the feelings I had for him? The answer was simple: I couldn't.

I climbed out of bed in a fog. Everything I believed in had been turned on its ear. In that old story of girl meets boy, girl falls in love with boy, and they both lived happily ever after, nowhere did it say the boy's brother would try to sweep girl off her feet with his dangerous charm.

And worst of all, I suddenly had no idea what to believe. Maddox promised to explain, but according to him, he needed to do something first. *Story of my life.* That boy *always* had something to do. Or somewhere to be.

After the requisite time spent feeling sorry for myself, I pulled on a pair of loose-fitting jeans and one of my dad's faded blue Hoyas sweatshirts, tied my hair into a high ponytail, and wandered downstairs to eat something. I couldn't think on an empty stomach.

Mom and Josh were both in the kitchen, deep into the usual Sunday morning ritual of breakfast and cooking experiments. Josh would eat sugary cereals while Mom concocted some new recipe that she'd inevitably spring on us later for dinner, often with disastrous results. Like food poisoning. Mom was always quick to remind us, though, *that* only happened once, and it was the store-bought salsa's fault, not her cooking.

I dropped into the chair across from Josh and reached for the box of Lucky Charms.

"You look like crap," my brother informed me before stuffing a heaping spoonful of rainbow marshmallow bits into his gaping mouth.

"Josh!" Mom swung around and swatted him with a potholder then went back to her bubbling pot on the stove.

It was obvious from the way her shoulders practically vibrated she was trying not to laugh. Maybe I did look like crap. Hell, after the night I'd had, I figured I had a free pass.

"Tell your sister you're sorry." Once she'd gotten her seizure under control, she gave him a stern glare.

He opened his mouth again, and green-tinged milk dribbled down his chin. "I'm sorry you look like crap."

I giggled.

Then the giggles turned into a full-on belly laugh. In the next moment, I'd doubled over with tears streaming down my face as I convulsed in hysterics.

"It wasn't that funny," Josh muttered, and I laughed harder at the twisted look on his face.

Mom put her hand on my shoulder. "Honey, are you okay?"

As if a giant switch had flipped inside me, my laughter abruptly turned to sobs. "Yes. No. I don't know."

She rubbed soothing circles over my back the way she used

to when I was six and had a skinned knee. "Did you have a fight with Maddox?"

"Not a fight. Not really. But..." I sat up and pulled my heels onto the chair, wrapping my arms around my knees. "Why is life so complicated all of a sudden?"

She nodded, and a faint smile crossed her lips. "You're an adult now and in college. I hate to tell you this, but it doesn't get a whole lot easier."

I choked out another laugh. "Great. Remind me again why I was so anxious to grow up."

"Aww, sweetie." She pressed a kiss to my forehead. One of those "all healing" kisses that only a mother could administer. "It'll get better. It really will. You're just overwhelmed right now. It happens to all of us at one time or another."

I used the back of my hand to wipe tears from my eyes. "I wish Dad were here."

"Me too." She swallowed hard, and I could tell she was fighting back tears of her own. "Your dad would be so proud of you."

"Uh, Mom?" Josh dropped his spoon, and it landed in his bowl with a splash.

Whatever concoction Mom was cooking had boiled over, and white frothy foam had cascaded over the sides of the pot onto the burner.

"Shit!" Mom hurried back to the stove, using the dishtowel to carry her pot to the sink.

Josh shot me a grin and reached across the table to give me a high five on the sly.

So much for Sunday surprise.

———————◆———————

After polishing off the last slice of Papa Mario's Buy One, Get One Free pizza, I wandered out to the porch in a bit of a daze. The sun had almost gone down, and Maddox still hadn't called me. I'd sent him at least a dozen messages without a single reply.

That alone would have had me worried, but coupled with what I'd discovered last night... I was frantic.

Where could he be? I'd spent my entire day imagining scenarios that would keep him from contacting me: his motorcycle mangled on the side of the road, a gas leak trapping him in his house, his crazy brother shoving him into a well. Every conclusion ended up being worse than the one before it, even if several of them were pulled straight out of the latest episode of *The Vampire Diaries*.

Part of me hoped I'd hear the growl of his motorcycle as it came flying down the street, but other than a few kids on bikes and the guy with his lamppost-marking Pomeranian, the street was quiet.

The chains groaned as I eased myself into the ancient porch swing. Mom said my grandmother used to come out here when she needed to think, and that was a good enough reason for me. I gave a gentle push with my toes to test it out before relaxing all the way into the seat. But staring at the leggy vines climbing up the rotting posts only made me more anxious. Grandma would have never forgiven Mom for letting the house go.

In desperate need of a distraction to snap me out of my misery, I snatched up my phone and dialed Sam's number. I hadn't talked to her since she went to get me a drink at the party. It barely rang once before she picked up.

"Oh, my God, Ava! I've been worried sick about you. You ditch me without saying goodbye, then you don't call, you don't text. I thought you were dead, washed out to sea or something. Is it because I never came back with your drink? I swear to God, I was bringing you one when someone told me Maddox showed up, and you were making out on the deck. And *trust* me, that was the *last* thing I wanted to see. But I looked for you a little later, and you were gone. Poof. I was beginning to think you'd teleported out of there."

She stopped long enough to take a breath, and I broke in. "Whoa, slow down. I'm fine. I just wasn't feeling well. It came over me so quickly I-I needed to go home, so I caught a ride."

"Oh." She giggled. "I thought maybe you were pissed at me for ignoring you at another party. I met the cutest guy. Ryan. He's a sophomore. And a frat boy. And oh my God, so cute! Anyway... do you swear you didn't leave because you were mad at me?"

I rocked back in the swing. "Honest. Really. It was nothing you did."

"Okay, good. So did you hear about what happened after you left? Oh. Em. Gee. It's going to be the talk of the school tomorrow..."

I sat back and let the rocking motion lull me into a state of calm. I must have drifted off because the next thing I knew, the sky had turned pitch black, and my phone was silent in my hand.

Before getting up to go in, I checked my messages again. The only text was from Sam, asking if I needed a ride to school in the morning.

Thankfully, Sam didn't ask me about my weekend when she picked me up the next morning. Instead, she blathered on about some couple who'd hooked up at the party. I nodded my head and pretended to listen when all I really cared about was what had happened to Maddox. I'd stayed awake half the night waiting for the damn pebbles to plink against my window, and I'd woken up stiff and restless. During the night, worry had morphed into dread. He'd promised to call me sometime Sunday, and Sunday had come and gone with nothing to show for it.

Sam pulled into our usual spot a few minutes early, but all hope of seeing Maddox waiting for me faded faster than Hannah's blue hair. I wanted to believe it wasn't like him to ditch, but that had been his MO from the moment I'd met him.

Part of me wondered if his disappearance had been planned, if maybe he'd never intended to call me on Sunday, if the whole thing had been an elaborate plan to break up with me. Was this what it felt like to be blown off? If so, I didn't like it one bit. I wanted to be sick.

As if the past few weeks had never even happened, Abercrombie came strutting his way across the quad, still wearing his stupid hoodie and heading in my direction. My skin bristled at the goofy grin plastered on his face. I really wasn't in the mood to give him the brushoff yet again. *But a girl has to do what a girl has to do.* Then in an unexpected turn of events, he walked right past me and planted a big sloppy kiss on Hannah's burgundy lips.

What in the eff?

"Did I miss something?"

Sam shrugged and leaned in to whisper. "I've decided to just go with the flow."

"Will's party," Paige said, as if that explained everything.

I did a double take, giving Paige a quick once-over. She didn't *look* any different, but it wasn't like her to speak to me without throwing in an insult or two.

"What?" She glared at me followed by a discreet wink, and I choked back a laugh. I decided our secret detente must have still been in effect.

"Nothing." I pressed my lips into a thin line and diverted my attention to a group of guys arguing over who would win in an epic battle between Anakin Skywalker and Harry Potter.

Harry Potter, of course.

"You look beautiful."

I spun around at the sound of his voice and froze. *His* voice. *His* face.

Laith was the exact image of Maddox—from his messy hair to his Doc Martens. All that was missing was the leather jacket… and the *soul*. But he was decidedly *not* Maddox. I saw that now.

"Act natural," he whispered, circling me like a shark, his bright white teeth glinting in the sun.

He leaned in to brush his lips to my ear and growled deep in his throat like a predator about to attack. I sucked in a jagged breath and stepped back. The boy was like an angry god, and I felt unworthy standing in his presence.

How had I failed to notice the subtle differences between

the two of them the other night? Laith's hair, while still artfully disheveled, seemed to follow a more formal style as if he'd somehow been transplanted from another era and only just decided to loosen up. And his scent—peppermint candies and lavender—was a far cry from Maddox's fresh rain smell.

I clenched my jaw and tried to speak through my teeth. "What are you doing here?"

He shrugged. "I wanted to see you." He easily disarmed me with his smile, and I had to shake off the urge to lean into him.

"Laith, I—"

"Maddox, remember?" His eyes sparkled as he glanced at my friends. No one seemed to notice anything out of the ordinary. They had no idea a stranger had invaded our little group. Laith had them completely fooled. His eyes landed on me. "Don't tell me you've forgotten your boyfriend so soon." The smirk was identical too.

I forced a smile of my own. "No, of course not."

"Good. Is this how you usually greet him, or rather *me*? Or do you..." He invaded my personal space, resting his large hands on my hips before surging in for a breath-stealing kiss.

Damn him for being such a good kisser. And damn my body for reacting to him without my permission. And I did react. I melted into him, my heart banging out a tango as our lips moved together in a choreographed dance. I felt the loss immediately when he stepped away, looking quite happy with himself, if his face-splitting grin was any indication.

He licked his lips. "Mmm, better than I remember." Then he stole another quick kiss before turning, taking my hand in his, and towing me toward my retreating friends.

———◆———

I took one look at the greasy piece of pizza and dropped the uneaten slice onto my plate. Without missing a beat, Laith reached over and picked it up, finishing it in a few bites.

I narrowed my eyes at him. "Why are you here?"

"It's Monday. We have classes on Mondays." With his ever-present smirk firmly in place, he kept up his side of the charade with impressive precision.

"That's not what I mean, and you know it." I shot a nervous glance over at Sam, who sat directly across from us. She seemed too involved in her conversation with a dreamy-eyed Hannah to notice our bickering. I almost wished I were part of *that* conversation.

He leaned in, bringing his face dangerously close to mine, and let his words feather out over my lips. "I'm here to get to know you better."

The memory of his rough fingers rasping against my softest parts played on a loop, and my face flamed. My traitorous hormones craved his proximity as vehemently as my logical side fought to repel him. "Why would you want to do that?"

He sat up again, reaching for the apple on my tray. He brought it to his lips then seemed to change his mind. "I would think you'd want that, too."

I scoffed at his arrogance. "Why would you think that?"

"Because that's what soul mates do." He took a huge bite of the apple, crunching loudly as I choked on his words.

"Soul mates? We're not soul mates." I wanted to laugh at the ridiculousness of that statement. A stab of something that tasted like regret twisted in my gut, and I lowered my voice. "I love Maddox. Your *brother*. Why can't you see that?"

He wiped the juice from his lips with the back of his hand then laughed, studying me with eyes that looked too much like Maddox's for my comfort. "But we're twins."

"So?" As if being twins explained anything. My hands trembled with anger, and I had to sit on them to keep from throttling the guy.

The more time Laith and I spent together, the more differences I discovered. For one, Laith seemed to have a chip on his shoulder the size of Virginia. Yet something about the way he gazed at me with that antagonistic grin set my skin on fire. I didn't want to be attracted to him. I fought it with every fiber of my being, but it continued to fester like an open wound.

His hazel eyes sparkled as they locked on mine. "*So...* twins share *everything.*"

The casual way he'd tossed out that statement horrified me. The legs of my chair scraped across the concrete floor as I scooted back, snapping the invisible tether connecting us.

Being that close to him was too much. I had to get out of there. I couldn't sit in the dining hall with him, discussing some sort of perverse arrangement I'd neither signed on for nor condoned.

Unfortunately, I didn't move fast enough, and Laith was out of his chair before I could blink. His hand wrapped around my upper arm, stopping me in my tracks. "Where do you think you're going?"

"I'm not having this conversation in front of people." I snatched my arm back and proceeded to the exit with Laith close on my heels. His hot breath fanned across my neck, sending goose bumps down my spine.

"You want privacy? Fine." He dragged me into the men's restroom and pushed me into the closest stall. "Is this private enough for you?"

I snapped my mouth shut and avoided looking down at the rust stains in the toilet. At least I *hoped* they were rust stains.

"Well?" Laith glared at me as if he were reading my thoughts through my eyes. "I'm assuming you have something to say."

I cleared my throat and hoped my voice didn't crack. "*I* won't be *shared*. And believe me, if Maddox feels the same way you do, he can find a new girlfriend. I'm not going to be passed around between a pair of asshole brothers who get their jollies competing for affection like it's a game."

"Is that what you think this is?" His teeth gnashed together, and his brows furrowed until the skin between them puckered. "A game?"

I gave him a weak nod, remembering Maddox's promise to the contrary. But Laith made me feel like a rabbit trapped between the paws of a feral cat. I'd do almost anything to break free of his hold. I could almost feel his teeth sinking into my neck.

"Well, I'm sorry to disappoint you, Ava, but it's much more

involved than that. I'm surprised my *brother* hasn't explained anything to you yet." He sighed as he muttered to himself. "I suppose I have to do everything."

I took half a step back and bumped into the cold metal stall divider. "Explain what?"

"The curse."

CHAPTER FIFTEEN

1655

"IT'S A BOY!" THE MIDWIFE wrapped the screaming baby in a fine linen blanket and handed him to Lady Catherine.

"A son." The new mother smiled down at her baby as her handmaiden mopped the sweat from her brow.

"He's a fine, strong boy with a good set of lungs." Mary laughed and dipped the cloth into the cool water again before cleaning her lady's face. "Do you know what you'll call him?"

Lady Catherine gazed at the child at her breast. Dark tufts of hair swirled over his delicate crown. "I'll call him Maddox."

Mary nodded her head and smiled. "A good name."

"Oh my, I didn't expect this." The midwife frowned as she attended to Lady Catherine's nether regions.

"Why does it still hurt?" Lady Catherine questioned as a new wave of pain gripped her. "Do tell me what's wrong."

The midwife took her position again. "Not so much wrong as unexpected. It's another baby."

"What?" Lady Catherine's shoulders tensed, and she leaned forward in the birthing chair as the shock ripped through her.

"Sit back. He'll be coming soon. Be patient, and you'll see."

"But... it can't be. There can't be two."

The woman chuckled. "Oh, but there can. And there is. Twins, I dare say."

Fear twisted Lady Catherine's insides as she panted through another jolt of pain. "I need to speak with Mary, alone."

Shock registered on the midwife's face. "What? Now? But...
the second baby is coming."

"I only need a moment. Please." Catherine grimaced as
another wave of pain consumed her.

"As you wish. I'll wait in the other room." She turned to Mary.
"Come get me if her pain worsens."

"Yes, of course." Mary stepped back to allow the woman to
pass then hurried to her lady's side. "What is it, Lady Catherine.
What do you need?"

"I need to see the old woman you bid me go see for the
blessing, Bess Floyd. You must send for her immediately."

Mary's eyes stretched wide. "And if she won't come?"

"Force her. Do whatever must be done." Catherine gripped
the bedding in her hands. "I don't care what the cost."

"My ladyship, there are few I would trust with such a task.
The penalty for—"

"If you must go yourself, so be it."

A gasp ripped from Mary's throat. "But ma'am, it's half a
day's ride there and back."

"Then I suggest you hurry." Lady Catherine cried out, and
Mary backed away as the midwife barged her way into the room.
"Please, Mary. Please don't let me down."

"It will be done."

The midwife waved Mary from the room. "Enough talking.
This baby is coming now. Push, Lady Catherine."

Catherine's body shook from the effort as the midwife ripped
a second baby from her body.

"Another boy!" The midwife held him up.

Tears blurred Catherine's vision as she gazed at her newborn
son. "Laith. I shall call you Laith."

Evening shadows etched the walls of her chamber as worry ate
away at her soul. Mary had been gone too long. What if the
guard had detained her? What if the old woman had resisted her
pleas to come? What would happen to her boys then?

A loud bellowing outside her door drew her attention away from her thoughts. Was that Mary's voice she heard?

"Lady Catherine bid me bring her here. You must let us pass." It *was* Mary, and she must have the old woman with her. Then the door was wrenched open and Mary strode through, followed by a small woman in a dark cloak.

"Mary, you've returned. I was so worried." Catherine waved the young woman in but kept her eyes fixed on the figure in the cloak. "I trust your journey was uneventful?"

The old woman laughed, tugging away her cloak. "You mean to ask if we were questioned, and the answer is no. That is, until we arrived here. It would seem your household is more distrustful than the guard."

"My apologies for not greeting you myself. But as you can see, I've just given birth." Catherine turned to the cradle beside the bed where the boys slept, tangled together like two sides of a coin. "I wouldn't let the nurse take them. I wanted to watch them sleep for a while."

"Them?" The woman scowled as she came around the bed to inspect the babies. She gasped and whirled back to face their mother. "Twins!"

That one single utterance caused fear to rise anew. "Yes." Catherine bowed her head before the woman in a show of respect. She could scarcely afford to offend her now. "Please, can you tell me if the blessing you bestowed upon them includes them both? I worry that one of my sons might be left out."

"You should worry more that he won't be." The woman shook her head, a look of great sadness passing over her features. "Your boys look to be a matched set."

"Yes, the midwife said they were."

"It's as if the one is a mirror image of the other." The woman pressed her hands together then turned them open, both palms laid bare. "Yes, these boys are but two halves of the same whole."

Catherine squirmed in her bed. "I don't understand what you mean. Can't you simply erase what's been done...

or perhaps modify things so that each boy would be given a *separate* blessing?"

"You still don't understand the implications of what has been done." The woman stared down at her with cold eyes. "These poor innocent babies share a soul. They each have one half."

"But that would mean..." Catherine gasped. "No. It can't be."

"It is. You have asked for their soul to be bound to its mate. And it has."

"But *both* bound to the same one? You must undo it."

The woman laughed, but it was without mirth. "Oh dear lady, would that I could. I would sooner cut out my own heart than see this happen. But my hands are tied."

Catherine reached out and grasped the woman's wrist. "Please! Oh please, I beg of you to fix it."

"I warned you this could happen. You accepted the responsibility willingly. What was done cannot be undone." The woman carefully extricated her arm from Catherine and stepped back.

"You cursed my babies!"

"I did nothing of the sort! *You* set this in motion. I tried to tell you. I begged you to reconsider, but you wouldn't listen." She shook her gray head. "You have no idea what you've done. The obsession to possess the other half of their splintered soul will drive your boys to destroy each other. Neither can be happy while the other draws breath."

"No!"

"I'm afraid it's true. I'll go to my grave wishing I'd turned down your gold... *and* your avarice."

Tears ran down Catherine's cheeks as she shrank into herself on the bed. "Dear God in Heaven, what have I done?"

CHAPTER SIXTEEN

AFTER LAITH DROPPED HIS LAST little bombshell on me, I laughed. It had been close to a decade since I'd believed in Santa Claus or the Easter Bunny. And I certainly didn't believe in witches or curses. The concept of Maddox and Laith's mother making a bargain for their futures seemed *plausible*. What mother wouldn't want some guarantee for her child's safety and well-being? But the idea of her seeking out a witch and inadvertently cursing her unborn sons to a life of misery? Instinct told me that was impossible. But I couldn't deny the certainty in his eyes. True or not, *Laith* believed it. And apparently, Maddox did too.

So why hadn't Maddox told me? How could he keep something as life-changing as that from me? I walked around for the rest of the day in a daze. Had I really been cursed before I'd even been born? Wouldn't I feel different, somehow heavier, with the burden of a curse weighing down on me?

I thought of the prickling sensation I felt when either Maddox or Laith were near. It happened so frequently, I barely even noticed anymore. Maybe Laith *was* telling the truth.

My empty stomach churned like a boat at sea. This revelation was all too much for me. I was only nineteen. Too young to be cursed. Too young to have my future set in stone.

I needed space and time to let everything sink in. But Laith wouldn't give me either. Instead, he smothered me. He wouldn't let me out of his sight for a minute, as if he feared I'd take that opportunity to disappear. And maybe I would have. The idea certainly had merit. But when it came right down to it, I had no place to go.

When our professor dismissed us at the end of French, I jumped out of my seat and bolted for the door. He could follow me all the way to the parking lot if he wanted, but unless he'd planned on kidnapping me, that was as far as he'd get.

"Ava, wait!" Laith called after me, and I heard his heavy breathing behind me.

"What do you want?" I kept moving, weaving in and out of the crowd.

"I think we need to finish our conversation." He was too close, his voice acting like a cage ready to trap me.

I surged forward. "I have nothing else to say to you."

"Well, I have plenty to say, and you should probably listen. I haven't even made a *dent* in everything you need to know." His anger snaked toward me like icy fingers as he closed in on me.

"I don't need to know anything else, Laith. I'm going home." I stumbled over my own feet, and he caught up to me, wrapping his hand around my arm and tugging me back.

"Then I'll drive you. We can talk on the way."

I wriggled out of his grasp. I couldn't be that close to him without wanting to kiss him. And I most *definitely* did *not* want to kiss him. "No, thanks. I already have a ride."

"Maddox won't show up." He chuckled darkly. "Not knowing I'm already here. He'd blow our cover."

I laughed. "What cover? You're not Tom Cruise, and this isn't the newest *Mission: Impossible*."

"I don't think you're grasping the severity of the situation." He didn't seem to grasp the *humor* in the situation. We were standing in the middle of a college campus, arguing about covers and secret twins and curses.

"Listen, Laith. I need time to let things sink in." Since nothing else seemed to work with him, I tried to appeal to his humanity. I only hoped he still had some. "I'd rather do that in the safety of my own home, if you don't mind."

He shoved a hand into his hair as I turned to leave. "I almost forgot how stubborn you were."

That stopped me in my tracks, and I whirled on him. "What do you mean, how stubborn I *was*?" Maddox's comment from the other day came back to me full force.

"Never mind, Ava. Just go home and wait for your precious Maddox. Let him be the bearer of bad news for a change." With that, Laith spun on his heels and went back the way he'd come, leaving me standing in the middle of the quad with my mouth hanging open.

"You and Maddox have another fight?" Sam came up behind me and nearly stopped my heart.

I clutched my hand to my chest, feeling the out-of-control thrumming beneath my fingers. "Shit, Sam. You scared me."

She giggled. "Yeah, I have that effect on people. You need a ride home?"

"God, please." I flashed her a smile. "I'm exhausted. I just wanna go home and sleep for a few days."

"Well, don't sleep too long. We have a French test tomorrow."

———◆———

Maddox was waiting on the curb when Sam pulled into my driveway. She stared at the flame-orange motorcycle and scratched her head. "Geez, he must drive really fast if he beat us home."

"Yeah, he's a regular Doctor Who." I frowned as he climbed off the bike and made his way toward us.

Sam pulled down her sunglasses and spread her bubblegum-pink lips in a wide smile. "Maybe he'll give you a ride on his TARDIS."

"Shut up!" I swallowed a nervous giggle then glanced back at Maddox. "I guess I'd better talk to him. I'll see you in the morning?"

Sam slid her glasses back into place. "Bright and early."

I climbed out and waited for her to back out before acknowledging Maddox—all the fear and anxiety that had been building since Sunday finally bursting like a dam. I made an attempt at replicating the Joanie Flynn patented bitch brow. "So... where have you been?"

He flashed me a sad smile. "I got stuck in an elevator."

"What does that even mean?" I sighed and let my shoulders sag. "You promised to call me Sunday, and you didn't. Then you didn't show up on campus again, but of course, everyone *thinks* you did because your duplicate turned up in your place."

The muscles in his neck stiffened as he clenched his jaw. "Yeah, well, that's why I wasn't in class. The asshole beat me there."

When he mentioned Laith, I was reminded of the "twins share everything" comment. I crossed my arms tightly and stood stock still in the middle of the sidewalk, directly between Maddox and my house. "Whatever sort of messed-up game you two are playing, you can leave me out of it."

Maddox glowered at me. "I've told you once already: this is no game. But if it *were*, my brother wouldn't be playing by the rules. He has his own code of ethics. And he doesn't seem to be that familiar with this century quite yet." He mumbled the last part, and I couldn't quite make sense of it.

His riddles were giving me a headache. "I have no idea what you're talking about."

Another grim smile. "I know."

I tried to hold onto my anger but caved to the sadness I felt instead. God, I was such a girl. "Why didn't you tell me?"

"About Laith? I told you the other night. I honestly hoped you'd never have to meet him."

"No, not about Laith. About the curse."

A look of horror washed over his face. "He told you?"

"*You* should have told me!" I snapped. His reaction told me he'd had no intention of telling me himself.

He took a step toward me. "I know what you're thinking, but I *had* planned on telling you Sunday, before Laith—" He shook his head. "It doesn't matter now. I would have told you eventually."

"You should have told me that night at the lighthouse or when

I found out about Laith. You had plenty of chances, Maddox. But you didn't."

He barked out an empty laugh. "And you would have believed me?"

"No!" I plopped down on the damp earth. "I still don't believe it. Not really. How is it even possible? How is any of this possible? Witches don't exist. People don't go around cursing each other."

"Maybe they don't *now*." He eyed me cautiously, as if gauging my reactions.

"What does that mean, 'they don't now'?" Comments the two of them had made swirled in my brain, making me dizzy. "Maddox, what's really going on?"

He reached his hand toward me. "Come take a ride with me."

"Why should I trust you?"

His eyes locked on mine. "Because I love you, and I'd never intentionally do anything to hurt you."

My mouth went dry. His admission left me speechless. I loved him too, God knew I did, but this was all too much to handle.

"Please." The sincerity in his expression got to me.

"Fine."

He zipped me into his leather jacket and fastened the strap on my helmet before climbing onto the bike in front of me. Despite everything going on, I felt perfectly safe with my arms wrapped around him as we flew down the highway.

I knew without asking where we were going. The lighthouse. This time, when we snuck into the tower, we made the daunting climb up the curving staircase, all the way to the top.

"Was this your intention?" I gazed out at the panoramic view of the bay.

He came up behind me and snaked his arms around my waist, resting his chin on the top of my head. "Was what my intention?"

"To distract me from the issues with this amazing view?" I let my body melt into his.

"It is stunning, but no. I just wanted to take you somewhere we could be alone." His lips latched onto the sweet spot behind my ear, and I swallowed a moan.

"Laith kissed me." I hadn't intended on telling him, but when I opened my mouth, the words just seemed to tumble from my lips.

His body went rigid behind me. "I kind of figured he would."

"I didn't stop him." Admitting that to him was the hardest thing I'd done since packing my stuff and moving to Maine.

He held his breath, and his heart thundered against my spine. "It's okay."

"It's not." I turned in his arms. "None of this is okay."

The corners of his mouth curved down, pain etched across his features. "No. No, it's not. But what else can I say? Damn you for kissing my brother? I know you feel the bond with him, too. And I know you can't help it."

The bond? Is that why I'm so drawn to Laith? To both of them? I buried my face in his chest. "I don't want to feel... *that* with him. It goes against everything I know, and yet I can't seem to fight it. Why didn't I feel it before? Why now?"

He tried to hide it, but I heard the agony in his voice. "It's always been there. You just didn't realize it. He can get into your dreams, work his way into your heart through your subconscious."

I pulled my head back, horrified at this new piece of information. "He can do that?"

Maddox exhaled loudly and nodded. "We both can. But I was *with* you, so I never needed to."

"I. Don't. Understand." I stepped away, but he followed me, taking my face in his hands.

"I'll explain everything. You need to know what you're up against. I should have told you before. I-I just didn't want you to hate me."

My eyes glazed over with tears as I searched his. "Hate you? Why would I hate you?"

"My family did this to you." His voice cracked, his eyes glistening with unshed tears. "I'm so sorry, Ava."

Something about his reaction nagged at me. I had to know if

what I felt was real or simply one of the side effects of the curse. "If not for the spell, would we have still been soul mates?"

"Yes."

I reached up and tugged his face down to mine, bringing our lips together. The kiss was desperate, like the first gulp of oxygen after almost drowning. My lungs filled with him, and I could finally breathe. The draw I'd felt toward Laith all day shifted, and suddenly, my soul yearned for Maddox. I wanted to grab him and disappear where no one could find us. Yet in the back of my mind, the bond pulled me toward Laith. My heart had never been so full. Or so confused.

My lips were tender and swollen by the time I tore them away from his. "What are we going to do?"

His forehead rested on mine. "I don't know."

"Let's just stay here forever."

He smiled. "Okay."

We stayed in the observation deck of the lighthouse long after the sun went down. I curled up on Maddox's lap, listening to the sound of his heart and the waves beating against the rocks beyond the brick walls. We both fell asleep at some point, but thankfully, Laith had steered clear of my dreams for once.

"We're going to have to go back." His voice was scratchy from sleep.

"I know."

"But, Ava, there's so much more I need to tell you. You have to be prepared, so Laith can't take you by surprise again."

I nodded against his shoulder.

He scrubbed a hand over his face. "God, I have no idea where to begin with this."

"Start at the beginning." My pulse raced as I waited for him to speak the words that would change my life forever.

He nodded and cleared his throat. "After Laith and I were born and our mother realized she'd, uh…"

"Cursed you?"

"Yeah. After that, she went crazy. Some said it was because of the consequences of the spell. Some said it was guilt."

"Who else knew what she did?"

"Just a few people. A woman who worked for her. My father. But he was away when it happened, so he didn't find out for a long time. The woman helped her keep a journal of everything. I think they knew we'd have questions when we were older. Thank God, they did, too. By the time I was a teenager, my mother's ramblings were barely coherent." Maddox stared at his hands, tracing the lines in his palm with a finger as he spoke. "After she..." He closed his eyes and swallowed. "After she was gone, I read her journal over and over again, trying to make sense of things. Apparently, as babies, Laith and I were inseparable. We'd cry if we were apart for even a moment. But as we grew older, things changed. By the time we were five, we couldn't be in the same room together for more than a few minutes without trying to hurt one another.

"Our mother grew afraid we'd harm each other like the witch said, so she decided to send one of us to live with our aunt in the south. It broke her heart to be separated from either of her children, but she didn't know what else to do." He didn't say which of them she'd sent away, and I didn't dare ask. I did notice neither of them seemed to have a Southern accent.

I wanted to understand their strange relationship, why Maddox's brother hated him so much. "So you and Laith grew up separately?"

"Yes." His face was devoid of emotion, as if the weight of his disclosure had stripped it away.

"But you know each other now, so you must have reunited at some point."

He nodded. "After our mother died, I grasped onto the journal like a lifeline. I read it from cover to cover so many times the pages were tattered and worn. I memorized the contents as a small child might a favorite book. I didn't believe anything she'd written down, mind you. Like you, I couldn't imagine things like witches and curses existing. I grew up believing she was insane, so anything she'd written in her journal could only be the ramblings of a woman out of her mind. Once I became of age, I set out to find my brother."

"But you knew where he was, right?"

"I had a good idea. I just had to track him down." He chuckled darkly. "But when I found him, he wasn't happy to see me. He'd grown up believing our mother had sent him away because she couldn't handle two boys, and she'd chosen to keep me rather than him. It didn't matter that he was raised in a happy, loving household. He was well cared for, even loved, whereas I grew up surrounded by lunacy and anger."

My heart broke for him. My fingers itched to reach out and touch him, but he was too wrapped up in telling his story, and in my own need to satisfy my curiosity, I didn't want to interrupt.

"Our relationship became exactly what our mother feared, especially after *she* entered our lives."

"She?" An uncomfortable sensation twisted my stomach, and I squirmed where I sat.

"Our soul mate." He shifted his attention to his palm again.

I sucked in a breath, the pieces suddenly falling into place. "You mean me."

He lifted his eyes to meet mine. "No, Ava. This happened way before you."

"What?" As if the romantic soundtrack looping in my head had come to a screeching halt, I sat up straighter and shook my head. "You're not making any sense at all. How could you have met your soul mate way before me? That's impossible. That would mean you'd met her before I was even born."

He watched me cautiously as he nodded. "It was the spring of 1675."

CHAPTER SEVENTEEN

TIME SEEMED TO GRIND TO a complete stop. Even Maddox had frozen in place, eyes wide, as if staring down a dangerous predator—as if *I'd* been the one who'd claimed to have been born over three hundred fifty years ago. He seemed to be waiting for a reaction from me, but I couldn't move. Couldn't think, not after the grenade he'd just detonated.

I waited for him to laugh—to say, "Gotcha!"—but that never happened. And the discomfort in his expression spread through his body like Ebola. He was a spring, wound too tight and ready to snap. I heard the rapid hammering behind his ribs as his pulse raced out of control.

My own heart ceased to beat, and I refused to breathe until he put an end to the insanity and told me the whole thing was all a horrible joke. In my head, I heard my mother's ridiculous clock, ticking off the seconds until my lungs burned, and I had no choice but to suck in a breath. "No," I murmured, still unable to move.

"I was…" His voice came out hollow, as if I was hearing it from the end of a long tunnel. "Laith and I… we were born in England. In 1655."

I scrambled from his lap and backed into the rough texture of the curved wall. "Stop!" He *had* to be lying. *1655.* Hundreds of years before my parents—my *grandparents*—had even been born. My head turned from side to side of its own accord, as if it were trying to detach itself from my shoulders.

"Please, hear me out." His voice cracked, and he seemed to be on the verge of crying.

"No!" Tears stung my eyes as I gripped the railing, easing my feet backward until I reached the next step. Then the one after that. I was prepared to take them one at a time until I reached the bottom.

Maddox wiped the moisture from his eyes with the back of his hand and moved slowly toward me. "Ava, you're gonna fall. Please, sit down, and let me explain."

"It's not possible. That's... you're talking about *centuries* ago. You'd be long dead by now. Unless you're immortal. Oh my God, are you immortal?" My tears flowed freely as the realization sank in. "Of course you are. You were cursed to a life of immortality so you could keep finding and losing your soul mate forever, right?"

"No, that's not it." He shook his head vehemently. With every step I took, inching my way down the stairs, he followed, keeping just two steps behind me. "I promise that's not it."

"Then what? How can you be from the seventeenth century? How can you not be a bag of bones blowing in the wind? If you're not immortal, why do you look my age?"

We'd only made it one full revolution on the spiral stairs before he grasped my hands in his, slowing my descent. "Because every time we jump, it resets our clock to the same age as the day we first jumped."

My mind raced as I tried to process the information. "How old are you?"

"We'd turned twenty that June."

Not so much older than me in physical years, but in actual time... "But I don't understand." I'd gotten so tired of that phrase. I wanted to understand just one thing—one thing in this crazy, messed-up situation I'd found myself in. "Normal people can't travel through time."

"I did." His lips curved up in a sad smile. "Laith did. For you."

My heart jumped, stealing my breath and sending my head into a dizzying flat spin. Every word coming out of his mouth overwhelmed me. "But it wasn't really me, was it? I wasn't around back then. I'm not the girl you lost. I'm not from another time.

I'm from the here and now, twenty-first-century America. And if you're telling the truth—if you're not both delusional sociopaths who need to be locked up for your own safety—you're from seventeenth-century England."

There must have been something seriously interesting about the tops of his boots, because he couldn't tear his eyes away from them. "Your soul is an old one. When it, uh, ceases to exist in one time, it comes back in the next. It's still you. Just a little different." He raised his eyes to mine. "If it makes you feel better, I like *this* you best. You're smart and feisty, and you might be young and inexperienced, but you aren't weak."

Every ragged breath I sucked in burned my chest and made my lips tingle. If I had to listen to even one more bit of information, my head would surely explode. Did he not understand how utterly insane it all sounded? "This is crazy. Too crazy to be true."

"Too crazy to be a lie," he said with a bitter smile.

A cold laugh burst out of me. "No, I think it's just the right sort of crazy for a lie or a paranoid delusion. Mine or yours, I'm not entirely sure which."

"But you feel it." He reached out to me, and the prickle flared, proving his point. "You feel the pull of the bond. I don't have the power to make you feel something you don't."

A million different scenarios floated through my brain like helium balloons. "How do I know you haven't drugged me? Maybe... *maybe* I'm not even here. Maybe I'm tucked into my bed dreaming right now." I snapped my fingers and pointed at him, feeling the first few balloons popping in my head.

He took my hand in his and gave it a reassuring squeeze. "Ava, you know better."

"I don't know anything anymore." Part of me wished *I* could go back in time to when I first saw him. I would have avoided making eye contact. Hell, I would have stayed away from that damn window altogether. But the instant the thought formed, I knew it was a lie. Even after hearing his outrageous story. And even though I was half sure he was as nuts as his mother, I would have done it all the same—pursued him every bit as relentlessly.

"This is a lot to take in. A day ago, I was an ordinary college freshman with a normal boyfriend. Today, I'm some kind of splintered soul, tracked through time by a pair of identical time travelers. It's like the plot of a bad movie, and I still don't really understand it all."

"I know. I'm sorry." He sat on the step and tugged me down beside him. "I'll tell you whatever you want to know."

What did I want to know, besides how I factored into the whole thing? "For starters, how do you—what did you call it—jump through time?"

"You don't go for the easy questions, do you?" He chuckled. "Time jumping is… *complicated*. I don't know how to explain it, not in a way anyone would understand. Can I think about that for a little while, and you ask me something else?"

"Fine… if you can travel anywhere in time, why can't you just go back to before your mother made the bargain with the witch and stop her?"

He shrugged. "Because we can't jump into a time where we already exist."

I shook my head as another wave of confusion shot through me. "What does that mean?"

Maddox took my hand and traced the lines in my palm, the way he'd done with his. "It's complicated, but basically, Laith and I existed in 1654. We weren't born yet, but we existed. If we tried to jump into that time while our younger selves were there, the jump wouldn't go through. Essentially, time would reject us."

"Time would reject you?" I blinked at him, completely stunned by what I was hearing.

He didn't explain. He simply nodded. "Now, if we try to jump into a time we've already been to, but maybe didn't stay very long, we'd go into what I call a holding pattern. Sort of like being stuck between floors in an elevator. We'd have to wait until we weren't there anymore to jump in. So when we're talking about the time before we initially jumped, there would never be that opening. We existed there until early autumn of 1675 when we made our first jump, so we can never go back to any time before that."

"So there can never be two of either of you in one place?"

"Exactly. So if I wanted to, say... go to June of 1855, but back in 1743 I made a jump there from the fifteenth until the twenty-third—this actually happened, so I'm using that example—the jump would put me in the elevator until the other me jumped out again."

My head spun with the intricacies. "So that's what you meant when you said you were stuck in an elevator?"

"Yes. When I got home Sunday morning, Laith was waiting for me. He grabbed me and jumped to a place I'd already been. I got caught in the elevator and had to wait."

"But Laith?"

"He'd never been there, so he went straight in and was able to come straight out again. Well, after the recharge period, but that's another story."

"You could potentially be trapped for *years* if you forgot you'd already jumped into the same place?"

He laughed. "No, not years. Time is a giant temporal fold, so it happens all at once. And time doesn't move at the same pace inside that imaginary elevator. Waiting for a particular time slot to open up could take as little as a few hours or as long as a few weeks. It all depends on how long I was there the first time. So to answer your original question, it wouldn't work to jump into 1654 before my mother went to the witch. I'd either end up right back where I was, or I'd get rerouted to another time."

Mind. Blown.

"At the risk of sounding like a broken record, do you realize how crazy this all sounds?"

He squeezed my hand. "Yeah. I mean, can you imagine what it was like for us? Figuring it out along the way? I had no idea what I was doing. I can only compare it to driving at night without headlights. I was totally flying blind. It took me more than a decade to figure out there was a recharge period. A waiting period before you can jump again. I kept thinking

I'd broken time. The first time I jumped, I thought I was permanently trapped in the middle of the French Revolution. Then I realized I just had to wait to recharge. Still, it was years of sleeping in stables and stealing food to survive while I figured everything out."

I tried not to think about him having to *survive* that way. "If it was so horrible, why didn't you go home?"

"After everything that happened, going home didn't seem like an option. There was nothing left for us there. Especially after..." He looked away, and I suspected he was thinking about *her* again.

"What happened to her?"

He swallowed and played dumb. "Who?"

"The girl with my soul. You never mentioned her name."

"Elizabeth. She, uh..." His shoes suddenly became of vital importance again.

"Did she... die?" I regretted the words the instant I'd spoken them. It was clear he wasn't ready to talk about her.

He nodded.

Sensing his discomfort, I changed the subject, knowing I'd circle back to it later. "You keep saying you have to recharge, but what does that mean?"

"It means we can't go from one jump directly into the next. I honestly don't know why, but I have a theory."

"Well?" I motioned for him to continue.

His mood did a complete one-eighty, reminding me of Josh when the subject of video games came up. "When we travel through time, we're surrounded by this massive static electric charge—like a bubble of current. Anyone standing too close at the exact moment we jumped would probably even feel it. So I figure this bubble creates a ripple, like when you throw a rock into still water."

"And you think you need time for that ripple to smooth out before you can create a new one?" Finally, something I understood.

"Exactly!" He lit up. "I mean, it's just a theory, but it makes sense."

"Does jumping through time work like it does in the movies? Do you show up crouched down naked in an alley?"

He laughed. "No, thank God. In fact, we can bring more than just our clothes with us if we're careful. I started picking up little trinkets from the eighteenth and nineteenth centuries and stashing them so I could dig them up and sell them to antique dealers in the twentieth. I bought stocks when they were new and sold just before they peaked. I picked up my motorcycle brand new in 1969 and rode it right through time to bring it here."

"You're not only a time traveler, but you're rich too? I guess I hit the boyfriend lottery, didn't I?" I didn't know what else to do but joke about it. He'd lived an amazing life, and I couldn't imagine him wanting someone as inexperienced as me.

He smiled. "I have enough to get by without working, if that's what you're asking. I even own a house. Once I'd tracked you to Maine, I went back to the seventies and bought the house down the block. It was destined to sit vacant for decades, so I bought it and locked it up tight before jumping here to move in."

"I guess you can see tomorrow's lottery numbers." The minute the words passed my lips, I felt my cheeks flame. The last thing I wanted was for him to think all I cared about was the money.

He reached up and coiled a lock of my hair around his fingers. "I could, if I was so inclined. I actually think that's how Laith gets by. He plays the lottery, bets on sporting events. He likes to live on the edge a bit more than I do."

Laith. Just thinking about him opened up a new line of questioning. "Can you tell me how Laith enters my dreams?"

He nodded. "Aside from the obvious drawbacks of having your brother haunt your girlfriend, it's actually pretty cool. While we're in that imaginary elevator, we can break through time by entering into your dreams—or occasionally your subconscious. I don't think it always works, but it's a way to communicate when we can't get to you."

"You said *my* dreams. Just mine?"

"Just yours or each other's. We all share a soul connection." He grinned. "I sat in on a lecture back in the 1970s—seventy-four, I think—where the professor was talking about Plato's theory on soul mates. But he called them 'twin flames.' And though I have to say, I think he was totally off the mark where the original material was concerned, he had his own little theory about twin flames being able to reach out over space and time to connect with each other. It was all very New Age. The guy was probably dropping acid—it was the seventies, after all—but I think he might have been onto something. And I kind of like the term 'twin flames.' It seems slightly more apropos than simply 'soul mates.'"

"So this, whatever it is..." I waved my hand as I struggled for the words. "This soul-mate connection, twin-flame mumbo jumbo, is real? You're not just making up some elaborate story to draw me into some kinky relationship with the two of you? You know, polyamorous couplings, ménage à trois, the stuff of *Penthouse Magazine...* "

He threw his head back and barked out a laugh. "It's real. No kinky polyamorous relationships. *Definitely* no three-ways." He shuddered. Like a switch flipped inside him, he got quiet. Serious. "This bond... this *curse*... it drives us mad sometimes. Seeing you anywhere near him is unbearable. Believe me. If I could keep you all to myself, if I could run away so Laith couldn't find you, God, Ava, I would. In a heartbeat."

As if responding to the desperation in his eyes, my pulse quickened. There was no question in my mind. If he asked me to, I'd go. "If you can travel through time, why don't you just find my soul in different times and both live happily ever after?"

Maddox gave me a sad smile. "I wish it worked that way."

"Why can't it?" I had to believe there was a way to make it work out for all of us.

"Much like I can't be in two places at once, our split souls can't bond with more than one of yours at the same time. It's that pesky paradox again. When either of us finds your soul, the other is automatically drawn toward it, almost as if you don't exist anywhere else but that place and time."

"Is there no chance for us, then? It's all hopeless? We're all three bound to each other in some witch's curse from another time?" A tornado of emotions swirled through me. Hurt. Devastation. And finally understanding. "So there's nothing I can do? I'm cursed to love both of you for all eternity while you destroy each other competing for my love?"

His eyes welled up again, his Adam's apple bobbing as he swallowed. "I'm so sorry, Ava. I wish it were only that. I'd like nothing more than to let you go on thinking we can just live out this crazy love triangle until we're old and gray, but it's so much worse."

"Worse?" My voice rose at least an octave, the sound little more than a squeak.

He cupped my face in his hand, and I leaned into his touch, craving the skin-on-skin contact. "Our love for you will end up tearing you apart. It's happened once already."

I knew he'd been hiding something. Self-preservation warred with my perverse need to know. "Elizabeth. What happened to her?"

His hand dropped away from my face, and his entire being seemed to shift from carefree college student to war-weathered soldier in a nanosecond. It physically hurt me to look into his angst-ridden eyes. "We both had to have her. Couldn't just let her go. Couldn't put her happiness first. I don't even know if it had anything to do with the curse or if it was just plain sibling rivalry. Jealousy so vile it didn't think twice about destroying the most beautiful soul I'd ever known."

I choked back a sob. My head knew the soul he was talking about was mine, but my heart—the heart that had so completely fallen for him in such a short time—couldn't see her as anything more than a rival for his affections.

Maddox heaved out a breath. "She found out the man she'd given herself to, the man she'd married under cover of night and willingly surrendered to—body, mind, and soul—wasn't the man she'd fallen in love with." His voice dropped so low I had to strain to hear him. "When she discovered she'd been tricked, she hanged herself."

I gasped, and my hand flew up to cover my mouth to keep from blurting out my thoughts. I wanted to ask him which of them had been so treacherous, but I knew. In my heart, I knew Maddox would never do something so ruthless. But Laith—the same brother who'd tried to have sex with me against the side of Will Clark's house—had already proven how cold-blooded he could be.

"Laith and I found her in the morning, her amber hair glinting in filtered sunlight as it always did. But her eyes... they were empty." He exhaled a ragged breath, his body deflating with the effort, and leaned hard against the curved brick wall. "We blamed each other, both of us certain the other was at fault, neither willing to accept a modicum of blame."

I grabbed his hand, clutching it between mine. "My God, Maddox. What did you do?"

"We went to find the witch who'd cursed us. Remember I told you I had my mother's diary? It was all there, her name, where she lived, other assorted clues to guide us on our path."

"And did you find her?"

He gave me a single curt nod. "We did. And she told us the soul had been released and would await its chance to be reborn. The soul—*your soul*—continues to do that until it binds with its mate."

A sliver of dread worked its way under my skin. "How do soul mates bind together when there's more than two halves to the soul?"

The undiluted anguish radiating from his expression would have answered my question even had he not spoken the words. "They don't."

CHAPTER EIGHTEEN

A PAIR OF NERVOUS HORSES EYED *a storm on the horizon, snorting out puffs of hot breath as they pawed the damp ground. They took turns trying to yank free of the tethers holding them to a thick tree trunk, as if they knew the tempest would be heading their way.*

"*You brought this upon yourself, brother.*" *Laith pointed to the fresh mound of earth and the plain wooden marker, decorated with bright-blue flowers, as he paced over newly trampled grass. His clean-shaven face twisted in rage as he balled up his fists at his sides. Despite his high-bred appearance—fancy buckled shoes and the finest silk and velvet clothes under his long wool coat—he looked like a soldier, ready to do battle.*

For his part, Maddox stood from where he'd been kneeling and turned his back on the fresh grave. His coat hung loose on his shoulders, his shirt dirty and untucked, and he didn't bother to brush the mud from his black velvet breeches. "I did this? I dare say not! I loved her with every fiber of my being. Her death lies at your feet. Not mine." Even several days' growth of beard couldn't hide their resemblance, and yet this brother's handsome face distorted in pain rather than rage.

Laith continued to paw restlessly at the ground like his horse. "She was as much mine as yours. And she married me."

"*She wasn't yours to marry. She was betrothed to me!" Maddox's voice rang out over the wind. "You tricked her."*

"*So she was. And so I did. And for that, I should be sorry." Laith turned to hide a smirk but wasn't fast enough.*

His brother gritted his teeth. "But you're not."

"*Of course not.*" Laith *whirled around to face his sibling.* "*Would* you *have been had I found her first? I think not.*" *A large drop of rain splashed against his cheek, and he wiped it away with the back of his hand.* "*Now what, brother? We have lost our great prize, our eternal love, and now we have nothing. Though it was destined for one of us to end up empty-handed, wasn't it?*"

A look of horror crossed Maddox's face. "*How can you be so callous? How can you speak of her as if she were nothing more than a prize to be won? To me, she was everything.*"

"*My heart is broken too, brother.*" *Laith lifted his eyes to the darkened sky, stretching his arms out to the sides until he resembled a giant cross.* "*God could strike me down where I stand, and I would not feel it. Our mother cursed us to this life. What can we do but her bidding?*"

"*We could part ways again and pray we never cross paths hereafter.*" *Maddox shook his head at his brother.* "*If I never see you again, it will be too soon.*"

Laith sneered. "*Or we could find that witch who cursed us and seek our revenge on* her *soul.*"

"*What are you saying?*"

"*I'm saying, I'll do whatever it takes to have Ava... even if it means killing everyone who stands in my path.*"

My eyes snapped open, and I swallowed the scream building in my throat. The nightmares seriously needed to give it a rest.

Filtered daylight streamed in through slender windows high above me, and I struggled to sit up in the dim light, but an arm wrapped around my waist held me down. For a half a second, I freaked out while I tried to work out in my head where the hell I was.

Then I heard the waves shattering against the rocks outside, and it all came rushing back to me. *We fell asleep in the lighthouse.*

"Maddox. Wake up!" I nudged him with my elbow, but he only grunted and held me tighter. My body ached from lying half on the hard floor and half on Maddox. My neck had a crick in it from where my head rested on his chest. After struggling for what seemed like hours, I managed to wriggle an arm free to dig my phone out of my pocket.

Dead. No wonder I hadn't received a single call, or even a text, from Mom. It had most likely died sometime in the night. As far as I knew, Maddox's was in his pocket, but I couldn't reach it without waking him up. And he wasn't cooperating.

"Come on, Maddox. My mom must be freaking out by now. She probably called the cops and put out an Amber alert on me or something."

He stirred beneath me. Adorable groans emanated from his throat as he struggled to wake up on the cold, hard floor. "I think you're too old for an Amber alert. She probably thinks you ran away from home."

That one little thought opened up a floodgate of emotions, and my eyes filled with tears. "*Damn it.* She just lost my dad. I can't let her think she's lost me too."

"Okay, I'm up." He released me and sat up to rub his eyes. "What time is it?"

"I have no idea, but it's daytime. And my phone died. I need to use yours."

Maddox fished into his pocket and handed me his phone. "What are you going to tell her?"

"I don't know. The truth? We had a fight, you brought me to the lighthouse to talk, and we fell asleep." I keyed in my mom's cell number.

"You're gonna tell her we broke into the lighthouse after hours?" he whispered.

I frowned at him and shook my head while I waited for the call to connect. It rang several times before she answered.

"Hello?"

I swallowed down my nerves and cleared my throat. "Hi, Mom, it's me."

"Ava?" She didn't *sound* all that frantic, just a bit suspicious maybe. "Is everything okay?"

"Uh, yeah? Just, you know, checking in." From my illegal location in the restricted lighthouse.

"Whose number are you calling from?" Definitely not frantic about my whereabouts.

"Oh, this is, uh, Maddox's phone." I shot him a quick glance. "I forgot to charge mine last night, so it died."

"Oh." I could hear her rushing around, shuffling papers. "I guess I need to get you one of those emergency chargers. Did you get a lot of studying done last night? Sam said you had to prep for a big French test when she called to say you'd be staying over. I have to tell you, I'm not thrilled about you having your friend call me with a guilt trip. You could've called me yourself. You're not a kid anymore. And honestly, I was always horrible at French. If your dad was still alive, he could have helped you, but I'm glad you at least have Sam."

"Yeah, uh, definitely." When what she'd said finally sank in, I let go of the breath I was holding. I relaxed back into Maddox's chest and shot him a grin over my shoulder. "Thank God for Sam. I honestly don't know what I'd do without her."

"Listen, sweetie, I need to run. I have a client coming in early this morning. Will I see you for dinner?"

"I-I don't know yet. I'll let you know." I couldn't think that far into the future, not when I was so completely wrapped up in the past.

"*Josh!* Come on. We're leaving. Okay, just let me know before it gets too late. Oh, and good luck on your test."

"Thanks, Mom. Bye," I said, but she was already gone.

"Holy shit." I dropped my head between my knees and took a few cleansing breaths.

"What was that all about?" Maddox rubbed circles on my back.

I sat back up and turned to face him. "How she knew I needed her to save me, I have no idea, but Sam called Mom last night and told her I'd be staying over to study."

A few days ago, I would have been majorly weirded out by Sam's apparent psychic abilities. But a little ESP had *nothing* on the other revelations I'd had to accept over the past several hours. Still... I owed her. Big time. And now that she'd dug me out of a major hole, she'd be like a shark on a paper cut. She'd expect juicy tidbits, and the only juicy thing that had happened last night was the drool I left on Maddox's chest.

He looked incredulous. "That's... *strange.* And your mom just bought it? Didn't ask to speak with you or anything?"

"So it would seem. Either she's relaxing the reins a little bit now that I'm in college, or my years of toeing the line worked in my favor for once, though it would seem my reign as the resident good girl has officially ended."

He flashed a wide smile and leaned in for a quick kiss. "I think I might like you as a bad girl."

"Don't get your hopes up too high. That much innocence is hard to shed overnight."

"Well, if you decide to turn to the dark side, let me know. I'd be happy to help."

For an instant, I saw Laith in his eyes, and it brought everything tumbling back down on top of me in a flash. The curse, the time travel, the other me who'd taken her own life rather than be torn between the two of them.

"Hey." He held my face in his hands, concern radiating from his eyes as he gazed into mine. It was as if he thought he could pluck my thoughts out, one by one, just by willing it. "You were just smiling, and now you look like you're about to have a panic attack."

"You're very perceptive for someone who just woke up." I reached up with both hands to grasp his wrists, but I didn't pull his hands away. Instead, I savored the skin contact for as long as I could.

He gave me a sad smile. "Centuries of practice."

"Well, Mister Time-traveling Soul Mate..." I forced a smile and gave his wrists one last squeeze before using them to haul myself up. I had to look away or risk breaking down. "We need to go to class and at least pretend my life isn't hanging by a frayed thread."

"Ava."

I turned toward the somber tone in his voice and looked down at him where he still sat on the brick floor of the lighthouse, hugging his knees to his chest, his handsome face illuminated by pinpricks of light from above. "You don't have to say anything."

"But I do." He jumped to his feet and circled me in his embrace. "I may be able to travel to the future, but I can't predict it. The one thing I *can* do is promise you I'll do whatever it takes to protect you. I won't let what happened before happen to you." He kissed the top of my head. "I love you, Ava. I truly do."

"I love you, too." My voice barely made a sound with my face buried in his shirt.

He pulled back to look at me, his cocky grin right back where it belonged. "What did you say?"

I slapped his shoulder. "You heard me. I said, 'I love you.'"

"Yeah, I did." He pulled me back against him, tucking my head under his chin while he held me. "You have no idea how happy I am that I heard you."

I cleared my throat and pressed my lips against his chest. Part of me hoped he wouldn't hear what I had to say next. "I'm not gonna lie. I still feel the bond with Laith. But it's not him I want, just that piece of his soul that binds me to him. With you, it's different. I love you for the things I see inside your soul. You're inherently good. And you make me smile. And I've never known anyone who likes the Rolling Stones as much as me."

"Well, I am from England... originally."

I threw my head back and laughed. "Yeah, I guess you are. Too bad you lost the accent. British guys are hot."

"Damn it. Do you have any idea how long I worked to shed that accent?"

That only made me laugh harder. "Well, maybe you can practice a little. For me."

"You know I'd do anything for you." He stopped laughing and rested his forehead on mine as he stared down at me. "I mean that, Ava. Anything. If it means I have to go back to see the witch again, I will. I'll force her to remove the curse, somehow. Whatever it takes. I'd gladly go back and undo every single thing from my past to ensure you'd be safe in the future."

When we pulled into the campus parking lot, Sam was waiting for us by her car. "Well, there she is." She grinned. "I'm glad to see you're alive. I have to admit, I was a little worried."

I gave her a hug, squeezing the life out of her for being there for me when I needed her. "How did you know I needed to be bailed out?"

"He, uh..." Sam glanced at Maddox then tilted her head as if she was waiting for him to interject. When he just stood there looking as confused as I did, she went on. "Maddox showed up at my house and begged me to be your alibi." She turned to him. "You didn't tell her?"

He frowned but didn't say anything. I saw the wheels turning in his head. Maddox had been with me the entire time since Sam dropped me off from school. It had to have been Laith. But why?

I draped my arm over her shoulder and led her toward the school, leaving Maddox behind. "Well, thank you. You totally saved my ass."

"What's going on with you two? It's weird. One minute he's the dark romantic hero, and in the next, he's... I don't even know how to describe him. Just a little scary."

I nodded. I knew exactly what she meant. Laith was more than a little scary. "Did Maddox tell you why I needed an alibi?"

"Uh, yeah. He said he was going to surprise you and take you somewhere. He looked super excited, especially when he said you probably wouldn't make it back in time for curfew. It was almost creepy. If it had been anyone other than Maddox, I would have sworn he'd planned to kidnap you." She glanced over her shoulder and frowned. "Seriously, though, what's going on? He looks mad as hell that I told you he came to see me."

I peeked back at Maddox, who paced the quad with his jaw clenched, having what appeared to be a heated conversation on his cell phone. "I promise he's not mad at you. But I'll tell you later. Right now, I'm gonna go see who he *is* mad at." Or rather, what Laith had done this time. Maddox's brother was obviously up to something, and that could only mean trouble.

"Okay, fine. I'll catch up to you at lunch, but when I do, you'd better be ready to dish, girlfriend." She laughed as she backed away from me. "That's the price for bailing you out. I want full disclosure on the details."

"I never expected anything less." I shot her a grin and fell into a full-on sprint over to where Maddox stood, half hidden by the sign.

Before I'd even reached the corner, I felt the static charge in the air. The force of the jolt kicked me back the instant I stepped around the sign. My entire body lit up as if I'd tossed a toaster into the bathtub. And as I hit the ground, I saw Maddox's horrified face before he completely disappeared into thin air.

I was too calm. I must have been in shock. But things could have been worse. At least my heart was still beating. I tried to roll over from where I lay on the ground with the wind knocked out of me, waiting to regain the use of my limbs. My head buzzed as I tried to make sense of what had happened. I must have stepped into the jump zone as Maddox was on his way out. I could only hazard a guess as to what had prompted him to jump. *Laith.* I just didn't know the reason.

"Hey, are you okay?" A boy in a blue windbreaker crouched down beside me, looking at me as if he were inspecting roadkill. "You pass out or something? My sister passes out all the time. You should eat. Girls never think they need to eat." He reached a hand out to me, and I grasped it, letting him haul me to my feet.

"Thanks." I kept things short and sweet. I didn't need to get into the hows or whys of my current predicament.

"Yeah, sure." He scratched his blond head, looking at me like I had rabies. "You need to go to the clinic?"

I shook my head.

"Okay, well, I'm gonna go. You're lucky I was already running late."

"Yeah, lucky." Maybe my head *was* still a little fuzzy. Maybe I did need to see a doctor. "Thanks."

"You said that." He smiled that time—a crooked grin that made him a lot cuter than I'd first realized.

If I hadn't already been spoken for, twice over, I might have let this one flirt with me. "I'm gonna..." I pointed toward the science building as I willed my feet to move forward.

"Yeah, me too. Chem lab."

"Molecular bio."

"Nice." His head bobbed a few times as he backed slowly toward the building. "You know, I think I'll go ahead and walk with you. Make sure you don't take another dirt nap on the way."

"Sure." I shrugged, keeping pace with him. I caught him shooting glances at me every so often as we crossed the quad.

He reached the door first and held it open for me. "You sure you're okay? You look like you've seen a ghost."

"I'll be fine. Thanks." The instant the words passed my lips, I knew I was lying. I'd just seen my boyfriend disappear in front of me, presumably so he could travel to another place and time. And even if I *could* contact him there, my phone was still dead. Maybe I had seen a ghost after all.

Or maybe what I saw was way worse.

The boy nodded a few times then turned and vanished around a corner the way normal boys do when they disappear.

I didn't think I'd ever be able to settle for normal again.

CHAPTER NINETEEN

A FTER MAKING SURE MY WOULD-BE savior wasn't coming back to check on me, I wandered the science building in a daze. Since I was already late, I figured I might as well skip the entire class. Thanks to the anticipated "recharge period," I had doubts Maddox would make it back in time for our European history class, not that he'd miss much. As it turned out, my boyfriend was a bit of an expert on the subject.

Boyfriend. The word didn't seem to do justice to the entire scope of our relationship.

When he still hadn't come back by the time class ended, I wandered off to the library to study for the French test Sam had told my mom I'd already studied for. Instead, I directed every bit of my focus on the entrance. My weak attempts to *will* Maddox to step through the glass door with nothing but sheer determination didn't pan out, but that didn't stop me from trying.

I'd officially become a zombie. The zap I'd taken from his time jump ripple and the sense of loss I always experienced when he wasn't around left me with a fuzzy head. Even halfway through the day, I couldn't seem to shake the feeling.

My need to talk to Maddox bordered on desperate. I spent my entire lunch break making a mountain out of my mashed potatoes like a crazy person and staring at my dead cell phone, willing it back to life.

By the time I sat down to take the test in French, I would have settled for seeing Laith, not that I had any idea how to reach him. I certainly didn't have his number, if he even had a phone.

If Sam was concerned about my odd behavior, she didn't say anything. And I barely saw Paige or Hannah, who appeared to be surgically attached to Abercrombie's hip these days and didn't seem to notice me at all.

In fact, the only person who acknowledged something might be wrong with me was the guy who'd found me sprawled out in the grass under the sign. He stopped me in the quad before French to ask if I was still in shock. The guy had no idea how right he was.

After finishing my test, I decided not to wait for Sam and slipped out quietly, walking the six blocks home for the first time since I'd started at the Port Michael campus.

"Mom?" I tossed my keys on the kitchen table and listened for any signs of life other than that damn clock. "Josh?"

I jogged up the stairs and pushed my brother's door open. *Empty.* Mom hadn't mentioned it, but I figured Josh must have had one of those after-school things again.

"Guess I'm on my own for dinner," I muttered as I took the attic steps two at a time.

I'd gotten used to being on my own in the afternoons, but even after living in my grandmother's house for over a month, it still freaked me out to walk into my room with no one else home. I just couldn't shake the feeling I was being watched.

The shadow of a face that wasn't mine formed in my mirror, fading almost as quickly as it appeared, and I nearly came out of my skin.

Laith.

Maddox had told me they had the ability to reach out to me in creepy ways, but I still swallowed a scream when I glanced at the window and watched as my name appeared then disappeared in the condensation. "I'm not paying attention to you, Laith!" I yelled into the empty room and plugged my phone into the charger and flopped down on my bed. I must have dozed off because the next thing I knew, the battery was full, and the sun was going down. I switched it on, and less than a minute later, a series of chirps went off as several texts came in all at once.

Sam: Where are you? Covered for you with your mom. You owe me!

Sam: Am I picking you up this morning, or are you riding with Romeo?

Mom: I have a work thing for dinner tonight. Stouffer's lasagna in the fridge! Just heat it up.

Mom: Dropped Josh off at Mrs. Crane's house around the corner. Can you walk over and get him when you get home? I told her you'd get him by 5.

Mom: Did you get my messages?

Mom: It's almost 5. Don't forget your brother.

Mom: Remind me to get you that emergency charger. Please don't forget your brother!

I checked the time. *Shit!* Five forty-five. I grabbed my sneakers and left my phone charging. Hopefully Mrs. Crane hadn't sold the peanut to the circus yet.

I grabbed my keys on my way out and walked around the block where I figured Josh was deep into a game of *Grand Theft Auto 99* or whatever he and his friends were into this week.

The porch lights were already off when I rang the bell.

A little girl no more than six or seven came to the door in a shimmering blue Disney princess dress with a fat ribbon holding her auburn curls out of her face. "Who is it?"

I crouched down to her level. "Hi, I'm Ava Flynn. I'm here to pick up my brother, Josh."

"He's not here," she said and slammed the door in my face.

Once the initial shock wore off, I rang the bell again.

This time a much older version of the little girl opened the door. Mrs. Crane, I presumed. "Hello, can I help you?"

"Yes, hi. I'm Ava Flynn. My mother told me to pick Josh up at five, and I'm so sorry it took me so long to get him, but I just got her message a few minutes ago."

The woman blinked a few times then wiped her hands on a red-and-white-striped dishtowel. "Oh! Well, I'm afraid someone already picked him up. H-he said he was doing you a favor." She scrunched up her face as she studied me. "You *do* have a boyfriend, don't you? He's a good-looking boy. Hazel eyes. Messy brown hair. Josh seemed to know who he was."

I sucked in a breath. "Maddox picked him up?"

"Yes!" Her face lit up, and I could see how she might have been pretty, once. "I think that's what he said his name was. I hope it's not a problem that I let Josh go with him. The boy arrived right around the time I expected you, and Josh said he knew him."

I smiled, but on the inside, I was on the verge of panicking. How could she just let my brother leave with someone else, even if he *was* my boyfriend? "Oh, I'm sure it's fine. He's a good guy. He probably knew I was a little out of it. My phone died, and I didn't realize I was supposed to pick Josh up until a few minutes ago." I wondered how Maddox knew to pick Josh up when even I didn't. I guessed if he could travel to the future, it wasn't so farfetched to think he'd known this would happen. I needed a crash course on all things time related.

But what if it wasn't Maddox? I shoved *that* thought right out of my head.

"Did you need anything else, dear?" Mrs. Crane's artificially sweetened voice startled me out of my thoughts.

"Oh. No, thank you." I gave her another forced smile and turned to walk back home.

An eerie feeling festering just below the surface of my skin had me practically running the entire way. I raced up the porch steps and had my key ready to slip into the lock when I came to a screeching halt.

A bloodred tack held a white envelope to the door with my name scrawled across the front in bold black ink. With a shaky hand, I plucked out the pin, letting it fall to the ground as I retrieved the note. I ran a finger over the indentations left by the pen. Something about the swirling script seemed familiar, yet I couldn't place it. A gust of wind rustled my hair, and I spun around to search the darkness behind me.

"Maddox?" When no one answered, I hurried inside, closing and locking the door behind me before tearing open the envelope.

Ava,

Don't worry about me. I'm fine.

Josh

"What the hell?" I sat down on the bottom step and read the note again. *Don't worry about me. I'm fine.* Fine, but where? And why hadn't Maddox called me yet?

I realized I'd left my phone upstairs and dashed up two flights to snatch it off the charger. "No messages?" I sat down, scratching my head.

Where would Maddox take Josh?

The doorbell rang, and I let out a burst of nervous laughter. "Oh, thank God. That must be them."

I hadn't even made it to the steps when the banging started. Whoever was at the door alternated between holding down the doorbell and pounding on the door as if they couldn't wait another moment to get inside my house.

By the time I reached the bottom of the stairs, the hair on the back of my neck stood on end. My brother didn't have the strength to pound the door that hard, and I couldn't imagine Maddox being that aggressive unless the situation warranted it.

"Who is it?" I yelled, keeping myself to the shadows and out of direct sight of the door.

"Ava?" It *was* Maddox, and he sounded frantic. "Jesus, Ava, open the door."

I practically vaulted to the door, sliding the deadbolt out of the way, and all but tore the damn thing off the hinges opening it. "Where have you—"

"Has he been here?" Maddox nudged me out of the way, and the instant he'd made it inside, he quickly closed and locked the door again.

"Has who been here?"

"Laith." Maddox grabbed both of my shoulders and held me still. His eyes were wild as he ran them over me, presumably making sure I was in one piece. "Has my brother been here?"

He had me completely confused. "No, I mean, I thought I saw him in my mirror earlier, but in the flesh? No. Why? Where have you been all day? And where's my brother? Mrs. Crane said you picked him up at five."

Maddox turned into a statue in front of me. I could have planted him in the middle of the quad, and birds would have used him as a perch. That's how still he went. His face morphed into abject horror. "I'm too late. Damn it! I let him play me, and now I'm too *late*!" Maddox shouted the last word as he turned and pounded both fists into the wall. "That sonofabitch!"

I stepped back and let him get himself under control as my blood turned to ice cubes in my veins. Whatever had him so worked up could only be bad. "Maddox, please, you're scaring me. Tell me what's wrong."

He spun away from the wall and began pacing circles over my grandmother's Persian rug, running his bruised hands through his hair as he walked. "It's Laith."

"What's Laith?" A list of possibilities, each one worse than the one before, ran through my head.

"Ava, I'm so sorry." He abruptly stopped pacing and pulled me into an awkward hug. "I tried to get here as fast as I could. I thought I had his plan figured out. I thought I'd gotten the jump on him. That's why I came here first. I should've known better." He released me and went back to pacing. His emotions ran the gamut between fear, guilt, and anger, as if even *he* couldn't decide how he felt. But the look of absolute panic in his eyes terrified me more than anything else. "Laith knew I'd protect you and leave your brother vulnerable, God damn it, and I fell for it." The more he tortured himself, the more of his anxiety I felt coursing through me. Maddox didn't have Josh.

Which could only mean Laith did.

My heart skipped so hard it made me cough. The cough turned into a broken sob. "H-he left me a note. Josh left me a note on the door, saying he was fine." I grabbed the paper from the side table where I'd left it and shoved it into Maddox's hand. "He has to be fine. He wouldn't hurt him, right? Laith wouldn't hurt Josh, would he?"

Maddox shook his head, but the action did nothing to

convince me, especially when I dared to look into his glistening eyes. "He doesn't want Josh, Ava. He wants you."

———◆———

"He sent me a text this morning just after Sam's little revelation about *me* asking her to cover for you." Maddox had finally calmed down enough to sit on the sofa and explain what had happened, starting with his unexpected time jump that morning. "He was taunting me. About you. He told me how I'd ruined his perfect plan to grab you by hiding you out in the lighthouse all night. God, Ava, he had this whole thing worked out. He'd gotten Sam to cover for you, and he intended to jump with you. To disappear."

Hearing the pain in Maddox's voice made it that much more real. "You would have come for me, though. Right?"

He grabbed my hand and squeezed. "Of course I would have, but it's not that easy. It's not as if we have a tracking beacon embedded in us somewhere. We get a feel for where you are. We can sense when you're near."

My hand instinctively went to the back of my neck. "You mean like the prickling sensation I feel when you're around me?"

"Yes." He swallowed hard. "Exactly that. And if one of us is with you, that sensation is even more intense. The more pieces of the soul that come together, the more powerful the draw is to join it."

"But you can't see exactly where I am?"

"Not exactly, no. We have an advantage over you because we can search while we're in that holding pattern."

"The elevator?"

He smiled. "Yes. From inside the elevator, we can *see* more clearly into time's wrinkles to find you. But it's not an exact science. It's more like a scavenger hunt through the centuries."

"So finding Josh would be..." I couldn't even say the word.

He squeezed my hand again. "It's not impossible. It's just not going to be easy. And the one thing we have going for us is that

Laith doesn't want Josh. He wants you. So he's going to contact us to make the switch. I'm certain of it."

"That's what he implied earlier?"

"The asshole flat out told me he was going to do this. That's why I jumped. I figured I could stop him before he had a chance to do it. But what I didn't count on was that this was his plan from the beginning. He *knew* I'd try to stop him, so he took advantage of the fact that I couldn't be two places at once. When I jumped here earlier and nothing was out of the ordinary, I went back, which is why I couldn't get here when he actually *was* grabbing Josh. I'd basically created my own paradox by trying to get the jump on him. I played right into his hands. It was a bloody brilliant ruse. I wish I'd thought of it."

I glanced at the clock. "My mom's gonna be home soon."

"Laith knows you're frantic. He can feel your emotions just as easily as I can. He'll use that to his advantage. He's going to wait until the most intense moment to get a message to us."

"So he didn't jump into the future with him?"

"He wouldn't take him into the future. It could potentially create a paradox down the road. He'd take him into the past. Somewhere safe. He's not going to want to lose his only bargaining chip. But he won't care if he makes everyone insane with worry while he's at it. Will your mom check on Josh when she comes in?"

"She still checks on *me* most nights." I smiled at the memory of her standing in the doorway, thinking she'd been stealthy. "But she just sticks her head—" I jumped to my feet and clasped his hand in mine. "Come on, I have an idea."

I towed Maddox up the stairs and into Josh's room. "Go grab a pair of jeans and a shirt out of his drawer. Turn them inside out and ball them up on the floor. Oh, and don't forget two mismatched socks."

Maddox stopped and made a face. "Mismatched socks?"

"Josh never wears matching socks. Trust me. We're about to pull the oldest trick in the book." I peeled back Josh's blankets and lined up his pillows so it would look like a body under the covers. I grabbed his old teddy bear from under the bed and arranged it to resemble the back of Josh's dark head resting on a pillow. With the lights off, Mom would be fooled into thinking Josh was asleep. Or so I hoped.

Maddox did as I asked then stood back to scratch his head. "And you think this'll work?"

"Oh, absolutely." I shot a grin over my shoulder as I put the final touches on our plan. "I can't even count the number of times my brother's managed to pull this off without getting caught. I think he likes getting away with the deception more than anything else. He never goes farther than the backyard. Mom let him watch *Ferris Bueller's Day Off* one too many times, if you ask me."

Once we had Josh's room set up, we shut off the light and headed to the attic.

"He should have contacted us by now." Maddox checked his phone for the umpteenth time then looked around my room as if searching for something. "You said you saw a face in the mirror earlier. Did you see anything else that may have been Laith trying to get a message to you?"

"Just my name on the window."

"Didn't you say he wrote on your bathroom mirror once?"

"Yeah." I shrugged. "While I was in the tub."

Maddox's face flashed with anger. He quickly tamped it down.

"Stop imagining him seeing me naked." I slapped his arm. "It's bad enough I have to think about it. I need you to focus."

He pressed his lips into a tight line and nodded. "Yeah, okay. Sorry."

"Hey, what if we filled my tub with hot water and let the bathroom steam up? If he's trying to send me a message, maybe he's waiting for a place to put it."

Maddox reached out and grabbed me, pulling me in for a quick kiss. "You're brilliant. You know that?"

I couldn't hold back the smile.

"Lead the way." He followed me into the bathroom and quickly opened the hot water taps on the sink and tub until the water came out full blast. "Come on, come on..." He paced in the small space, waiting for the cloud of steam to fill the bathroom and fog the mirror.

"Look!" I pointed at the swirled script forming on the glass.
Comiskey Park October 3, 1919
See you after the first pitch.

CHAPTER TWENTY

"**O**CTOBER THIRD, 1919? 'SEE YOU after the first pitch?' Is he referring to a baseball game? Does that mean anything to you?" I stared at the words on the mirror, trying to make sense of the message.

"Yeah. Apparently, my brother has a twisted sense of humor." Maddox chuckled but didn't elaborate.

"Comiskey Park? Why does that sound familiar?"

He caught my eyes in the mirror. "Because that's where the Chicago White Sox used to play."

I pulled my attention from Maddox's reflection and turned to face him. "Why is he sending us to a baseball field?"

He shrugged but made a point of looking everywhere but at me. "I'm guessing he wanted to catch the game."

"There's something you're not telling me." I watched him carefully as he walked out of my bathroom.

I followed him into my room, catching up to him beside my unmade bed.

He completely ignored my comment but turned to face me. "You're going to want to change your clothes."

"What?" I peeked down at my *Tattoo You* T-shirt and favorite jeans. "But we're going to a baseball game."

"We're going to a baseball game in *1919*. You can't go like *this*." Maddox brought his lips to my ear as he trailed a finger over the exposed skin at my collarbone, sending a delicious shiver down my spine. "Not that I'm complaining about how you're dressed because you look fantastic. But you'd create quite the scandal in pre-1920s Chicago."

I shook my head to clear it. "Oh. Right. Of course. I wasn't thinking." If he didn't stop touching me, I doubted I'd ever think straight again.

He kissed the sweet spot behind my ear then flopped down on my bed, staring up at the cracks in my ceiling as if trying to solve an equation. "Does your mom have anything you can borrow?" He picked up my pillow and brought it to his face.

"Anything from that era? I doubt it." I bit back a smirk. "Did you really just smell my pillow?"

He shrugged then smiled and shoved the pillow behind his head. "Well, we can't just show up in regular clothes. We'd never get through the gate looking like a couple of vagrants."

I wasn't sure how I felt about that statement, but I let it go. "So you're saying Laith has a stash of clothes from the early twentieth century?"

"I'm certain he does. I know I do."

My eyes popped wide as his words sank in. "You have clothes from the twenties?"

"And the thirties, forties, and fifties, actually. You can get away with a lot of the same stuff for the sixties and seventies, and I avoid the eighties like the plague."

I nodded. It made sense.

"Do you have any long skirts or—"

"Oh my God, I can't believe I forgot!" I shot a glance at the narrow storage closet on the other side of my room. "When we first moved in, I discovered these trunks filled with old clothes. I think they must have been my grandmother's, maybe even my great-grandmother's. I'd planned on selling them on Etsy or taking them to a vintage shop, but I got distracted." My cheeks heated up as I thought of exactly *who* had distracted me.

He gave me a knowing grin. "Well, what are we waiting for? Let's see what's inside."

Maddox helped me drag the first trunk out of the closet, and I carefully removed the floral silk dress I'd seen that first day.

I stood in front of the full-length mirror and held it up to me. The long-sleeved dress looked to be about ankle length with a pattern of pale pink and white flowers repeating over a delicate cream background. As far as I could tell, it was absolutely perfect. "Do you think it'll fit?"

Maddox's eyes seemed to glaze over as he watched my reflection. "I guess there's only one way to know for sure. Why don't you try it on?"

I nodded and disappeared into the bathroom, hanging the dress on the back of the door. I yanked my T-shirt over my head and shimmied out of my jeans. "Laith, you'd better not be watching me," I whispered into the mirror before slipping the dress over my head.

My grandmother must have been about my size because the dress not only fit, it fit as if it had been made for me. The high-waisted skirt and the thick lapels of the wrapped bodice accentuated every barely-there curve of my body.

I grabbed a few clips from my sink and swept my hair back, twisting and rolling it into a haphazard up-do before pinning it in place. I took a deep breath and stepped out of the bathroom.

Maddox was stretched out across my bed, but when he saw me, his mouth fell open, and he jumped up and crossed the room as if he'd time-jumped to me. "Ava, you..." He took my face in his hands and without breaking eye contact, he slowly closed the distance between us until his lips barely brushed mine. "You take my breath away."

Just when I thought he'd take a step back, his eyes flashed with need. He slid one hand behind my back as the other fought against the pins to snake into my hair, tilting my head slightly so he could really kiss me. Without asking for the permission I would have willingly given, his mouth claimed mine, setting off a chain reaction of fireworks through my body.

The entire house could have fallen down around us, and I wouldn't have noticed. Every bit of my attention focused on Maddox. Our lips moved together as if they'd known each other in a past life. And in a way, I guessed they had.

My arms went up to wrap around his neck, and he responded by pulling me flush against him. I couldn't tell which heartbeat was his and which was mine. His hand skated around to rest on the slippery fabric at my hip, and my pulse spiked. He swallowed my moans, capturing my bottom lip between his then releasing it with a pop before going in for more. Every touch, every sound drove me past the point of rational thought.

We were both breathless when he finally pulled away, putting a little distance between us. "I-I almost forgot..." He didn't finish the sentence, but we both knew what he meant. *Josh.* Laith still had my little brother.

"Let's go." I slipped my feet into a pair of pink ballet flats and grabbed Mom's tan London Fog overcoat on the way downstairs. We hurried out of the house before my mother got home and made things even more complicated. Instead of taking Maddox's bike, we walked the less than half a block to his house.

All that time wasted searching for him when he'd lived just four houses away—if I'd only known.

"I'll only be a few minutes." He gave me a quick kiss before disappearing down a dark hallway.

I waited in the empty living room while Maddox changed into something more appropriate. His house was stark in comparison to mine. He'd said the place had been abandoned for years, and it showed. The old vine-patterned wallpaper had peeled away from the corners, and dark stains made random patterns on the ceiling like a giant Rorschach test. But it had good bones. It could be a nice house if he fixed it up.

I sat in the only chair, a stiff high-backed thing that must have been designed for looks, because it was most definitely not made for comfort.

"Ready?"

His voice startled me, and I nearly capsized myself out of the chair. "Uh huh."

Maddox laughed. "Are you sure?" He looked different in a suit, with his messy hair tamed into a neat style. Older. But very handsome.

I kept my eyes down so he wouldn't notice how much he affected me. "Shut up. You scared me. This place is sort of creepy."

"Yeah, sorry. I've never had much need to fix it up. My room is nice, if you..."

My head snapped up, and even in the dim light from the old chandelier, I noticed his face flush to his hair.

Maddox rubbed the back of his neck. "Uh, never mind."

I crossed the room to stand in front of him and gazed up into his hazel eyes. "I'm ready."

He cleared his throat, but his voice still came out a little husky. "Ready?"

"Yeah." I reached up to straighten his tie. "To, you know, time travel with you."

"Oh, right." He shook his head. "I don't know what I was thinking." He took me in his arms so we were chest to chest and placed his palm against the bare skin at the back of my neck, making me shudder. "We need to have skin-on-skin contact for you to... so I can bring you with me."

I didn't even want to ask how he knew that, but I nodded and slid my hand into the back of his hair, where I could feel his pulse thrumming against my fingertips. "Is this good?"

He dropped his forehead to mine and let out a half-groan, half-whine. "Yeah. It's, uh... it's good." Then he took a deep breath. "I'm sorry."

"What for?"

"This is going to be disorienting."

I felt the room swirl around me, pulling me in all different directions until a deep, dark hole sucked us in.

Just like in my dream, I spiraled down a dark tunnel with an icy wind whipping around me, threatening to rip me to shreds. Only this time, Maddox held on to me as we dropped into the abyss. And instead of grasping at the air, my hands held tight to him like a lifeline. With my face buried in his chest, I couldn't see. I could barely breathe. And just like the dream, it took so long to reach the bottom, I feared we'd fall forever.

I bit back the scream building in my throat as we landed with a thud. Maddox was right. We didn't end up crouched down or naked in a dark alley. But we weren't at the ball field, either. Instead, we clung to one another in the middle of nowhere, a glowing ripple of energy dissipating around us.

"Where are we?" I gaped at the trees and rolling hills. We were a few yards from a small pond with a wooden bridge. "Is this even Chicago?"

Maddox did a quick scan of the area and laughed. "Well, this is ironic."

I untangled my fingers from his hair and stepped out of his arms. "What is?"

"We're in Washington Park."

"Did something go wrong? Weren't we trying to hit Comiskey Park?"

Maddox laughed again. "Totally different kind of park. But to answer your question, jumping isn't an exact science. We can get close, but to my knowledge, neither of us has yet to jump on a giant X marking the spot."

"Oh. Then what about Washington Park is ironic?"

"Well, we're not too far from the spot where the Fountain of Time sculpture will be erected about a year from now."

"That's interesting, I guess." I failed to understand the significance of the sculpture.

"You don't know it?"

"No."

He frowned and took a tentative step toward me. "Come here. You're all... windblown." Maddox spun me around then took his time tucking my hair back into the pins. With meticulous precision, he wound each lock around his finger before securing it into place. The sweet gesture took me off guard. "You've never heard of the Fountain of Time?"

I started to shake my head, but his hands in my hair prevented me from moving. And his warm breath against my neck banished all thoughts of sculptures, parks, and baseball games into the fringe of my consciousness.

He secured the last pin and turned me around, a slight smile curving his full lips. "Henry Austin Dobson's poem 'The Paradox of Time' inspired it. A personal favorite of mine, actually."

I caught the sweet scent of fresh-cut grass as I stared up at him and cleared my throat. The urge to kiss him overwhelmed me. "I don't know it."

"'*Time goes, you say? Ah, no! Alas, Time stays, we go.*'" Maddox kept his voice low, seductive, locking his eyes on me as he recited the poem. "'*Or else, were this not so. What need to chain the hours, For youth were always ours? Time goes, you say?–ah no!*' Fitting, wouldn't you say?"

"Hmm." I gulped, and something intense crackled between us, making my stomach flutter.

"We'd better hurry." Maddox dropped his eyes to the gold watch on his wrist. "We don't want to miss the first pitch."

I nodded and took his outstretched hand. "What time does the game start?"

"Two-twenty, and it's already almost one."

"Is it far to the field?"

"Far enough by foot."

———◆———

We arrived at Comiskey Park with ten minutes to spare. Maddox picked up the tickets waiting for us at the gate, and we made our way to our seats.

The stadium was way smaller than the modern venues I'd been to with Josh and my father, and crowds of people settling into the teal seats looked as if they'd be more comfortable in an office building than a ball field, or maybe the set of a movie. Men in fancy three-piece suits escorted women in long, narrow skirts and wide-brimmed hats. I didn't see a single kid in baseball attire. No one ran up and down the stairs shouting with team spirit. The stadium was as serene as a church. Maddox was right; I would have stuck out like a sore thumb in my jeans and concert tee.

"What do we do now?" I leaned over to whisper, and he met me in the middle.

"We wait." He reached out, taking my hand and lacing my fingers with his. "Cincinnati's up to bat first. Dickie Kerr's about to throw the first pitch and get the first three batters out in a row."

"Have you been here before?"

He laughed. "I can't be in two places at once, remember? Though I *have* seen newsreels and read articles about it. This series is pretty infamous, historically speaking."

"What happened that made it so infamous?" I leaned into him until our shoulders pressed together.

"Are you kidding me?"

I gave him a look.

"Have you ever seen *Field of Dreams*?"

The mere mention of my dad's all-time favorite movie brought tears to my eyes, and I blinked them back. "Uh, yeah, I've seen it several times."

He put his lips closer to my ear. "Ray Liotta's character, the ghost of Shoeless Joe Jackson, got sent to the cornfield because he'd been banned from baseball for life after *this* World Series."

"So Ray Liotta's playing in this game?"

He laughed. "No, but the real Shoeless Joe is."

"Oh, right." I giggled. "This time travel thing is so confusing. I mean, logically, I know we're sitting here, nearly a hundred years in the past, but I keep forgetting. Everything looks so crisp and real."

Maddox squeezed my hand. "Believe me, I understand."

"Hello, brother."

I whipped my head around at the sound of Laith's voice. Part of me itched to slap the grin from his lips. The other part yearned to kiss them. I hated that my body responded to him at all.

"Laith." Maddox gritted his teeth, and I could tell it was taking everything in him not to attack his brother.

"Oh, come on. Don't tell me you aren't enjoying the game." Laith kept his eyes trained on the field. "Kerr just struck out the third batter. I imagine Rothstein's seething right about now."

"You know that's just a rumor." Maddox looked around before answering in a whisper. "No one knows for sure if Arnold Rothstein had anything to do with the fix."

"You know what they say: where there's smoke, there's fire." He grinned down at me. "It's a shame we won't be here to see the end of the game, but I'm afraid I have other plans."

"Where's my brother?" I asked. "Where's Josh?"

"Josh is perfectly fine. In fact, I'd say he's quite enjoying himself. Come on, I'll take you to him." Laith held out his hand and waited.

"She's not going with you!" Maddox snapped, tightening his grip on my hand almost to the point of pain.

I glanced around us and tensed to my toes. We were beginning to draw a crowd. The last thing I wanted was to get arrested in a time when women didn't even have the right to vote.

"Maddox, please." I rested my hand on his arm. "I need to see my brother."

"Fine." He clenched his jaw and nodded. "But we're sticking together."

Laith rolled his eyes, looking too sure of himself for my comfort. "Whatever. Come on."

We followed Laith through the stands until we reached the vacant seats at the very top. Josh stood a few feet away, leaning over the railing, watching the game through an ancient pair of binoculars. "Can we go back to the good seats, now? I can hardly see anything from here." My brother turned to us with a sour frown. He looked frustrated but fine. At least Laith seemed to have taken good care of him.

"Josh!"

I moved toward him, but Laith stepped between us. "Not so fast. Josh wants to stay and watch the game."

"I don't care what Josh wants!" I hissed, working against my own emotions to keep my voice low. "My mother is going to freak out when she realizes he's gone. He needs to come home with me. Now."

Laith smiled. "You see, that's where you're missing the point.

There's absolutely no reason Josh can't stay to watch the whole game and still get home before your mother realizes he's missing. It's called 'time travel.'" He actually made the quotation marks in the air.

"I'm guessing you didn't drag us all the way here just so Josh could watch a ninety-five-year-old baseball game." Maddox squeezed my hand until I felt the bones compress.

"Well, no. Not exactly. I'd like Ava to come with me while you stay here with Josh. You can make sure he gets home safe and sound, and we can take a little time to get to know each other." The smile Laith directed at me made my mouth go dry.

Maddox pushed me behind him. "Absolutely not."

"Fine," Laith snapped. "I'll just take Josh, and we'll leave."

"Wait!" I stepped around Maddox. "I'll go."

"Ava, no!" Maddox looked horrified, but I had to make sure my brother got home safely. "You can't go with him."

"Maddox, I have to. I can't do that to my mother. She'd never recover."

Maddox scoffed. "He's not going to keep Josh."

"Oh, I dunno. He's a great kid. I'll bet we'd have loads of fun jumping around time. I can take him back in say, twenty years. I mean, he'll still be eleven, but at least he'd be home, right?"

Now I *really* wanted to slap the smirk from his face.

"You wouldn't do that!" Angry tears sprang into my eyes, but I blinked them back.

"I wouldn't *want* to, but trust me. I *would*." Laith turned toward Maddox, and his eyes flashed. "I refuse to end up on the short end of things this time."

The pain of his threat felt like a dagger plunged between my ribs. "What are you talking about?"

"Ask your boyfriend." Laith's features hardened as he glared at Maddox then softened again as he turned back to me and held out his hand. "Well? Are you coming?"

"Can I at least say goodbye first?" I wiped the first tear as it fell.

"Fine." Laith exhaled sharply. "Be quick. This era bores me."

Laith walked over to Josh, ruffling his hair as the two of them shared a joke.

How dare he laugh while he tears out my heart?

"I can't simply let you go, Ava." Maddox's face blurred from behind my tears as he cupped my cheek and leaned in. His mouth came down on mine in a desperate kiss. He held still with our lips pressed together for several beats then released me. "My heart is breaking, and you haven't even left me yet."

I licked the salt from my lips. I wasn't sure if the tears were his, mine, or maybe a combination of the two. "I know. I feel it, too."

He choked back a sob. "I'll find you. I promise, if it takes another three hundred and fifty years. If it takes a hundred thousand years. I'll never stop looking."

"I love you, Maddox." I pulled him in for one last kiss before tearing my lips away. "I'm ready." Even as the words came out, I knew I was lying. I would never be ready to leave him.

Maddox put on a brave face as he walked over to Josh. I couldn't hear what they said, but Josh shrugged and went back to watching the game.

"Just waiting for you." Laith took a step toward me, and I held my hands up.

"Can I—"

"No. You've said your goodbyes. Now it's time to go." He almost sounded sad, as if he knew I was leaving against my will.

"You won't let me give my brother one hug? I don't know when I'll see him again."

His jaw clenched, but he managed a stiff smile. "Josh. Can you come say goodbye to your sister, please?" Laith stepped to the side. "Quickly."

"Hey, Ava. You look weird all dressed up." Josh met me halfway between the brothers, and I wrapped my arms around him in a crushing hug. "Geez, what the heck? I was trying to watch the game, you know."

I laughed through my tears, resting my head on his small shoulder. "I know. I just wanted to say goodbye."

"Okay, well... goodbye."

He turned to walk away, but I grabbed his hand. "Josh, wait. Tell Mom I—"

"Don't let go!" Maddox shouted as he dove toward us. His hand wrapped around my neck, and he jerked me toward him at the same time as scooping Josh up with his other arm.

Laith shouted out a string of obscenities, rushing toward us just before an energy ripple propelled him backward, and the abyss sucked us in yet again.

CHAPTER TWENTY-ONE

A GUST OF ICY WIND SWIRLED around us as we spiraled through the dark tunnel. Even my hair got caught up in the cyclone, ripping free of the pins and slapping me in the face as it whipped through the air. The sound reminded me of the waves breaking against the rocks at the lighthouse, and I shuddered.

My hand had gone numb from my death grip on Josh, but I was terrified of what would happen if I let go. I had no idea if Maddox had a grasp on him or if my connection was the only thing holding him to us. Maddox said there had to be skin contact to make the jump, but he never said what would happen if we lost contact during one. After everything we'd been through that day, I couldn't allow my inability to hold on to ruin it all.

The churning made me seasick, and I swallowed back the urge to empty my stomach. The mere thought of puking in a pitch-black vortex made the queasiness so much worse. I wondered if Alice felt this way tumbling down the rabbit hole. Then I remembered Alice was a character in a book. The sickness in my stomach was *real*. The wind rushing in my ears was real. I was real.

Everything went as quiet as death, and we landed in a cold, dark place with a jolt. For a moment, none of us moved. Then Maddox tightened his hold on me as if he couldn't believe we were safe. He kissed me—my forehead, my eyelids, my cheeks—as if the thought of *not* touching me caused him pain.

I wrapped my arms around his neck, meeting him in the middle with my lips. His mouth closed over mine, and we were kissing. I couldn't get enough of him, and if his enthusiasm was any indication, he felt the same way.

"Really? Can you two get a room?" Josh's snarky tone burst our blissful little bubble. Then he let out a squeal of delight. He'd clearly enjoyed the trip. "That time jump thing rocks! Can we do it again?"

Maddox ignored Josh's question, untangling my body from his as he examined me with his hands. "Are you okay?" His voice still carried the anguish from our almost parting, and the need to comfort him overwhelmed me.

"I'm fine." A little white lie. I couldn't have gotten any farther away from *fine* if I tried, but Maddox didn't need to know that.

Laith had almost succeeded in kidnapping me. He *had* taken my brother. And if not for Maddox's quick thinking, I might never have seen either of them, or my mother, again.

Mom.

"Wait." I turned in his arms to survey my unfamiliar surroundings. There wasn't much light, but as far as I could tell, we were in some sort of tomb or dungeon. I could barely make out the dirt floor, and wispy spider webs stretched across the low, wood-beam ceiling. The stone walls looked sturdy but damp, and the stale air smelled like mildew and decay. "Where are we?"

"Oh, cool!" Something caught my brother's attention, and he scurried off like a rat on a sinking ship.

"Josh, wait!" I had no idea what condition the space was in or how safe it was to go wandering around. "Stay where I can see you. We don't even know where we are. Or when we are." I mumbled the last part, not really intending it to be out loud, but Maddox had said time travel wasn't an exact science, so we could literally be anywhere.

"We're back." He pulled me into another hug. "It should only be a few minutes past the time we left, actually." Logically, I understood him, but I couldn't seem to wrap my head around it. We'd been gone for hours. How could only a few minutes have passed? And what difference did it make how long it took if we were trapped below ground?

"But where?"

"It's the basement," Josh shouted from the shadows. "I came down here the day we moved in, but Mom told me to steer clear until she had someone check it out. Do you think there might be bats hiding down here? That would be so cool! Or maybe there's a body buried under the floor."

"God, I hope not." I looked up at Maddox, and he shook his head, biting back a grin. "So how do we get out of here?"

"Stairs, duh." Josh answered as if it were obvious, and I guess it was, but I didn't see any stairs from where I stood. As if he'd read my mind, he wandered back into the open and grabbed me by the hand. "This way, spaz."

"Gee, thanks, jerk." I gripped his clammy hand as he towed me to an even darker corner of the basement.

"*These* are the stairs, but I'm not going first. Who knows *what's* up there," said the kid hoping to find bats or a dead body.

"Way to be brave." I gave him two thumbs up, but I doubted anyone saw in the dark.

"I'll go." Maddox took the lead up the creaking steps but had to use force and his shoulder to open the swollen old door at the top. When it finally gave way, the three of us burst into the kitchen like a set of dominoes.

One look at Maddox sprawled out on the floor under me and I broke out in a fit of giggles.

"What on *earth* were you three doing down there?" Mom appeared in the doorway with her hands on her hips and her bitch brow firmly in place. "Josh, didn't I already tell you the basement was too dangerous?"

"Sorry, Mom." Josh scrambled to his feet, a hundred-watt smile lighting up his face. "But we just got back from time traveling to 1919 to watch Shoeless Joe Jackson play baseball!"

"Shoeless Joe, huh? Have you been watching *Field of Dreams* again?" Mom tried to hide the grin, but she didn't do a very good job of it. Ever since Dad died, Josh had worn out our copy of the movie, watching it at least once every weekend.

"No! And I can prove we went to the game." Josh fished through his pocket and pulled out what looked like a yellow business card. He held it over his head with pride. "See?"

Mom took the card from his fingers and flipped it over to read it. Her eyes snapped up to mine. "Where did he get this?"

"What is it?" My stomach rolled as I imagined the possibilities.

She held it out for me. "It's a ticket for game three of the 1919 World Series."

I swallowed, and my saliva went down the wrong pipe, making me choke and cough, thankfully saving me from having to answer.

Maddox had my back, literally, whacking me until I could breathe again. "We, uh, went on a little scavenger hunt and found a trunk of stuff from the early nineteen hundreds in Ava's closet. It must have been in there."

I sucked in an uncomfortable breath. "Yeah, that's where I found this dress. And Maddox's suit. We were just playing with Josh until you got home." It was amazing how well I lied once I got going.

It didn't escape me that Maddox could be considered an expert in the art of deception.

"Did not!" Josh stomped his foot and pouted like a toddler. "We went to the baseball game. But I only got to watch the first half of the first inning before Maddox grabbed me and made me come back."

Mom flashed an apologetic smile at me then steered Josh toward the stairs. "Okay, that's enough adventure for one day, kiddo. Time for bed."

"Where's my ticket? I want my ticket back."

"Here!" I waved it in front of me, and he darted across the kitchen and snatched it out of my hand before heading upstairs with Mom close on his heels.

"Quick thinking." I rested my head on Maddox's chest, melting into him as he wrapped his arms around me.

He rested his chin on the top of my head. "Occupational hazard."

"I'll bet." I pulled back to look into his eyes. "What the hell was your brother thinking, bringing a kid on a time jump? Did he think Josh could keep something like that a secret?"

"I don't imagine he cared. It's not as if anyone would believe Josh. He didn't see anything that couldn't be researched on the Internet, and even the ticket stub is something you can get from collectors here and there. Luckily, you happened to have a stash of things from that era."

"And if I hadn't?" I tucked myself under his chin again, listening to the rhythmic beat of his heart.

"I would have said I found it in the basement. Relax." He kissed the top of my head. "People are always willing to discount the unbelievable. You'll see."

"If you say so." I had to wonder how often he'd had to distract people from the truth. How many times had I let things slide because they seemed impossible?

He chuckled. "I do."

"But what do we do now? What's stopping Laith from coming back and grabbing Josh again?" The question sat like a stone at the bottom of my stomach.

"Laith didn't grab me. I went with him because I wanted to."

I spun around in Maddox's arms to find my brother standing at the edge of the kitchen in his pajamas, a sour scowl pasted on his face. "Josh, Laith isn't like Maddox—"

"You're right." He stepped forward, his dimpled chin pointing at Maddox like an accusation. "Laith *isn't* like Maddox. I like Laith. He's a nice guy. He likes baseball... like Dad. And he's like Shoeless Joe. Everyone thinks he did something bad, but he didn't. He got blamed for what someone else did. Laith should be your boyfriend, Ava. You're stupid if you think Maddox is the good brother."

With that, Josh turned around and ran out the way he came, leaving me in total and complete shock—and Maddox restless and tense.

Maddox tried to convince me to let him sleep on my floor that night. His reasons hinged on watching over me in case Laith showed up to grab me in a fit of frustration, but I suspected it had more to do with my little brother's smear campaign. For whatever reason, Josh's dislike of Maddox had gotten under his skin.

My brother had it in his head that Laith had his reasons for doing what he did. And maybe Josh was right. Maybe Laith believed he was doing the right thing, but believing something didn't make it true.

Unfortunately, that went for Maddox, too. I believed in him wholeheartedly, but after our trip to 1919, I wondered if there weren't layers of the story I'd missed, nuances he'd left out along the way. The problem was I didn't want to think of either of them as all bad. Maddox owned my heart, but my soul belonged equally to both of them. And as I lay there, studying the cracks in my ceiling, I realized how much I wanted Laith to be as good as Josh believed him to be.

Unfortunately, history told a different tale.

I couldn't sleep. Instead, I tossed and turned, desperate to shut off my brain, but the events of the day continued to replay through my mind like an old newsreel. Only the colors were all wrong.

In my head, the past had always been faded, the color leached away until it resembled a lifeless sepia print. But standing there in Comiskey Park, with people walking around me in the flesh, turned out to be a totally different story. Like in what I considered *real life*, the colors were rich and vibrant. Today was like Dorothy walking through the door into Munchkinland. It was the difference between black-and-white and Technicolor—the difference between Laith and Maddox.

Night and Day.

One thing I knew for sure: I couldn't wait to jump through time again.

Josh sat in his usual spot, shoveling brightly colored cereal into his mouth, when I wandered down to the kitchen the next morning, looking like a junkie jonesing for a fix.

"You look like crap." He enunciated each word around a mouthful of Trix.

I grabbed a bowl and filled it up halfway with the cereal *du jour* before dumping in enough milk to make the colored balls float. "Yeah, well, today I *feel* like crap. How do you like *that*?"

He swallowed his food then licked his lips. "Good. You deserve it."

I paused with the spoon inches from my mouth. "I know you think Laith is a good guy, but trust me, he's not. You hung out with him for all of a few hours, but I've known him long enough to know better. And I've known Maddox even longer than that." Speaking in a purely cosmic sense, I'd known them both for an eternity. And in the back of my mind, I knew Laith would do whatever it took to get Josh on his side, like in the movies, where the bad guy always found time to recruit minions. "Laith wanted you to like him, Josh. That's all. He's not your friend."

"Well, I do like him. And he *is* my friend. And for your information, I spent a whole lot more than a few hours with him. We watched the first two baseball games before you showed up and *ruined* everything. I liked Chicago. I wanted to stay longer. There were a bunch more games, you know. But you just *had* to leave with Maddox." He stuffed another load of Trix in his mouth, and I had to look away while he chewed.

But something he'd said nagged at me. "What do you mean you watched the first two games? They played three games that day?"

"No, stupid." Pink milk dribbled down his chin, and he wiped it away with the back of his hand. "The first two games were in Cincinnati."

My mouth fell open, and I quickly closed it. "You were in Cincinnati?"

"Yeah." He shrugged. "We were in some other city, too, but I don't remember which one. Laith said he needed to do something, so I listened to the man playing piano while I waited."

"So... how long were you and Laith gone, exactly?"

He shrugged again, chewing with his mouth open. "I dunno. A week or two, maybe longer. You'd have to ask him to be sure."

The spoon slipped from my fingers, hitting the side of my bowl with a loud clank. His words kept bouncing through my brain. *Maybe longer.* Laith had taken my brother and been gone for more than two weeks. "And he was nice to you the whole time?"

"Yeah, sure. We talked. Played cards. He took me out for ice cream and pizza." He giggled. "Dude's got it really bad for you. And he does *not* like his brother very much. He said Maddox took you from him once, but that won't happen again. When did you know them before?"

I had no desire to get into a philosophical discussion with an eleven-year-old. "I didn't."

"Oh. Laith said he's known you forever."

Forever. I didn't even know what that meant anymore.

CHAPTER TWENTY-TWO

I SPENT THE NEXT TWO DAYS waiting for the other shoe to drop. I'd basically floated through my classes in a daze, failing two quizzes and forgetting to hand in a homework assignment in history. I could actually *feel* my grades falling along with the barometric pressure. The way things were going, I'd be lucky to pass, come midterms.

Instead of focusing on school like the straight-A student I was supposed to be, I divided my attention between Maddox and his unpredictable moods... and Laith—mostly, wondering where Laith had disappeared to. We hadn't heard from him since Chicago. And I felt certain the not knowing was driving Maddox crazy, which in turn drove *me* crazy.

"I'll wait for you." Maddox planted himself against the wall directly outside the ladies' room.

"You don't have to. Just head to the cafeteria and get us a table. I'll catch up in a minute."

He crossed his arms and stared over my head toward the exit.

I exhaled. "Maddox, he's not hiding in a stall waiting to grab me."

"He could be."

"But he's not. You said yourself it's not that easy to hit an X when you jump. What are the odds he'd randomly end up in a random restroom in the Commons?"

He shrugged. "It'll make me feel better to wait. Okay?"

"No. It's not okay." I pulled myself up to my full height to stand toe to toe with him. He ran a hand through his disheveled hair. "Maddox, I can't pee with you right outside the door."

"Geez, what are you two bickering about? And don't even try to say you're not. I'm pretty sure everyone in the Commons can read your body language." Sam crossed her arms and ran through a veritable array of mock scowls as she approached.

I couldn't help laughing at her over-the-top expressions. "Maddox's just being ridiculous."

He gave me a sweet smile but kept his thoughts to himself. He wouldn't dare tell Sam *why* I thought he was being ridiculous. "Why don't you girls do your thing in the restroom and meet me in the cafeteria when you're done?" It seemed as though he was fine as long as I had *someone* watching over me.

"Brilliant plan." Or an acceptable compromise. I'd take what I could get. "We don't need a guy hovering while we do our thing. Right, Sam?"

Her eyes bounced between us as if she were watching a tennis match. "I have no idea what the hell either of you are talking about."

"That's probably for the best," Maddox muttered.

I reached up on my toes to plant a kiss on his lips. "See you in a few minutes."

He gave me one of those looks, the ones where he was obviously trying to convey something wordlessly. So I scrunched up my face as I tried to decipher the hidden message, mouthing out guesses as if playing charades. But based on his reactions, I hadn't figured out what he was trying to say.

Finally, he gave up and rolled his eyes. "Don't be too long, okay?"

"Oh! Yeah, we'll be right behind you." I gave him a quick salute and watched him leave.

Sam waited until Maddox was out of earshot before opening her mouth. "Okay, what the hell was *that* all about?"

I laughed as we made our way into the restroom. It wasn't as if I could tell her about Laith's kidnapping attempt or Maddox's concern for my safety. Not exactly, anyway. But I could definitely bend the truth a little. "Maddox caught some guy flirting with me, uh, outside of our Euro history class, and he's convinced the guy is working up the nerve to try something."

Sam laughed. "Does he think your would-be stalker is going to kidnap you from the bathroom?"

I shrugged. That was exactly what he thought.

Sam pulled out a tube of bubblegum-pink lipstick and brought it to her lips while staring at her reflection. "Well, he's clearly channeling every overprotective, controlling boyfriend character ever created. Next thing you know, he'll be sparkling in the sun." She lacquered her lips then proceeded to fluff her blond hair.

"Shut up." I hip-checked her and took her place in front of the mirror. "He's a little protective; I'll give you that. But he's not deranged."

"Hey, I'm just saying, you need to remind him that you're a modern woman, and you don't need him to protect you from every guy on the planet. In fact, I've got just the thing to put him in his place." Sam turned on her high heels and strode halfway down the hall before spinning back around. "Are you coming?"

<hr />

"Tomorrow night? A double date?" I could only imagine the look on my face as I gaped around the table. Shock? Disbelief? Horror? Probably all of the above.

"A triple actually." Sam flashed a closed-lip smile. "Me and Ryan, you and Maddox, and Hannah and Aaron. But who's counting?"

Who *was* counting? Not me. I'd run out of fingers to count on. There were *infinite* reasons why her idea was ridiculous. Not even *my* wild imagination could come up with a scenario where that would have been a good idea.

"Oh, come on, Ava. It'll be fun," said the blue-haired girl with the hoodie-wearing boyfriend. The very *same* hoodie-wearing boyfriend who'd found himself sprawled out on the floor by *my* boyfriend for trying to kiss me, not so long ago.

Yeah, brilliant idea. "Fun. Right." I shoved a fry between my lips to keep my mouth busy. The less I said the better.

"What's fun?" Paige dropped into the open seat across from me.

"We're all going on a group date!" Hannah beamed. She was entirely too excited for my taste.

"Oh, I wanna come!" Paige picked the vegetables out of her salad until she had nothing but plain lettuce in her bowl. "I met a new guy." She glanced at Maddox as if they shared a dirty secret. Some deep dark side of me I never even knew existed ached to rip her throat out. Was she trying to make him jealous because he'd ignored her attention? Or did she still think she had a chance with my boyfriend?

"Ohhh, a new guy? Why haven't we seen him around?" Sam leaned in on her elbows, eager for all the juicy details.

"He keeps a low profile." Paige glanced my way again. "I'm surprised you'd agree to go on another outing with this crowd, Ava." I couldn't tell if she was keeping up the facade or if we'd gone back to being adversaries.

I forced a smile. "Sam doesn't take no for an answer."

"Don't I know it!" Paige laughed, and I decided our tenuous friendship was still intact. "So where are we going?"

Sam practically bounced in her seat. "There's a new club in Portland—Kryptonite. I heard it's all high-tech futuristic. We should go there."

"All the way in Portland? That's like... an hour away."

The sound of Abercrombie's voice made the hair on the back of my neck stand up, and Maddox reached for my hand under the table as if he'd felt a disturbance in the Force. He'd stayed quiet through the entire exchange, and I couldn't tell if he was for or against the group-date idea.

"It is not." Sam scoffed. "It's like thirty-five minutes, tops."

"It'll be fun, Aaron. Can we go? Please?" Hannah batted her eyelashes at him, and the guy melted like a puddle of goo. It was disgusting.

"It's settled." Sam clapped her hands together. "Now we need to figure out who's driving."

◆

"You're sure you don't mind?" I bit my lip as I looked up at Maddox's stiff expression. He might have said otherwise, but I had a feeling he wasn't thrilled with the travel arrangements.

The threat of rain had derailed our plan to take Maddox's motorcycle to Portland, so instead, we waited on my front porch for Sam to pick us up in her bright-yellow Mini Cooper.

"I'm positive." He gave my hand a squeeze. "You look gorgeous, by the way."

"Thanks." I fidgeted under his scrutiny, feeling naked in the leather miniskirt and red sparkly crop top Sam insisted I wear. *You can't wear denim to a nightclub,* she'd said. And apparently, the sky-high stilettos were a *must* with the outfit. "I feel a little under-dressed." *As in undressed.*

He brought his mouth down to my ear. "I like it."

"I'm sure you do." I trembled as he caught my earlobe in his teeth then worked his way down my neck. I melted into him as the ever-present prickling flared and spread through my entire body. It didn't hurt that Maddox looked positively edible in his dark jeans and black button-down.

A loud honk interrupted what might have been an embarrassing make-out session, and Maddox pulled his lips away from my throat. "She has shitty timing."

I jumped out of his arms, cooling my flaming cheeks with my palms. "At least she's consistent."

"Enough with the PDA!" Sam snapped her fingers as she shouted out her window. "Let's go. Portland awaits."

The ride to Portland took exactly thirty-seven minutes. Thirty-seven minutes of Maddox's hot palm pressed against the inside of my knee to keep me from strangling Sam while she went on and on about Kryptonite. For someone who'd never been there, she seemed to know a whole lot about the place—from the alien-planet décor right down to the techno song list we should

201

expect to hear. By the time we arrived, I felt as if there couldn't possibly be any surprises in store for me.

"Oh my God, Ava. You look amazing!" Hannah dragged me into a bone-crushing hug. "I'm so effing excited. My brother's girlfriend's cousin said this place is sick."

"Sounds like a glowing endorsement to me." Maddox winked at me then turned to glower at Abercrombie. "Aaron."

"Hey, Maddox." Abercrombie gave him the guy nod then grabbed Hannah's hand and pulled her to the door. "See you guys inside."

"Where's Paige?" I asked Sam as I scanned the faces in the crowd out front.

"She said she'd be a little late, something about making an entrance. You know how she is."

Unfortunately, I did.

"Why don't we just go in and wait for her inside?" Thank God, Ryan had the good sense to bring it up before I did. Sam seemed to be putty in his hands.

"Brilliant plan." Maddox wove his fingers between mine and led me to the entrance, where most of us were denied the red paper bracelets reserved for the over-twenty-one crowd.

Sam's secondhand description didn't quite do the place justice. Rather than the stark alien landscape I'd expected, Kryptonite looked like something out of a sci-fi vampire movie—like *Star Trek* meets *The Lost Boys*. Long strips of strobing white and purple lights lined the ceiling, casting an otherworldly glow over the stainless steel and red leather covering every surface. Electronic dance music thumped through the speakers, changing the pattern of my heartbeat. The volume was so high I could practically taste the sound on the tip of my tongue.

I followed Maddox to a crescent-moon mirrored table in the back of the room, and he motioned for me to slide into the bench seat along the concave side. "What do you want to drink?"

I shrugged. "Something fruity?"

"Really?" He looked shocked but pressed a quick kiss to my lips. "Fruity it is."

"Wait for me." Not to be outdone, Ryan kissed Sam then ran to catch up to Maddox as he headed for the bar.

"Hey, babe," Sam called after him. "Find Hannah while you're over there."

"I'm glad you talked me into coming," I said. "I've been a bad friend lately. I'm sorry."

"Hey, don't worry about it. Boyfriends take up a lot of time." She winked. "In fact, I'm hoping Ryan takes up the rest of my weekend."

"Hey... it's you. The girl who passed out in the quad."

I turned at the sound of his voice—the blond guy who'd helped me after Maddox's jump ripple zapped me. He looked different in a pair of black jeans and a white T-shirt, less studious or something. "Ava. Hi. I'm sorry. I don't know your name."

"Ethan." He held out his hand, and I awkwardly shook it.

"It's nice to finally meet you, Ethan."

"It's nice to meet you too, Ava." He grinned, creating a dimple in his left cheek.

"I'm Sam." Sam flashed him a wide smile then turned to me and mouthed, "He's hot!"

And I had to admit, he looked sexy without the blue windbreaker and the L.L. Bean backpack. But when he didn't leave after a long minute of awkward silence, I didn't know what to do. "Are you here with friends?"

"Who, me?" He looked around as if he didn't realize I was talking to him. "Yeah. I'm here with a couple of friends. They're talking to a few girls over there." He nodded toward the bar, where Maddox and Ryan still hadn't gotten our drinks.

"Oh."

"So yeah..." He rested his palms on the reflective surface of the table, invading my personal space as he leaned in until I could smell his rosemary and sweet mint cologne. "I was wondering if maybe you'd like to dance."

I swallowed hard and sat back until I hit the cold leather of the bench seat. "I'm sorry. I can't. I'm here with—"

"She's here with her boyfriend." Pure, unmistakable hate dripped from Maddox's voice.

My eyes flickered up to his face, and I actually flinched from the palpable rage pouring off him. I'd only seen him that angry once before, and that was only a dream.

Ethan stood back from the table and held up his hands. "Oh, hey, no problem, man. I didn't know. I'll see you around campus, Ava. Have fun." He turned to leave, but Maddox grabbed his arm.

Maddox maintained an icy calm demeanor that had me riveted in place. "Stay. Away. From. Ava."

"Jesus, chill out." Ethan pulled his arm out of Maddox's grip and backed away slowly. "All I did was ask her to dance."

"And I said to stay away from her."

Ethan looked shaken, but he played it off the way guys do. "Yeah, whatever."

Once Ethan disappeared into the crowd, Maddox turned to me. "May I have a word with you?" He hadn't lost a drop of the venom in his tone.

I cleared my throat and willed my legs to move, sliding slowly from the booth. "Yeah, sure." Once I was on my feet, he grasped my arm and towed me away from the table to a dark corner in the back of the room. "Maddox, what the hell has gotten into you?"

"Who was that?"

I wrenched my arm free and took a steadying breath. "Who was who?"

"Very funny." A sinister smile slithered across his face. "The guy, Ava. Who was the guy? How do you know him?"

"He's just a guy from school. He helped me up after I got caught in the wash from your jump the other day. I didn't even know his name until just now."

"You looked awfully chummy from where I was standing." He shoved his hand into his hair, making a mess of the artful disarray.

I laughed. "Chummy? Are you serious? He asked me to dance. I said no. That's all there was to it."

"Well, I didn't like it."

"Clearly." Something about him seemed off. I stepped toward

him on wobbly legs and gazed into his eyes, as if I might see something looking back that would explain his behavior. I'd been fooled by the brothers before. Had I been fooled again? Was he really—

He blew out a breath and pulled away, horrified. "Jesus, I'm not Laith."

"I-I know that." I crossed my arms as a chill rolled through me.

"But you were checking to make sure, weren't you?"

I rested my hand on my stomach to steady the churning. "Let's go back to the table before Sam sends out a search party."

The last thing I wanted to do was tell him I'd doubted him. Hell, the last thing I wanted to feel was doubt. But over the past several days, Maddox had not been himself. It had me wondering if something had happened when we made that jump from Chicago. I didn't understand enough about the time travel thing to know how it worked. Maybe the jumps affected him more than even he realized.

"I'm not Laith," he said once again. This time his tone had softened. He looked almost apologetic. "I'm nothing like him."

I wasn't sure about that at all. The more I got to know them, the more I noticed both the differences *and* the similarities between them.

"We can talk about it later, okay? Let's go salvage the evening. Let's have a little fun. Things have been way too tense for far too many days."

He nodded, the ghost of a smile on his lips. "You're right. I'm just wound up. Maybe a night of dancing is exactly what I need." He held out his hand, and I took it, letting him weave our fingers together as we walked back to the table.

From across the way, I could see that Hannah and Abercrombie had found our group, and Paige had finally arrived. I recognized her long, silky black hair as it cascaded over her shoulder. She was huddled deep in conversation with her mystery guy, but the way they had their heads together made it impossible to tell what he looked like, especially from behind.

"What's going on over there?" Maddox whispered in my ear.

It took me an instant to figure out what he meant. Then I saw it.

All the color had drained from Sam's face. Even Hannah and Abercrombie looked uncomfortable. Hannah fidgeted with her hair while Abercrombie—for once without his trademark hoodie—bounced his leg up and down, making the entire table shake. In fact, everyone but Paige and her date looked like they'd just witnessed a vampire attack at the next table.

"Are you kidding me?" Maddox choked out the words as he came to a screeching halt steps from the group.

Everything happened in slow motion like a scene from the movies. Paige stopped laughing and turned to face us just as the rest of the group gasped. Her date turned, and my stomach dropped to my toes.

"Laith."

CHAPTER TWENTY-THREE

MY BREATH CAUGHT IN MY throat, his name still tingling on my lips. Seeing him again made my heart race. I swear I could feel my blood pumping faster through my veins, and I wanted to slap myself for letting him get to me that way. Stupid soul connection and its power over me.

"What are you doing here, brother?" Maddox vibrated with anger beside me, but he played it off well, pretending to be merely surprised instead of horrified.

"Oh, don't sound so happy to see me." Laith beamed, clearly delighted with himself.

"Wait. So…" Hannah's eyes darted so fast between Laith and Maddox I worried they might roll right out of her head.

The color flooded back to Sam's cheeks. "So you guys are what? Twins? How did I not know Maddox had a twin?" She gave me a look that said we'd be talking about this later. Apparently, I'd broken the friend code by keeping Laith a secret.

"No shit, man. Why keep it a secret? Unless… have you guys been swapping back and forth this whole time?" Abercrombie asked Laith the million-dollar question, and I scrambled to come up with an answer in case neither of my soul mates did.

As if he'd heard the gears turning in my head, Laith shot me a quick grin before turning back to Abercrombie with his watered-down version of the truth. "Nah, we just aren't that close. Our parents split up when we were young. We each went to live with one. So even though we're brothers, we didn't grow up together."

"You mean like in *The Parent Trap*?" Sam asked, and everyone laughed. Everyone but me. And Maddox. Maddox seethed quietly beside me. His fingers bit into mine, he held my hand so tight.

"So how did you and Laith meet?" I directed my question to Paige, who sat uncharacteristically silent beside her *date*.

Paige gave me an icy smirk and slid her arm around Laith's shoulders. "It's really funny actually. We met at Will Clark's party. We only spoke for a few minutes. I thought he was Maddox at first. Then we ran into each other Thursday afternoon at Bullfrogs. I guess it was fate." She leaned over and kissed him, and my blood pressure shot through the roof.

Fate? What did Paige know about fate? And why did Laith let her put her bitchy lips all over his? More importantly, why did I *care* if she kissed him? Maddox glanced at me and frowned as if he could read the fury in my eyes. The night had been a total disaster—first Ethan and then Laith. I was afraid to ask what more could go wrong.

"Let's go dance." Paige tugged Laith out of the booth, and he went willingly, following her across the room to the dance floor like a lovesick teenager.

He glanced my way a few times, but he was clearly interested in whatever Paige had to offer. I should have been glad. I should have thanked my lucky stars that someone had distracted Laith from his pursuit of me. But instead, resentment bubbled right below the surface, waiting to explode in a jealous rage.

❖

The evening fizzled out just before midnight. Between Maddox's mood swings and my unexplainable bouts of jealousy, we were miserable. And as they say, misery loves company.

By the time we left, Hannah and Abercrombie had mysteriously disappeared, Sam and Ryan weren't speaking to each other after Ryan's ex-girlfriend showed up in a sheer dress that left her practically naked, and Paige had all but mounted Laith in the booth, making everyone but the two of them uncomfortable.

Sam dropped us off at twelve-thirty, and after the night I'd had, I was only too eager to spend a few quiet minutes alone with Maddox.

"Walk with me?" Maddox reached out his hand, and I took it, letting him pull me to his side. "Next time Sam suggests a group date—"

"Trust me; there won't be a next time."

He exhaled loudly. "Thank God."

I giggled, cuddling into his embrace as we strolled aimlessly down the sidewalk. "I'm sorry I let Laith get to me. He's such a jerk. I hate that I feel so drawn toward him. When he's around, I can't seem to help feeling the pull. It's so confusing."

He kissed the top of my head. "It's not your fault. He did it on purpose. Trying to let us know he can get to us no matter where we are."

"Why? What purpose does it serve? I'm not going to break up with you for him. So why does he keep trying?"

The pained look on Maddox's face told me all I needed to hear. "He's not going to stop because he can't. And honestly, if the shoe was on the other foot, I wouldn't be able to stop either. Your soul binds you to us. We can't escape it."

"So it's going to be like this forever?"

He stopped walking and turned to gaze down at me. The spark was gone from his eyes. "As far as I know, there's only one way to sever the soul bond."

Death. He didn't say the word, but I felt it in the air around us like smoke, choking the life out of me.

"Don't think about that right now, okay? For the rest of tonight, let's pretend we're two normal college students out on a normal date."

"Normal, huh?"

The light was back in his eyes, and he grinned.

"Hey, isn't this your house?" I looked up at the stone steps leading to his front door.

"I thought maybe you'd like to come in. So we can spend some time alone."

Alone. I let the word sink in for a moment then nodded.

An awkward silence hung between us, making my face go up in flames, though I had no idea why. I'd been alone with Maddox before, but stepping into his personal space—*his home*—left me feeling exposed.

"Come on." Maddox led me up the steps and had the front door open before I even realized he'd pulled out his keys. He took my hand again and towed me through the dark rooms until we reached his bedroom. Soft candlelight flickered from every solid surface.

"When did you do this?" My cheeks burned with the knowledge that he'd planned this from the beginning, or at least from before we'd set out on our walk. I had no idea how he'd managed to light candles while we were out.

And apparently, he wasn't giving up his secret. "Normal, remember?"

The nervous energy coursing through me reminded me that, deep down, I *was* just an ordinary girl on a date. Sure, I carried a witch's curse on my shoulders, and I had two soul mates, but aside from that, I was just a typical nineteen-year-old girl, madly in love with her boyfriend and his covert romantic gestures.

Maddox watched me curiously as I walked around his room, inspecting the little trinkets he had sitting out on his dresser and bedside table: a small collection of jagged blue stones, a few pieces of jewelry that could have belonged to his mother, an antique pocket watch, and a small gold cross. "See anything you like?"

A smile was my only response as I sat at the foot of the large four-poster bed. Dark wood framed the crisp white sheets topped with two fluffy pillows and a heavy wool blanket. No decorative comforter. No frilly accent pillows. The bed itself was ornate, but the bedding just looked comfortable. I ran my hand over the expensive linen bedding, and Maddox groaned.

He crossed the room and stopped in front of me. "If I don't kiss you, I'm going to die."

"Then kiss me."

Pulling me to my feet, he surged in, winding his hands

around me as his mouth closed over mine. I felt the desperation as his lips captured and claimed. His hands held me close, never wandering below my waist, but his fingers dug into my flesh as if he feared I'd disappear if he let go.

I wrapped my arms around his neck and pulled him even closer. With our chests pressed together, I felt every breath, every beat of his heart.

"I want you so much." He moaned into my mouth.

"I want you too." I let him nudge me to the mattress until I was lying under him. Every inch of him pressed down on me as he kissed me, pausing just long enough to nip my bottom lip with his teeth, insistent but never pushing. Almost restrained. Unlike the reckless abandon of kissing Laith. Having Laith's hands on me. I'd come so close to shattering in those same hands.

Where had that come from?

I thought I'd pushed that memory from my brain. I had no business thinking of Laith, especially after what he'd done. And yet the kiss—*and everything else*—we'd shared against the wall at the party kept flooding back into the forefront of my mind.

Maddox propped himself up on one hand while his other hand skated down my side, stopping at my hip before sliding over my ribs then under my shirt. "Are you okay?"

"Mmhmm." I sucked in a breath as he traced the skin just below my bra with his finger.

"Are you sure?" he whispered, bringing his lips to run a path from my chin down my throat.

"Yes." I grabbed the front of Maddox's black shirt and yanked, sending the buttons scattering to the floor. I needed to feel the heat of his skin against mine. I needed—*no*—I was desperate to shed the images of Laith crowding my thoughts.

"I love you, Ava." Maddox's voice was frantic—out of control—though his actions seemed controlled—almost too controlled—as if he was forcing himself to go slow when that was the exact opposite of what he wanted. "God, I want you so much."

"I love you, too. And I want..." I couldn't even finish the

thought. Saying it out loud seemed wrong when I couldn't get his brother out of my head. *What the hell am I doing?* "Wait." The word slipped out of my mouth before I could stop it.

He stopped kissing me. "Wait?"

I shoved against his chest lightly and lifted my eyes to his. "Yes. Please. For just a minute."

He rolled to the side, propping himself on his elbow to study my expression. "I'm waiting."

"I can't do this. I-I'm not ready for..." *For what? To choose between them?* I wasn't sure exactly.

He frowned but didn't interrupt.

"I want to." I kissed him quickly to make my point. "I just don't want my first time—*our* first time to be overshadowed by—"

"*Laith.*" He grimaced as he voiced what I couldn't.

"Hear me out, okay?"

He nodded.

"You've lived with this—" I struggled to find the right words "—curse, for longer than I've been alive. But I've barely had any time to make sense of it all. And I know you don't want to hear about my bond with your brother, but I can't pretend it doesn't exist. Tonight was intense. There were a lot of emotions flying around even before Laith got there. I'd like to—no, I *need* to wait." His lips parted as if he might say something, so I cut him off. "Not forever. Just for a little while longer."

"I understand." Maddox nodded and gave me a smile, but I could tell it took a lot of effort on his part. He could pretend all he wanted; I knew my rejection hurt. That wasn't my intention, but it was necessary. I couldn't sleep with Maddox when I hadn't resolved my feelings for Laith.

He sat up and fixed his chaotic hair. "You want me to walk you home now?"

"Yeah. That's probably a good idea. If I stay, I might change my mind." I let him take my hand and help me from the bed before leading me back through his darkened house.

The cool night air helped chill my overactive hormones. By

the time Maddox kissed me goodnight at my front door, the slow burn I'd felt while in his bed had nearly faded into a memory.

Even though I'd made it home well before my curfew, I crept up the stairs, careful not to step on the creaky floorboards. As I passed Josh's room, I saw the light under his door and heard what sounded like him talking to someone. I told myself I wasn't being a creeper, just a concerned sister, when I pressed my ear to the door.

Josh cackled like an evil genius. "I can't wait until Ava gets home."

I pushed the door open, claiming self-defense in my head. He'd mentioned my name in what sounded like some sort of plot.

"Hey! Get out of my room." He kept his voice low but still managed to inject menace into the tone.

I narrowed my eyes at him and crossed my arms. "Give it up, peanut. I heard you planning something in here. Now who are you talking to? And what do you have up your sleeve?"

"That's for me to know and you to find out." He giggled again then flinched as a chime sounded from his back pocket.

"What was that?"

"Why do you care?"

I batted my eyelashes and gave him my sweetest smile. "Because you're my brother, and I care about you."

"Bullshit. You're in a pissy mood because your date sucked."

"What makes you think my date sucked?"

"I-I can just tell. You look mad."

"I'm not mad. Yet. But if you give me a minute, I think I might be. What are you hiding behind your back?"

"I told you, it's nothing. It's mine."

"Uh huh." I walked over to his game system and checked the messages on his PlayStation account. "Not chatting with some of your little idiot friends?"

He laughed as he snatched the controller out of my hands. "No. I'm not."

"Okay, I'm going to bed. Try to keep it down in here so you don't wake Mom."

"Whatever." He closed the door behind me, laughing again as soon as I was safely on the other side.

Then I heard the chime again, this time coming from my pocket. I pulled out my phone to find a message from Maddox.

Maddox: Already miss you. Sleep well.

I looked from the message to Josh's door. The little shit had a cell phone in there. I shoved his door open again, this time catching him in the act of sending a text. "Where did you get that phone? Mom said you couldn't have one until you're thirteen."

"She changed her mind." He fumbled with the device, trying to shove it into his pocket before I reached him.

"Not so fast there, kiddo." I grabbed his wrist with one hand and the phone in the other then backed away quickly to scroll through his message log. "What do we have here?"

"Give it back!" His face turned bright red, and he lunged toward me, but I dodged out of the way just in time.

Every message had come from the same person.

"Laith?" I choked out his name. "You're texting with my boyfriend's evil twin?"

"He's not evil. He's my friend. Now give it back!"

I clicked on the most recent message and read it aloud.

Josh: O.M.G. You were right. She's so pissed off.

"I take it you're talking about me."

"No I wasn't." He tried to grab the phone away from me again. "Now. Give. It. Back."

"I don't think I will. And I think if you even try to take it from me, I'll tell Mom you have it, and *she'll* take it away from you, and then you'll never see it again."

"Gah! You're such a freaking bitch. You can't read those messages. They're private."

"They're about me. So I'm going to read every one of them. And when I'm done, if I feel charitable, maybe I'll give this back to you." I waved the phone in front of him then snatched it back, shoving it into my pocket and turning to leave.

"I'm going to tell him you took it."

"I guess you'll have to wait until you get your phone back first. Won't you?"

He flopped down on his bed, defeated. "Just go. Read the messages then bring it back."

"Maybe." I walked out of his room then ran, taking the steps two at a time all the way to the third floor. I darted down the hall to my room and locked my door behind me. Residual excitement raced through my veins as I quickly shed my uncomfortable clothes. Once I'd changed into my favorite pajamas, I climbed into my bed to read. I'd barely settled in when a new messaged flashed on the screen, followed closely by the chime.

Laith: Good. I can only hope that's why she's home so early.

How dare he? I quickly scrolled through the old messages. The topics ranged from baseball to history to me. Laith asked a lot of questions. Where I was? What I was doing? How my hair smelled first thing in the morning? Eww. Why would he ask my brother that? He needed a dose of his own medicine. And I happened to have the perfect way to administer it.

I keyed in a new message and hit send.

Josh: What is it about Ava you like so much?

I fidgeted with the phone while I waited for his reply.

Laith: She's beautiful.

Of course, that's why. I wanted to slap him.

Josh: So you like her because she's pretty?

Laith: No, you don't understand. Not just on the outside. She has fire. I love that about her. Sometimes, I go out of my way to piss her off just so I can see her get angry. Like tonight. I could see the fury coming off her in waves. It's spectacular, and yes, beautiful. She's like Athena.

My heart beat faster as I read his reply. He had me speechless, but I needed to hear more. Everything I'd thought about him suddenly came into question.

Josh: ?

Laith: Goddess of war. All golden hair and fiery determination.

I didn't have a comeback for that. He'd stunned me. He really felt that way... about me? I had to say something.

Josh: So basically, you think she's beautiful but a bitch.

Laith: No, not a bitch. Fierce. She would have made a beautiful warrior, though. I would have loved to see her in battle. But I would have never allowed her to be in that much danger.

Time to change the subject before my opinion of him had completely changed for the better. I needed to keep my distance. Having warm feelings for him would be dangerous. And I was already confused enough.

Josh: Why do you hate Maddox?

He didn't respond. Several minutes passed, and I worried I'd crossed the line with my questioning. Maybe he'd already talked about this with Josh. Josh did seem to know an awful lot about their relationship. I jumped up from the bed and paced around my room, willing the phone to chime with a new message. Every second the phone stayed quiet added to my anxiety. And then there it was.

Laith: Because he had everything. Every opportunity, every convenience. He had the best education, the benefit of both of our parents, and he still chose to take the only thing in the entire world that mattered to me.

Josh: You mean Ava?

Laith: No. Not Ava.

Not Ava? I stared at the words for at least a minute while they sank in, each one like a sliver of doubt clouding my vision, changing the way I saw him. As I studied his message, a new one came in.

Laith: If you want more information than that, you'll have to ask him yourself, Ava.

I stared at the screen. At my name. He knew it was me. I dropped the phone as if it were a snake, rearing up to bite me. It bounced off my foot just as another text chimed in, and I couldn't help my curiosity. I crawled under the bed to retrieve it, quickly reading the newest message.

Laith: After you've deleted our conversation, please give the phone back to your brother.

Ava: Why? What do you want with my brother?

Laith: Because your brother is the only friend I have.

CHAPTER TWENTY-FOUR

1675

MADDOX FAIRCHILD SHOVED HIS BROTHER out of the way to pound on the splintered door. Inside the cottage, someone stirred. He smelled the faint aroma of a meal cooking, though it didn't smell like anything he'd eaten before. The sour odor turned his stomach.

Footsteps approached just before the door wrenched open. A small woman no older than their mother stood in front of him. A curious expression lined her delicate features, and streaks of silver shot through her raven hair, but neither took away from her beauty.

"Are you Bess Floyd?" Even as Maddox asked her, he knew she couldn't have been the haggard old woman from his mother's journal.

"No, she's my aunt. And whatever you want with her, you're too late. She's a few breaths from the grave. She wouldn't survive the trip." She moved to close the door, but Laith put his foot in its path.

"What trip?" Laith flashed her a devastating smile, and the woman flushed. "We have no desire to take her with us. We've simply come to ask a few questions."

"What kind of questions?" Her blue eyes narrowed as she studied them.

Maddox pushed Laith behind him again. "She cursed us."

The woman choked out a bitter laugh and pushed against the

217

door. "You've come to the wrong place. Aunt Bess never worked in curses. Only blessings."

Maddox chuckled darkly. "Trust me, this was no blessing. Our mother came for a blessing but left with a curse."

"Yes..." Laith sneered at her. "And as curses go, it's quite impressive. It would seem we're bound to the same soul for all eternity. And the poor girl hanged herself to escape us. But it would seem *we* can't escape *her*. I feel her all around me... with every breath I take. How can that even be? She's dead and buried almost a week now."

The woman gasped. "You! I-I remember your mother, Lady Catherine Fairchild. And I heard what happened to your blessing." She stepped back, and the brothers took that as an invitation to come in.

With Laith close on his heels, Maddox crossed the room, swatting the hanging bird carcasses out of his way like flies. "Is Bess truly as close to death as you implied?"

The woman laughed. "Closer than even that, I'm afraid. But she'll see you. Not a day goes by that she doesn't mumble about her greatest failure." Her voice dripped with guilt. "And may God take pity on me... I'm to blame for it."

"How so?" Laith asked the question burning in Maddox's mind.

"I'm the one who tricked her into agreeing to it." The woman pushed back a tattered red curtain to reveal an old woman asleep in a bed. "Aunt Bess, you have visitors. It's Lady Catherine's sons, come to see you all these years later."

The woman stirred, and her eyes snapped open as if someone had stuck her with a pin. "You've come to bring me my consequences—my threefold? After all this time?"

"No." Laith approached her cautiously. "We've come to ask for your help."

The old woman seemed to deflate in front of Maddox's eyes. Her chest rose with a shallow breath, and her head moved slowly from side to side. "I'm afraid there is no help I can offer you. I warned your mother of the dangers of dark magic, and she accepted responsibility for it. I told her then, and I'll tell you now, no good magic comes of fear. "

"That can't be the end of it!" Laith shouted, making the younger woman flinch. "Our soul mate is dead, but I still feel the burn of longing. How can she still haunt me after death?"

"I think you should go." The younger woman turned to push them back out the way they came.

"No, Jane." The aunt struggled to lift her head. "They have a right to be angry. I should have never agreed to Lady Catherine's foolish idea. But anger does nothing to solve an unsolvable dilemma. I cannot remove the blessing. Your souls are tied together, destined to form an unbreakable bond. And it would have worked if you hadn't been split into two pieces." The old woman dissolved into a coughing fit. Her face turned red, twisting with the effort to breathe.

Laith scoffed. "So we're still cursed, and Elizabeth is still dead. We're bound to a dead girl."

Bess raised her head and looked Laith straight in his eyes. "Her body may be dead, but her soul lives. And *that* is what you are bound to."

"I don't understand." Maddox looked at Jane for an explanation. Had her aunt gone as crazy as his mother had?

Jane pressed her lips into a tight line then looked down at her frail aunt. "When the body dies, the soul is free to move on. It will continue to search for its mate throughout time."

Laith shot a glance at Maddox then turned back to Jane. "Explain."

"A soul doesn't really die," Bess croaked. "It comes back time and time again. As will hers."

"So you're saying Elizabeth will live again?" Maddox's mouth dropped open.

"Of course she will. She already does." Jane patted Maddox's hand. "In another time."

"Death is the only possible solution." The old woman's chest rattled as another coughing fit consumed her. With one last gasping breath, she went silent, her gray eyes frozen.

"Aunt Bess?" Jane leaned down, pressing her ear to her aunt's chest. She listened for a moment, then with tears welling in her eyes, she stood. "She's gone." She draped a worn blanket over the old woman's face then shooed the Fairchilds out of the room. "I need a moment alone with her."

Maddox pushed through the curtain to wait in the main room. "Is this our doing?" he asked his brother.

"No. She was old and sick. Our coming here did nothing to change that."

"So you feel no guilt for hastening her death?"

Laith's eyes turned to stone. "None."

They waited in silence for several minutes before Jane reappeared from behind the drape. "I didn't want to say anything before, but there may be another way for you to reunite with your soul mate."

"What way? What do you mean?" Maddox asked.

"You must go to Wiltshire. To Stonehenge," Jane whispered as if the dead woman would disapprove of their conversation.

Maddox looked to Laith, whose confusion mirrored his own.

"There are many legends about the mystic power of Stonehenge. The druids. The elementals. We—I believe many of those legends are true. And I believe you can harness those powers... call on aether, the quintessence, by bowing down to the blue stones."

"You're saying we should beg the gods at Stonehenge?" Disbelief colored Laith's tone. "And then what? They'll send Elizabeth back for us to share?"

She shook her head. "Your Elizabeth is gone, but the power of the stones can help you reunite with her soul."

"And what of the curse?" Maddox asked.

Jane dropped her eyes. "As my aunt said, death is the only solution."

Laith grabbed her shoulders, shaking her lightly. "What does that mean?"

She lifted her face. "One of you must sacrifice your soul to the other."

CHAPTER TWENTY-FIVE

ESPITE FIGHTING BONE-DEEP EXHAUSTION, I didn't sleep at all that night. After reluctantly wiping the messages and giving the phone back to Josh, I stared at the ceiling, trying to make sense of what Laith had said.

Maddox took something from him, something he valued above everything else. As far as I knew, the only thing either of them valued was me. Or rather, my soul. And I already knew Laith had taken Elizabeth from Maddox. I'd seen that memory in my dream. So if it wasn't Elizabeth, and it wasn't me, what had Maddox taken from him? His family? Did he blame his brother for taking his parents away?

I would've been lying to myself if I said it didn't hurt a little, knowing he didn't mean me. But I had no idea why it bothered me that Laith valued something, or someone, more than my soul. Could there have been more to my feelings for him than I realized?

I didn't even like Laith. Aside from the soul bond, I found him completely intolerable. And yet for some reason, I wanted to know more. I wanted to explore the unknown with him.

Since sleep wasn't in the cards for me, I shook off the uncomfortable truth and abandoned my bed for a hot shower. Sunrise was still a few hours away, but my need to uncover the facts overwhelmed me—picking at me like a dry scab. Laith said if I wanted more information, I should ask Maddox, so that was exactly what I planned to do.

I crept out of the house and walked the half a block to Maddox's in the dark, debating my decision the entire way. I didn't know what scared me so much about asking him—maybe those annoying slivers of doubt festering below the surface. I rang the bell and regretted it immediately. Going there had been a mistake. At just after four in the morning, he would be asleep.

I second-guessed myself with every moment that ticked by. What if he was angry I didn't wait until morning? Would he feel as if I'd breached his trust by listening to anything Laith had said? And how could I ask him without it coming out as an accusation, especially when I didn't even know what I was asking *about*? What would he say if I just came right out and asked what he'd taken from Laith?

When he didn't come to the door after several minutes, I rang the bell again, desperate to wake him for answers and almost wishing I could jump through time to see things for myself.

Where is he?

Thunder rumbled in the distance, and I felt the vibration all the way to my soul. First one, then another large droplet of water splashed against my cheek. The rain had finally arrived.

I pulled out my phone and dialed his number. When it went to voice mail, I pounded on the door. "Maddox!" I waited for the prickling to announce his arrival, but it never came.

A flash of lightning lit up the sky like an omen. Panic swelled in me, clogging my veins with something that felt too much like *déjà vu*. I abandoned Maddox's front door and raced the storm back home, taking the stairs two at a time and running all the way to my brother's room.

Josh slept kitty corner across the mattress, his feet poking out of the blankets and his mouth hanging open. He typically slept like the dead, so waking him was the least of my worries as I searched under the comic books on his nightstand and on the floor under the bed.

"Where's your phone?" I hissed, careful not to wake my mother down the hall.

Josh blinked his eyes open and sat up. "Huh?" Under different circumstances, it would have been funny to see him all sleep rumpled and confused. But I had more important things to worry about.

"Your phone," I whispered as I slid my hand under his pillow. "I need to reach Laith."

Josh yawned and shook his head. "You can't."

"What do you mean, I *can't*?" Something in his tone sent a ripple of fear wriggling down my spine.

"I mean, he's not going to answer. He said he had to take care of something." He sounded irritated, and not just because I'd woken him in the middle of the night. I knew my brother well enough to know something else bothered him.

"What do you mean, *he had to take care of something*? Like what? Where did he go?"

He shot me a sidelong glance, the same expression as when he lied to Mom. The kid needed to practice his bluffing techniques if he ever wanted to play poker.

"You know something you're not telling me." I wanted to shake the truth out of him. Force him to tell me.

"Why do you care?" He scowled at me. "I thought you didn't even *like* Laith."

Did I like Laith? I wasn't sure anymore. My hands trembled as I continued to search the wadded-up blankets tangled at the foot of his bed. "I-I don't, but Maddox is missing, and Laith might know where he is."

"Yeah." Josh laughed. "Probably. Since Maddox is the *something* Laith was talking about."

"Oh, my God!" Frustration ate away at my patience, and I balled up my fists, plopping down on the edge of his bed. "Can you stop being cryptic for two seconds, and tell me what you're talking about?"

Josh reached under the mattress and pulled out the small cell phone, slapping it into my palm. "Here, read for yourself. Now get out. I'm going back to sleep." And he rolled over and flopped his head back onto the pillow, falling instantly back to sleep.

I stepped into the hall and opened the most recent message. *Laith: Your sister must have done something to upset my brother tonight. He just messaged me to meet him at the lighthouse to "finish" things.*

Another message was time stamped a few minutes later.

Laith: If I don't come back, tell Ava I've loved her from the first moment my soul found hers.

If I don't come back? Why wouldn't he come back? A sick feeling of dread formed at the pit of my stomach.

Without stopping to think, I bolted down the stairs and grabbed Mom's keys from the hook in the kitchen. I scribbled her a quick note and left it on the table then ran out the front door without bothering to lock it behind me. I needed to get to them before they did something even time travel couldn't fix.

Driven by fear—fear of not getting there in time, fear of losing one or both of them, fear of ending up like Elizabeth—I pushed the speed limit, racing toward the lighthouse, praying I wasn't already too late.

Laith's last message played over and over in my head. *Tell Ava I've loved her from the first moment my soul found hers.* Lightning etched through the darkness, followed by a loud crack of thunder. Then the sky opened up, and blinding rain pelted the SUV.

He loved me.

The car fishtailed across the road near the bay exit, and my pulse took off as if my heart was trying to keep time with the windshield wipers. They moved so fast, slapping erratically against the glass, I feared one or both of them would break free and fly away. I should've pulled over until the rain let up. I probably should've never gone after them at all in a storm. But I would've never forgiven myself if I hadn't.

I almost missed the turn from Shore Drive to the narrow lighthouse access road, taking the corner too quickly and almost flipping Mom's Durango into the boulders. I swallowed down another panic attack and parked near the locked gate to make a run for the building. Once I'd left the safety of the car, rain quickly soaked through my clothes, drenching me to the bone. Tremors wracked my body with what was probably the beginning of hypothermia.

Streaks of pink and red tinged the horizon where the rising sun tried to peek through the gray clouds hanging low over the ocean. I scanned the area, unsure of exactly where they might be, only certain they were somewhere close, when I saw Maddox's motorcycle parked haphazardly near the old caretaker's cottage.

Another flash lit up the sky, and I saw a glint of something near the cliff. I took off running, my Chucks sinking into the soft ground with a squish. Cold rain stabbed my skin, burning my eyes and blurring my vision. I could barely make out the two dark figures facing off between the lighthouse and the rocky coast. They were both dressed in black and soaked to the skin, holding what looked like long daggers in their outstretched hands. I couldn't tell them apart, but it didn't matter. I couldn't let them destroy each other.

The angry roar of the waves drowned out the sound of their voices as they yelled back and forth, and I realized they hadn't seen me yet. Fear paralyzed me. They were going to kill each other in front of me, and I could do nothing about it.

"Maddox!" I screamed his name, but the ocean swallowed up the sound. I willed him to turn in my direction, but nothing happened. A burst of adrenaline shot through me, and I started running again. My toe caught on a fallen branch, and I went down, hitting my head against the wet ground with a dull thud.

The fall knocked the wind out of me, stunning me into a silent stupor. While I lay there, fighting against my own limbs, a flash of memory—a vision, maybe—played behind my eyelids.

My soul mates were still arguing, but not along the seacoast. They fought in an open field, dressed in tight pants and loose shirts, looking as if they'd escaped from the pages of my European history book. Stalks of wheat blew in the wind as they clashed long swords against one another. Instead of waves crashing against the shore, the clang of steel on steel echoed through the air.

A girl with golden hair called their names as she rushed toward them from a stone house in the distance. "Maddox! Laith! Stop. Oh, please stop!" Her long, cornflower-blue skirt caught on a limb and ripped up the side as she ran. She ignored the tear and kept moving, anguish distorting her pretty features. She looked like me. Not an exact copy, but close enough to be my sister. And every stab of pain slicing through her wounded me. I felt her heart break seeing them fighting over her, and I knew she would do anything to stop them.

I sensed the instant the idea came to her—her plan to keep them safe from harm: her decision to end her own life. Not out of shame as Maddox had told me, but out of love. Her love for them was too much for one young girl to bear. I understood that infinitely too well.

"Stop, Elizabeth!" I screamed until my throat burned, but she turned and headed toward the barn. Then like a vapor, she disappeared. The barn, the wheat... Elizabeth... they were all gone, and only the rocky coast and the two boys battling for my soul were left.

Feeling had come back into my limbs, and I wrenched myself from the ground and took off running toward them again, desperation pouring off me like summer sweat.

"Maddox! Laith!" I screamed into the driving rain. "Please stop!"

Maddox... or was it Laith—I couldn't tell them apart soaking wet and covered in mud—turned to me in horror. "Stay back, Ava. Stay out of this."

"No! You don't understand. Please. Please let me explain." Wet hair slapped me in the face, but I kept going until I reached them. I stopped a few feet away, panting to catch my breath. "Elizabeth... she didn't want you to destroy each other. Not over her. She just couldn't stand by and watch anymore."

"It's that damn curse," one of them shouted. Maddox maybe. "It's ruined us all. There's only one way to end it."

"What are you talking about?" I gaped at him. His tone and the look of defeat in his eyes terrified me.

"One of us has to die," Laith—I think it was Laith—said so casually I almost missed it.

I darted my eyes between them. They both had shallow cuts scattered over their exposed skin. Their shirts were so soaked the fabric turned transparent. "I can't let you do that."

"We should have finished this the first time." Laith wiped a bead of blood from his lip with the back of his hand.

"And we would have, had we not been interrupted." Only Maddox could have felt that pain so deeply. His face twisted with what had to be the memory of Elizabeth's death.

With Elizabeth's sacrifice still fresh in my mind, I inched toward the rocks as they stepped toward each other, daggers at the ready once again. I turned to the boy who I was certain was Maddox. "Even if Laith hadn't tricked her, she would've still taken her own life. She did it to save you both. Can't you see that?"

Maddox's eyes locked with mine but he spoke to his brother. "Tell her."

"Laith, no."

Laith? I whipped around to face the real Maddox. His eyes clouded over with remorse and something else.

Fear.

"She deserves to know what you did," Laith spoke from my other side as they both flanked me, and though my eyes were trained on Maddox, I sensed Laith moving closer.

"I didn't do anything." Maddox's shoulders sagged, and he let the hand with the dagger drop to his side.

"Oh, come on." Laith seemed to get a sick pleasure from his brother's pain. "Tell her how you manipulated her dreams so she'd believe it was me who tricked Elizabeth."

"No!" I took a step back, loose earth shifting under my feet. Icy spray soaked my back with each wave breaking against the rocks. "That's impossible. I saw—"

"You saw what he wanted you to see," Laith snapped, and I flinched from the bitterness of his voice. He gave me a sad smile. "You don't need to be afraid of me, Ava. I've never lied to you."

"You don't understand." Maddox drew my attention back to him, a mask of pain changing his face. "What happened with Elizabeth... that was *centuries* before I met you. I've atoned for my mistakes."

"Mistakes?" Laith barked out a laugh. "You mean your calculated decisions. You've been manipulating her this entire time."

"Is it true?" The guilty expression on his face told me everything I needed to know. "How could you? I-I *loved* you."

"Loved?" Maddox's expression turned cold in an instant. "And now, what? You love *him*?"

I shook my head, stepping farther away from the two of them, confusion taking over my thoughts. The familiar prickling I felt in their presence had spread through me like a virus, illuminating my senses like a thousand strings of tiny white Christmas lights. "I can't. It's too much."

Maddox tore his eyes away from mine and charged his brother, grabbing him around the middle and dragging him to the ground with a sickening thud. Laith raised up to his knees to throw the first punch, then they rolled around pummeling each other, coating themselves in a thick layer of mud.

As if they'd pissed off the gods, a bolt of lightning streaked across the sky, making me flinch.

"Watch out, Ava! You're gonna fall." I wasn't sure which one of them had spoken, but the words didn't make sense. Was he really warning me now? Didn't he know I'd already fallen? Hard and fast. For both of them in their own way. What I needed to watch out for was getting my heart broken, to watch out that I didn't let myself get pulled into the madness surrounding them. His warning had come much too late for that. Too late for all of it.

My brother's words suddenly came back to me. *You're stupid if you think Maddox is the good brother.* Had I really been so wrong about them? Had I misjudged Laith's intentions from the first moment I'd met him? Maybe Elizabeth was right, and I needed to run from *both* of them.

I screamed as my foot slipped on loose gravel, and I felt myself sliding over the edge. A wave rose up to meet me as my feet disappeared over the side. My midsection slammed against the jagged rocks, forcing the air from my lungs in a whoosh. "Maddox!"

"Jesus, Ava!" He lunged toward me, sliding across the ground until his outstretched hand reached mine.

"I'm slipping," I cried, fumbling for a foothold on the slippery rocks. But I was too cold, and my body had already started to go numb.

"Don't let go of her!" Laith yelled as he scrambled toward us on hands and knees.

Maddox gave me a stiff smile then, gripping my fingers as tightly as he could, he struggled to haul me back up. "Don't worry. I'll never let go."

Another wave shattered against me like a million knives in my skin. In the back of my mind, I knew if I fell, the craggy rocks below would batter me until there was nothing left, but I couldn't hold on anymore. "Maddox, I can't—"

"Don't you dare let go, Ava!" Laith clenched his jaw, scraping his chest along the sharp corners as he reached for me, but it was no use.

Every drop of energy I'd had had been used up. I'd become one of those old rag dolls my mother collected when I was six. And if I didn't let go, I'd drag Maddox over the side with me.

Then Laith's fingers brushed against my wrist. "Do you trust me?"

"What are you doing?" Maddox gritted his teeth, trying to get a better grip on me. "You'd better not be planning what I think you are. I have her. I have you, Ava."

"Ava." Laith's eyes locked on mine. "Do. You. Trust. Me?"

"No!" Maddox shouted as he grappled to hold on to me, but I couldn't feel my fingers anymore, and Laith looked so certain.

I sucked in a breath and held it for a beat. "Yes." The word had barely passed my lips when Laith hurled himself over the side.

Maddox lunged, his eyes wild with horror, his hands grasping at empty air to reconnect with mine. "Oh, God. Ava. No!"

The look of desperation contorting his face when my fingers slipped from his in that flash of an instant before Laith snatched me from the rocks would be permanently branded in my brain. As long as I lived, I would never forget the emptiness in Maddox's eyes.

A scream bubbled up from the tips of my toes, but just as it was about to burst free, just as Laith and I were about to be crushed against the rocks, we were sucked into the vortex, falling through space and time as the abyss took us.

ACKNOWLEDGMENTS

First and foremost, I'd like to thank my diehard fans. You know who you are, and I really wouldn't be here without you. I could thank you every minute of every day, and that still doesn't seem enough. I hope you enjoyed reading this book as much as I enjoyed writing it. I promise not to leave you hanging on that cliff too long.

I'd also like to give special thanks to everyone who pushed, prodded, and helped me along the way:

To the people who take the time to leave reviews—yes, even the bad ones—because praise feeds a writer's soul, and criticism makes us work even harder the next time.

To my parents for planting the creative seed that grew into a lifelong passion and for never discouraging me from listening to the voices in my head. I wouldn't be the person I am today without your love and guidance throughout my life. I can't tell you how glad I am that you've managed to stick around long enough to see me realize my dreams. Now you need to hang out until I hit the big time. I think I still owe you money.

To Lauren and Alexa, for keeping me up on the latest lingo and making sure I never lost sight of the teen voice. And to Spencer for reminding me I'm not a teenager anymore and probably shouldn't flirt with his friends.

To Josh Hulsey for asking me every question imaginable to prevent the existence of holes in the world I'd created. I couldn't have traveled through time without you.

To Karen Allen and Jessica Anderegg—my top-notch editing

team—for making sure I never get away with anything cheap or easy.

To Louise Flynn, Marie Patchen, Mercy Pilkington, and Candy Johnson—some of the best beta readers ever—for taking time away from your own projects and commitments to help me with mine. And to J. Leigh for making sure Aunt Bess didn't stray too far from the truth.

To Red Adept Publishing—and the best publishing staff anywhere—for not letting me get my way all the time—even when I pout.

To Glendon at Streetlight Graphics for keeping cool under pressure when we couldn't seem to nail down a concept for the cover. It wasn't the idea I had going in, but I can't thank him enough for the final product.

To Mary Fan for helping me keep my sanity during the hardest parts, like picking the perfect hot guy for a cover that never got to see the light of day and encouraging me to keep going when I thought I might pack it in and give up.

To my family and friends for allowing me to bounce crazy ideas off them at the weirdest hours of the day or night.

And lastly, to my husband for allowing me to quit my day job all those years ago to become a full-time writer and making it possible for me to do what I love every day. Without you, I'd still be jotting down stories on bar napkins while waiting for my turn to sing karaoke or working in a bank, waiving overdraft fees even when I wasn't supposed to. I know you don't always love what I do—or don't do... like the cooking, the dishes, or the laundry—but you allow me to do it anyway, and you almost never complain about it. I love you.

MORE BOOKS BY ERICA LUCKE DEAN

To Katie With Love
Suddenly Sorceress
Craving Caine
Ashes of Life (with Laura M. Kolar)

Jewels of Desire DUO #1
Diamond Duplicity (Book 1) (with Elise Delacroix)
Ruby Ransom (Book 2) (with Elise Delacroix)

ABOUT THE AUTHOR

After walking away from her career as a business banker to pursue writing full-time, Erica Lucke Dean moved from the hustle and bustle of the big city to a small tourist town in the North Georgia Mountains, where she lives in a 90-year-old haunted farmhouse with her workaholic husband, her 180-pound lap dog, and at least one ghost.

When she's not writing or tending to her collection of crazy chickens and diabolical ducks, she's either reading bad fan fiction or singing karaoke in the local pub. Much like the main character in her first book, *To Katie With Love*, Erica is a magnet for disaster and has been known to trip on air while walking across flat surfaces.

How she's managed to survive this long is one of life's great mysteries.